Other Books by Frank McKinney

The Tap

Burst This! Frank McKinney's Bubble-Proof Real Estate Strategies

Frank McKinney's Maverick Approach to Real Estate Success:
How You Can Go from a $50,000 Fixer-Upper
to a $100 Million Mansion

Make It BIG! 49 Secrets for Building a Life of Extreme Success

To contact the author, please visit Frank-McKinney.com

DEAD FRED, FLYING LUNCHBOXES, AND THE GOOD LUCK CIRCLE

Frank McKinney

with Kate Mason

Health Communications, Inc.
Deerfield Beach, Florida

www.hcibooks.com

Library of Congress Cataloging-in-Publication Data

McKinney, Frank.
    Dead Fred, flying lunchboxes, and the good luck circle / Frank McKinney.
    p. cm.
    Summary: On her way to her new school over the Intracoastal Waterway in Delray Beach,
Florida, eighth-grader Ppeekk passes a neglected nature reserve and begins an unusual
magical adventure.
    ISBN-13: 978-0-7573-1382-0 (hardcover)
    ISBN-10: 0-7573-1382-5 (hardcover)
    [1. Magic—Fiction.   2. Fishes—Fiction.   3. Friendship—Fiction.   4. Nature—Fiction.
5. Delray Beach (Fla.)—Fiction.]   I. Title.
    PZ7.M1991 2009
    [Fic]—dc22

                                                                                    2008042730

Publisher: Health Communications, Inc.
            3201 S.W. 15th Street
            Deerfield Beach, FL 33442–8190
This book was printed on recycled paper.

The Leadership in Energy and Environmental Design (LEED) Green Building Rating System™ of
the U.S. Green Building Council encourages and accelerates global adoption of sustainable green
building and development practices through the creation and implementation of universally
understood and accepted tools and performance criteria. This book is part of Frank McKinney's efforts to
educate the public about these practices and standards.

Cover photos ©Robin Roslund
Cover design by Erik Hollander, Hollanderdesignlab.com
Interior design and formatting by Lawna Patterson Oldfield
Interior art by Lauren E. Barrow

To all who turn the pages of
*Dead Fred, Flying Lunchboxes and
the Good Luck Circle,*
may you never lose
the little girl or boy inside.

To my beautiful daughter,
Laura (Ppeekk), and our one thousand-plus
walks to school:
You made each step we took,
and each word I wrote, such a joy.
I love you.

Contents

Chapter One

Ppeekk's* Path

"**S**top honking the horn, Dad!"

Ppeekk Rose Berry tugged at her white blouse. Although it was still early in the morning, her bangs dripped sweat into her eyes. She hated hot, humid weather. But here she was, plunked down in the middle of a barrier island in Florida, surrounded by murky lakes, swampy waterways, and a whole ocean full of slimy, scaly things. She was deathly afraid of large bodies of water, especially the ocean and the crashing waves. But her father insisted it was "the land of opportunity."

Pronounced "Peekie's."

"Stop honking, Dad. I hear you!" Ppeekk clattered down the deck steps, dragging her new backpack behind her. Before she could reach the old Yugo, her dad beeped again, the horn sounding like an out-of-tune clarinet.

"I'm coming!"

Didn't he realize what she had to deal with on the first day of eighth grade at a new school in a new town? She wheeled her overloaded backpack down the rock-strewn driveway, but it kept tipping over. With a sigh, she stopped to shift her books and school supplies and set it upright again.

Her dad leaned out the driver's side window. "Hurry up! I've got an early meeting."

Ppeekk scrunched her face and mouthed, *I've got an early meeting.* "You always have an early meeting, Dad." She knew he hadn't heard her. When she finally struggled to the car, her dad was in his usual pose: cell phone plastered to his ear.

"Ouch!" The hot vinyl upholstery in the cramped backseat burned the back of her legs. She wished she were wearing jeans instead of a thin cotton jumper, her new school's uniform for girls. At least her kneesocks protected her lower legs.

She hauled her backpack and lunchbox beside her. She was beyond frustrated. "This car and this uniform and all this gear I have to lug around do not mix!" Ppeekk slammed the door shut, its screech like seagulls squawking for bits of food.

Dad slapped his phone shut, revved the engine, and ground the gears into first. They lurched down the rutted dirt driveway.

"The ol' Yugo has really held up." Her dad patted the faded dashboard with a heavy hand. "Can you believe it carried us all the way from Indiana to Florida without a breakdown?"

He'd made that same statement at least a dozen times. But he'd not said one word about her burning herself on the backseat. All he cared about was his car and his "vacuum business."

"But, Dad, all this stuff is awkward and the uniform is scratchy." She scowled at the blue plaid jumper, already rumpled. The starched white blouse felt like wet sandpaper on her arms and at her throat.

"You'll get used to it all. Once you get to school and make new friends, you'll be rolling right along." He began whistling a stupid old tune.

Ppeekk squirmed and yanked at the sleeves of her blouse. "I miss my old backpack. It was easy to carry. Now I have to wheel this huge thing everywhere I go! I think all these books mean more homework, a *lot* more homework."

"You're lucky to be attending St. Vincent's. It's the best school in Delray Beach. You're going to receive a first-rate education, young lady." Dad gulped his coffee. "Besides, this is our new beginning. We're in the Sunshine State!"

"But I don't know anyone in that school or this town. I don't know anyone in the whole state of Florida! I want to go back to Indiana. I don't care if it's sunny here or not." Ppeekk slapped the vinyl seat with both hands. A puff of dust shot into the air and made her sneeze.

"You'll make friends." Her dad tried to catch her eyes in the rearview mirror.

"Friends? What's the point? We'll probably just move again, and it will all be for nothing. I've never had any real friends. We've never lived anywhere long enough to make them."

"What about your cousin in Wisconsin? You and she still talk on the phone sometimes."

"We haven't talked in over a year, Dad."

"You need to have more confidence in yourself. Make the best of every new situation. Look at me. I go out every day and have to face the world to sell my vacuums and supplies!"

Her dad was so corny and so out of touch—such a nerd. He had no idea what her life was like or how all their moves affected her. They had lived in six different states in her nearly fourteen years. Her dad probably didn't care that she never had a social life, didn't have any friends. Anyway, what did she care? Friends were just a bother and a nuisance.

The car bounced down the driveway through a mass of over-grown trees and brush that slashed the sides of the car. Sharp spears of a tall grasslike bush scraped and poked through the open windows. It was like driving through a jungle.

"Well, you could make more of an effort and call her. You could try to make new friends here. This is Florida—the land of opportunity!"

Her dad flung his arms wide, as though showing her what could be hers. He caught the wheel as the car veered toward the side, but not quickly enough. The car hit a deep rut. A metallic shriek, a bang, and then a big puff of blue smoke whooshed out of the engine as the car shuddered and rattled to a halt.

"What?" Ppeekk's dad turned the key in the ignition and punched the gas pedal. "I can't believe this is happening."

Their old Yugo that had carried them over a thousand miles from Indiana to Florida had finally died. *Click, click, click, clank.* The engine wouldn't turn over.

Her dad pounded the steering wheel with the heel of his hand and then, like a madman, shot out of the car and popped the hood. He muttered some bad words and fiddled with several dip-sticks and wires in the engine. Flicking his tie over his shoulder, he lowered himself onto his hands and knees. When he reached under the car, he cut his hand on a sharp shell. Finally, he jumped up and kicked one of the wheels. Hopping on his left foot while clutching his right foot, he yelled more curse words.

Mom had obviously heard the ruckus and was rushing down the driveway toward the car as Dad limped around.

"Edward, settle down. You're going to have to walk Ppeekk to school or she'll be late. It's only a few blocks away, just down the street and over the Waterway. I can't do it because I've got four cakes to bake for a reception tonight."

Ppeekk's mom was a dessert caterer and already had a few jobs lined up. In Indiana, she had been well-known for her elegant cakes and yummy baked goods.

Mr. Berry slammed the hood so hard the whole car shook. He glared at the once-trusty vehicle and balled his fists, obviously wanting to punch it. Instead, he glanced at his watch, opened the car door, and began stuffing papers into his briefcase.

Ppeekk sighed, grabbed all her stuff, and clambered out of the car.

Mom planted a kiss on Ppeekk's forehead that smelled of sugar and vanilla. "Sorry, honey, got to go. Have a good first day at school!"

Ppeekk set off down the driveway, towing her backpack behind her, leaving her father to fuss with his papers. A breeze rustled the leaves and branches of the lush bushes and trees that stretched like a canopy over her head. It was like walking through a green tunnel.

She glanced back at the long-neglected wooden bungalow they'd moved into a few days ago. The house sat well back from the road on a little sandy rise. Vines and strange plants and trees surrounded it so densely you could barely see the grayed and aging house. Tendrils and trailing plants of all kinds seemed to creep and crawl everywhere. She was definitely not in Indiana anymore.

Ppeekk heard her father muttering and stumbling as he tried to catch up with her. She didn't look back; she knew what she'd see: dressed in his baggy old brown suit and a brown fedora hat pulled low over his eyes, he looked like a traveling salesman she'd seen in the old black-and-white movies her parents liked to watch. He even acted like one, too. She heard him yakking on his oversized and outdated cell phone while rustling with what was probably his pride and joy, his vacuum cleaner supplies.

Edward spilled coffee all over his hand. "Darn! This coffee's hotter than blazes!"

She was sure the neighbors could hear every word he said. "Yeah, yeah, I'm going to be late for our meeting," he barked into his phone.

But even with all the noise her dad was making, Ppeekk also heard rustlings in the surrounding landscape. Out of the corner of her eye, she thought she saw a large brown snake slithering along the underbrush, as if guiding her, but when she got closer she saw it was only a thick vine that had fallen off a tree.

At the end of the driveway, Ppeekk crossed the paved street to a path of crushed shells and sand where she had to tug harder on the backpack. The street was deserted this early in the morning. She knew houses lined her side of the street, but they were completely hidden by the abundance of trees, shrubs, and grasses.

But no houses were on the other side of the path—just more greenery: a bunch of scrub trees and bushes, palm trees and palmettos. The vegetation stretched farther than she could see. It looked sort of swampy and mysterious, too, especially with the early morning mist hanging above, like a scene out of one of her dad's favorite old horror films.

Ppeekk left the path and waded through some weeds and bushes to read a small sign posted at the edge of the swampy area. "Hey, Dad, there's a sign here. It says NATURE PRESERVE."

Her father glanced at her and shook his head. He pulled the phone away from his ear. "There could be a sinkhole in there. And snakes and alligators! Get away from there!" Barely taking a breath, he resumed his cell phone conversation.

"Figures," she muttered. As she turned her attention back to the nature preserve, she saw coconut palm fronds waving in the breeze and dew glistening on gold blossoms that looked like sunflowers growing on a sandy dune. She sniffed the air and caught the scent of sweet jasmine and gardenia. A buzzing and whirring of flying insects filled her ears. She heard distant waves breaking. Although her senses picked up nature's busyness, the peaceful quiet amazed her. Indiana, this wasn't.

Back on the path, she trudged through the deepening sand. She turned and called to her father straggling behind her. "Dad, this is the most beautiful path and walk I've ever taken!"

He glanced at her, and then continued his conversation.

"He doesn't ever listen to me," Ppeekk said to herself. There seemed to be no getting through to him. Still, she sort of wished she had someone to talk to.

She stumbled, but caught herself before she fell. Looking down to see what had tripped her, she found a perfectly formed, beautiful shell at her feet like a waiting gift. When she plucked it out of the sand, it fit perfectly in the palm of her hand. Ppeekk ran her fingers over the rough surface and turned it over, studying it. It was chalky-white on the outside, pale pink on the inside.

"Look, Dad. I found a shell. How can a shell get over here on the path when the ocean is on the other side of our yard?"

He snapped his cell phone shut. "Don't be picking up junk off the ground."

"It's not junk, Dad, it's a shell." She slipped it into her jumper pocket.

"Well, whatever it is, it was on the ground, and it's dirty and full of germs. And it could tear a hole in your uniform. I saw you put it in your pocket."

Ppeekk snatched the shell out of her pocket, closing her hand around it.

"That uniform cost me good money, young lady, and I have to sell a lot of vacuum cleaners to pay for it."

Ppeekk turned on her heel and stomped along the path, leaving her dad behind. As soon as she heard him in another cell phone conversation, she stuffed the shell into her backpack. *I'll collect shells if I want to. If I have to live in this place, then I'm going to take a small bit of it and keep it with me. I may not have any friends, but this is my path.*

The sandy trail and the nature preserve ended at the intersection of a much busier street. It was like emerging into a different world. Where her path had been solitary and hushed, on this street traffic whizzed by, cars and trucks rushing and vans and station wagons filled with chattering children all buckled into their seats. At the stop sign, one of the kids in a car put his fingers in his mouth, pulled it wide, and stuck out his tongue at Ppeekk.

If she weren't nearly fourteen, she would have stuck her tongue out at him, too. Who did these Florida kids think they were? Just because she was walking didn't make her less than them. Just because they were driving in fancy, expensive cars didn't make them better.

In fact, she was glad to be outside and walking in the early morning sunshine. She had a feeling of freedom and possibilities she'd never felt in Indiana or any of the other places she'd lived. She dared to hope that maybe something good *could* happen in the land of opportunity.

CHAPTER TWO

THE OLD DRAWBRIDGE

Ppeekk stepped onto the concrete sidewalk, her father trailing behind, still babbling on the cell phone. The wheels of her backpack made a steady whirring over the rough surface.

When she arrived at the drawbridge over the Intracoastal Waterway, an odd tingling ran up her spine, like a million marching ants. She studied the bridge. A bronze embossed plaque mounted on one of the concrete piers read CONSTRUCTED 1927 AD. If the bridge had once been painted, it was impossible to tell what color. The plain drawbridge had two sections that divided and rose in the middle to let tall ships pass. The waist-high metal side railings were tarnished brownish-gray and several orange rust spots showed through. She shuddered when she looked through the splintery driftwood-gray slats of the bridge to the deep, current-driven water below.

At the far end, on the mainland side, stood a small bridge house, an unpainted shack just large enough for one person to sit inside. Its faded old roof shaded a flimsy door and windows with shutters falling off. Ppeekk shielded her eyes with a hand and could barely make out a silhouette behind the dusty windows of the little hut.

"Here goes." Ppeekk gulped her fear and stepped gingerly onto the bridge. She tiptoed, not wanting to put too much weight onto the slats or alert whoever sat in the bridge house. When a car thundered past Ppeekk, the weight of it bounced her up and down as if she were on a pogo stick. She froze and grabbed on to the metal railing until the car reached the other side of the bridge, which rumbled and squeaked and rattled in a metallic cacophony. Ppeekk heard something splash *kerplunk* and feared the whole thing was about to collapse and be swallowed by the water below her.

The waterway was beautiful—but only from a distance. She didn't want to go any closer. She'd driven across it several times with her mom and dad, and they'd remarked on the boats tied up

at the marina, but they'd never stopped and gotten out to have a good look around.

Ppeekk shuffled to the middle of the bridge. She looked at the dark water stretched out as far as she could see to her left and right. She squinted into the brilliant blue sky, then back to the water, wondering why in some patches it was dark green, almost black with areas of murky brown. From where she stood on the bridge she had a clear view all around her. Along both banks of the river, houses poked through the thriving greenery. A few boats bobbed and tugged at their lines at the marina pier near the bridge house. Ppeekk spotted the church with its steeple and her school building just beyond the marina on the other side of the waterway.

Her father clomped up behind her and followed her gaze to the school. He smiled and waved at the figure in the bridge house, who did not wave back.

"Okay, Ppeekk, your school's just over there. I'm sure the bridge keeper will watch out for you till you get there. He *is* a government employee, after all. And you can see all the kids in the parking lot. So hurry and go on to school. Mom will pick you up this afternoon."

"Good-bye, Da . . ." Before she could finish, her dad turned and hurried toward home—phone glued to his ear. Tears filled her eyes, and a hard lump formed in her throat. Even though he got on her nerves, she wished he'd stayed with her a little longer. She didn't want him tagging along, yet she'd never gone very far by herself, and it was the first day at a new school. She rubbed her eyes and straightened her shoulders. *I just have to get across this old bridge. Don't look down. It's not so hard. I can do it.*

Ppeekk crossed the two sections of the bridge, her body rigid, her backpack clattering over the slats. As she passed by the bridge house, she saw someone sitting in there, but she couldn't tell whether it was a man or a woman. Whoever it was wore a heavy Army-type jacket and a poofy kind of cap pulled low over black eyes that followed Ppeekk. And something protruded from the person's mouth. Ppeekk averted her eyes, shuddered, and hurried along, catching a whiff of smoke and foul odor.

On the other side of the bridge house, she stopped and leaned over the railing to catch a parting glimpse at the water. She lifted her two long ponytails off her neck, hoping the breeze would cool her. She imagined the water's coolness on her skin and wished for the courage to go down those big stone steps and splash her face.

But she didn't dare. What if she were trespassing? What if she fell in that water? She closed her eyes and saw herself leaping down the boulders, as nimbly as a dancer, but she knew she didn't have the nerve. Why couldn't she have some of her father's confidence without all the nerdiness?

Splash! Splash! Her eyes popped open. Several fish leaped in and out of the water. Crabs scuttled over the rocks she had just imagined climbing. She caught a glimpse of a dark shadow moving slowly, as big as a school bus, under the water's surface.

How can an animal that large live in this narrow waterway? Must be just a shadow of a cloud passing overhead. She squinted to the sky. Expecting to see clouds, she broke out in a cold sweat when several squawking and wheeling pelicans and seagulls dive-bombed toward her. At the last moment, they veered and struck the surface of the water where the shadow glided. Her sweat turned cold. She didn't know a lot about sea animals, but she knew something strange was happening.

CHAPTER THREE

THE CIGAR CHOMPING
BRIDGE KEEPER

The window on the bridge house banged open. The keeper leaned out and glared at Ppeekk. "Hey, girl! Watch out! You gonna fall in and be snatched up by a gator." The voice scratched like sandpaper.

Ppeekk narrowed her eyes at the grizzled face beneath a tattered pink shower cap. Her dad was wrong. The bridge keeper looked more like a woman than a man.

"Ol' gator do swim this here waterway, missy." The old woman cackled at Ppeekk's alarm. "And he'd chomp your leg off quick as a wink." She grasped the hem of the grimy nightgown she wore under the jacket and wiped her hands. Ppeekk straightened and grabbed her backpack handle when the old woman walked onto the bridge, scowling under a heavy gray unibrow and chomping on an unlit cigar. *That lady, that thing, that whatever . . . scares me,* Ppeekk thought.

"Ol' Bridget sees things. Ol' Bridget knows things." The woman stepped closer and pointed toward the bank of the waterway. "See them mangrove trees? That's where little gators like to hide. And other things down in there, too. Bad things, missy."

Ppeekk wasn't sure if it was what the old lady said or if it was her raspy voice that spooked her. But she peered at the spot where the old woman pointed. Just as she was about to lean over the railing, a concrete truck rumbled across the bridge. Ppeekk jiggled as if she had springs in her shoes. The vibrations of the heavy truck on the rickety bridge shook both Ppeekk and the bridge keeper so much that the unlit cigar fell out of the old woman's mouth. But the woman just picked it up and bit down on it again without even dusting it off.

The truck traveled in the direction Ppeekk had come from. She'd seen a lot of cement trucks but never one with a little bearded man hanging on to the back with one hand and one foot, his other arm and leg dangling just above the ground. He was the most wrinkled adult she had ever seen, and he was even smaller than Ppeekk. She thought that if the Lucky Charms leprechaun had a grandfather, this little fellow would be him.

As the truck passed, the man looked directly at Ppeekk. He smiled at her with the biggest, happiest grin she'd ever seen. Then he tipped his hard hat toward her and winked, like he knew a special secret and dared her to guess it.

The bridge keeper shook her fist at the little man and growled, then she turned and glared at Ppeekk. Ppeekk grabbed her backpack and took off toward school.

CHAPTER FOUR

A GLITTERING
WREATH OF SMOKE

The next morning Ppeekk hurried out of the house, the torn screen door slamming shut behind her. Bent over the engine of the old Yugo, her dad didn't notice her sneaking by. It was the second day of school, and she hoped to walk on the path by the nature preserve, preferably without Dad tagging along.

Glancing over her shoulder, Ppeekk saw her mom take a plate of homemade doughnuts to her dad. Her parents were clearly discussing something, and when they both looked at her she knew what was coming. Dad rushed after her, holding a coffee cup in one hand and stuffing a powdered doughnut into his mouth with the other.

Darn it! At least she was halfway down the driveway and had a head start.

An early morning breeze brushed Ppeekk's face and arms as she scuffed along the sandy path in her new school shoes, liking the warmth but still hating the way it made her sweat. She noted a dozen shades of green in the trees, plants, and leaves. Even the shadows were green. The fog hovered over the nature preserve like a thin layer of white cotton candy under the blue sky. Another beautiful day.

"Things are starting to look a little better here," Ppeekk said to herself, pulling the moistening blouse from her body.

A tiny wave of happiness rippled through her as she meandered along the sandy path. Although some little kids had made fun of her, the first school day had been more interesting and less stressful than Ppeekk had feared. Maybe the beautiful shell she'd found on the path yesterday was lucky, like a talisman. She had felt protected by it somehow. Ppeekk sped up, eager to put as much distance as possible between herself and her father.

She scanned the ground, hoping to find another lucky shell. At first all she found were bits and pieces of broken shells and plain old rocks. Then it caught her eye. She bent down and uncovered another small but perfectly formed shell, this one a pale pink scallop shell. She sneaked a look behind her, checking to see what her dad was doing, then slipped it into her pocket. Yes, maybe this was going to be another special day after all.

Continuing down the path, she noticed a large sign propped on the side of the road: CAUTION. MEN AT WORK. Just beyond the sign, several trucks were parked along the street, including a concrete truck that looked like the one the strange little man had ridden yesterday. Then she saw wet gray ooze flowing down a metal chute sticking out of the back of the concrete truck. A small group of men wearing orange jumpsuits and wielding shovels and other tools pushed and smoothed the wet concrete over the very path she was walking on, her path, "Ppeekk's Path."

"Oh, no!" She barely whispered these words, but inside she screamed them. This was wrong. She'd hated having to move here, but at least she had found this beautiful, special path. Everywhere she'd ever lived someone had paved over places she'd loved. They changed meadows and green yards into parking lots, sidewalks, and tall buildings. In Indiana, the vacant lot where the kids had played softball was turned into a gas station.

And now they would concrete this path right beside a nature preserve across from her house? Shaking with anger, Ppeekk marched right up to the workers. "What are you doing here? Why are you doing this?"

Two men stopped working, leaned on their tool handles, wiped the sweat off their foreheads, and stared at the brown-haired, lanky girl who stood before them with balled fists on her hips. Her dark, almost black, eyes flashed. "Don't you know you're paving over a special place? This path is perfectly fine the way it is! And it's right beside a nature preserve."

"That's no nature preserve," a worker with dreadlocks said. "They can call it that if they want to, but it's just a piece of ol' south Florida swampland, good for nothin'."

The other worker shrugged and nodded.

"We're just doing our job," Dreadlocks continued.

"But there's no need to put concrete here. You're covering up beautiful shells." Ppeekk's eyes started to fill with tears.

"This concrete makes it easier for y'all to run when a hurricane comes," a man holding a shovel said.

Another worker pointed a stubby finger toward the swamp and grinned, revealing a gold tooth. "Yeah, and it helps y'all run away from them ghosts that live in the swamp. You heard about them swamp ghosts, them swamp spirits?"

"Sw . . . swamp sp . . . spirits?" The blood drained from her face, and the sprinkling of freckles stood in stark contrast to her paled nose and cheeks.

Ppeekk backed away and looked for her dad.

Gold Tooth began smoothing the cement. "I wouldn't live over here on this barrier island for nothin'."

"But . . . but look at those trees over there and all the plants. This place is unique, and you're ruining it!" Ppeekk choked back a sob.

Dreadlocks tilted his head toward the yellow concrete truck. "You want answers to your questions, girl, ask the boss man there."

Ppeekk turned and gasped when she saw the strange old dwarf from yesterday. He dangled from the back of the truck just as he had before. His eyes, a deeper blue than the sky, gazed steadily at her. He puffed on a pipe and blew perfect smoke rings that seemed to hang in the air. The smoke rings, at least a dozen of them, ranged in sizes from as small as a bottle cap to as large as a saucer.

For the first time ever, Ppeekk didn't know what to say. She was both fascinated and overwhelmed by this little man. As she stared at him, she felt funny, like a bunch of butterflies fluttered inside her stomach.

The sounds of the rumbling trucks and the chatter of the workmen faded when the little man spoke, smoke wisping with each word he chanted in a soft and soothing voice:

Waves of smoke

and fish that sing.

Silvery, shimmery,

glittery wings.

Step and dance within the ring.

Look to see

what dreaming brings.

Ppeekk's mouth dropped open. "Uh . . . Good morning . . . Um . . . What was it that you just said? I didn't quite get what you were saying."

The little dwarf man didn't answer. He just smiled sweetly and continued blowing smoke rings.

"Dad! Where are you, Dad?"

She was just about to ask the little old man what that worker had meant about swamp ghosts and spirits when her father showed up with the ever-present cell phone glued to his head, not watching where he was going and stumbling right into her. She grabbed her father's arm, partly to steady him, but also to reassure herself that he was there.

"Oh, there you are. Sorry to bump into you. Well, come on, come on. Don't want to be late," her dad said.

If he saw the little man, he didn't let on and probably didn't care.

Her father marched right on ahead of her, walking on the narrow patch of grass between the path and the street. Wet gray concrete completely covered the length of the path in front of them. Ppeekk stared longingly at the little piece of the path not yet paved over, sighed, and then followed her dad.

But she had to turn around and catch a glimpse of the little man one more time. As she did, the driver revved the engine of the concrete truck, threw it into gear, and started slowly pulling away. The dwarf man still hung on to the back. He blew a silver dollar–sized smoke ring toward her. But as it neared her, the ring grew first to the size of a dinner plate, and then of a steering wheel.

If that weren't enough, the extraordinary smoke ring sparkled like a giant wreath of diamonds. Ppeekk tugged at her father's arm, but he ignored her and kept shouting into the cell phone. She stared at the glittering smoke ring. It rotated like a wheel and grew larger as it moved toward her. She pinched her nose, sure the smoke was noxious. Even more than hot weather, she hated smoke.

But she didn't want to run away from this strange and beautiful ring. The smoke began to solidify, if that were possible, as it came closer, wafting like a cloud of dazzling diamond chips. Then the shining circle of smoke actually passed through her body and encircled her like a slowly revolving hula hoop. She felt as if she were swaying with the glittering mist, its movement slow and graceful. It was like the fog over the swamp but with tiny stars scattered in it.

A gust of wind picked up some loose sand and flung it at Ppeekk. She shut her eyes against it. When she opened them, the truck, the workers, and the little man, as well as the glittering wreath of smoke, had vanished. She turned in a full circle to see where they had gone, but with the exception of the drying cement, it was as if they had never been there.

Her foot kicked something. She looked down at a strange gnarled twig. *It looks like the handle at the end of one of those Irish shillelagh sticks we had over our fireplace in Indiana.* She picked it up and hefted it, finding it heavy like stone or petrified wood.

Ppeekk reached the end of the newly paved sidewalk where the bridge began. Her dad was waving and heading back toward home. She waved good-bye back, but she was out of sorts, as if she had just woken up from a dream.

She grasped the old twig and drew a sweeping circle in the wet cement, recalling the brilliance of the smoke ring. Inside the circle she carefully inscribed: P-P-E-E-K-K.

As she clutched the twig, a few clumps of wet concrete dropped off the end. *There, that will show them. This is my path.*

Ppeekk turned and hurried across the drawbridge. The bridge house was dark and quiet, and she couldn't see anything of the horrible bridge keeper woman, thank goodness.

Using the concrete-coated twig as a sort of walking stick, she thought about throwing it off the bridge into the water or onto the bank. Then as she passed the church, she had an idea. She dashed inside and into the ladies' room. At the sink, she scrubbed the twig with wet paper towels, but the concrete had set and wouldn't come off. The wetter it got and the harder she scrubbed, the lighter and brighter the stick became. In fact, it shone brightly.

She paused to study it. *It's just a hard old stick.* Ppeekk tossed it into the trash and switched off the light. But as she was halfway through the door, she looked back and a faint glow coming from the open trash can caught her eye. It looked like a flashlight had been turned on and dropped inside. She backed into the restroom and peered in the trash can.

The twig glowed with a silvery, glittery shine like nothing she'd ever seen before. Even the torn towels she'd scrubbed it with were aglow. The colors and shimmerings changed and shifted like a miniature light show. Ppeekk retrieved it using a handful of clean paper towels and wrapped it in another layer. Satisfied, she flushed the old towels down the toilet and placed the twig in her backpack.

As she left the ladies' room and headed toward the outside door, she thought about the glittery twig and the strange little man. Were they somehow connected? Didn't the poem he'd chanted have a line about something glittering? And something about a ring? Waves of smoke . . . fish that sing . . . She plopped down in the church hallway, pulled a notebook out of her backpack, and began to write what she could remember of the dwarf's chant. Questions tumbled in her mind like clothes in a dryer: Who was the little man? What does the poem mean? Why did the twig and the smoke ring glitter?

CHAPTER FIVE

THE GOOD LUCK CIRCLE

*L*eft. *Left. Left, right, left.* Ppeekk marched down the newly paved sidewalk. "Left. Left. Left, right, left."

Though it was still hot and she hadn't made any friends, she was glad to be walking to school alone. The blue sky hung above her like a swath of silk. The lush green trees and plants seemed to welcome her. Ppeekk raised her nose and sucked in air thick with the scent of flowers and the tangy salt smell of the sea. She was getting used to her new home, but every time she thought of her sandy path being paved, she huffed and groaned.

This morning she'd felt rebellious, mad about her path, so she'd made a large lime-colored water balloon and balanced it on top of her books in her backpack. She would throw it at any worker she saw messing with her path—or if she saw one of those kids from school who yelled at her or stuck out his tongue at her again, she was going to let him have it.

Or if Dad started hassling her, maybe she would toss it at him. She was determined to throw that balloon at someone or something.

Ppeekk rushed past the repaired Yugo and her father, who was loading vacuum cleaner parts and supplies into the little space behind the backseat he referred to as the trunk.

He yelled as he slid into the driver's seat and cranked the engine. "Ppeekk, where are you going?"

Without looking back, Ppeekk swatted at the air with her free hand as if shooing him away. "I don't need you today, Dad. Don't even bother."

She continued to walk, but he followed her in the car, driving slightly behind her, while also talking on the cell phone, of course.

Left. Left. Left, right, left. She stomped in cadence, her heels clicking on the new concrete. The wheels of her rolling backpack buzzed like a little machine as she lugged it over the hard sidewalk.

Now she would never find any more shells on her walk to school. They'd all been paved over, and her path had been destroyed.

Left. Left. Left, right, left. Waves of smoke and fish that sing.

That was how the little old man's poem had begun. No sign of him today. The trucks and the workers were gone. All that remained was some trash left behind by them, the stone twig sticking out of her backpack, and her memory of the smoke ring and the dwarf man and that strange poem he'd recited to her. She'd written it down, but she wasn't sure she'd remembered it right or even gotten the whole chant. It seemed almost like a riddle, like something she had to figure out. She needed to remember it. She just knew it had a secret meaning to it.

Ppeekk walked and thought, trying to remember. Perhaps it would come to her if she considered it piece by piece. The waves of smoke part, that was easy. That must be the smoke ring he blew at her, which had been amazing. Now that it was just a memory, it seemed almost like a dream. The smoke ring had been so large and so shiny and beautiful. It didn't even seem like smoke, but more like a misty cloud. But how could a fish sing?

Left. Left. Left, right, left. Silvery, shimmery, glittery wings.

This part was easy, too. You could see glittery wings in lots of places: dragonflies and hummingbirds, fairies and angels. They all had shiny wings. But what was the connection between these creatures and fish that sing and waves of smoke? Maybe the line referred to airplane wings. It all seemed like nonsense.

Her dad pulled up next to Ppeekk. He stuck his head out of the car window. "C'mon, now, and get into the car, Ppeekk honey. There's no need to walk to school."

"No, Dad, I want to walk. I have to walk."

Mr. Berry shook his head, settled back into his seat, and continued driving beside her.

Left. Left. Left, right, left. Step and dance within the ring.

Ppeekk thought of some of the games they played in school—circle games with balls and Ring Around the Rosy. Is that what the little man meant? She was too old for those kinds of games now.

Left. Left. Left, right, left. Waves of smoke and fish that sing. Silvery, glittery, shimmering wings. Step and dance within the ring. Look to see what dreaming brings.

"I got it!" Ppeekk said out loud as she snatched the three-ring binder out of her backpack, careful not to upset the water balloon. She scribbled the words as she walked.

When they turned the corner at the intersection, Dad and the Yugo ended up in the far lane, one lane away from Ppeekk. She approached the end of the paved walk and the beginning of the bridge. Here was where she might see some of her classmates riding to school in their parents' expensive cars.

Up ahead she spotted something shining on the sidewalk, like a light. At first she thought it was a mirage, one of those heat illusions she'd sometimes see on the street on really hot days. But it wasn't that hot yet. Could it be a reflection in a puddle from the sprinklers that ran every night?

Ppeekk stopped at the mirage or the light or whatever it was. Her jaw dropped, and she gasped. The place where she had drawn yesterday in the wet cement was now glowing and glittering. The circle with her name written inside it looked as if it had been sprinkled with tiny bits of gold and silver and diamonds and sparkling jewels, all set ablaze like a supernova.

Ppeekk dropped to her knees, unaware that she was scraping them on the concrete. She reached out both hands and touched the pavement with her fingertips. It was dry and rough, the texture of regular concrete, but it sparkled like rare treasure. Bits of shimmering lustrous pearl reflected the morning sunshine with pinks and purples and blues like the inside of that big shell she'd seen in her field guidebook. What was it called? Abalone? Mother of pearl?

When she turned her head slightly, the colors shifted. The silver flecks changed to gold, then to emerald, and then to sapphire. The sapphire changed to pink, which merged into purples and ruby reds. The whole circle seemed to be slowly spinning in a clockwise motion. But how could that be? This circle was drawn in cement. It felt solid under her hands. But in her eyes it became a swirling circle of rainbow colors, shining like gems, right there in the circle she'd drawn in the concrete! A hundred different dazzling hues shimmered and vibrated across its brilliant surface.

Waves of smoke and fish that sing. Silvery, glittery, shimmering wings. Step and dance within the ring. Look to see what dreaming brings. Was this circle she'd made with the strange twig the ring in the little man's chant? The sparkles in the circle *were* like those in the glittering wreath of smoke the dwarf had blown at her. They had to be connected.

She opened her backpack and removed the strange twig. The hardened concrete on its end glittered just as the circle in the pavement did.

When her dad saw her down on the ground, he pulled over and stopped the car. "What in the world are you doing now?"

Ppeekk jumped to her feet. "Dad, it's fantastic! Look at this! Look at all the glittering bits of shells or jewels or I don't know what in the concrete."

"It's just a sidewalk that's wet from the rain or something. I don't see anything."

Ppeekk retraced her steps several yards back, looking for more evidence of the glittering pavement. But there was none to be

found. The rest of the sidewalk was plain gray concrete.

"But, Dad, it only sparkles inside the circle I drew in the wet cement yesterday."

"If you say so. Listen, honey, here's the bridge and there's your school. Can you take it from here? I gotta go."

Ppeekk nodded, then crossed her arms over her chest and drummed her fingers on her elbows. She watched as he swiveled the little car around in a perfect three-point turn and puttered off in the opposite direction. Couldn't he at least have looked at the circle she'd drawn? She took the water balloon out of her backpack but fought back the urge to throw it at the retreating Yugo.

She turned back toward the circle. Ahead of her was the bridge and that horrible bridge keeper, but no other cars filled the intersection right then. She balanced the lime green water balloon in her hands, hefting its weight from hand to hand, listening to and feeling the water slosh.

Then for no good reason, Ppeekk hurled the water balloon into the circle. Strings of liquid light shot up in an explosion of multicolored sparks, like a miniature Fourth of July fireworks show.

Ppeekk nearly jumped into the oncoming traffic lane. Had anyone else seen what had just happened? Then the last lines of the old man's poem popped into her head: *Step and dance within the ring.* Did he mean this ring? How could he have known about it before she even drew it? Well, here was a ring and Ppeekk had always loved to dance.

She gingerly placed one foot into the circle. Holding her breath, she put her other foot inside. *I can't believe I'm doing this. If anyone sees me, they'll think I'm crazy.* She glanced around and saw no one. Letting out her breath, she did a quick electric slide step. Then she pounded her feet and scuffed her heels in the small puddle left by the burst balloon.

Finished with her short dance, Ppeekk stepped out of the circle. She felt good, really good. She glanced around and saw things she'd never noticed before—blue crabs scuttling in and out of their holes, a parade of snails, a small cloud of butterflies. She heard every seagull's cry, and even the leaves of the trees whispered to her. The world seemed altogether different, and she did, too.

Remembering she had to get to school, Ppeekk took one last look at the beautiful glowing circle before she continued down the concrete path and up one side of the old drawbridge over the Intracoastal Waterway. The sky had never seemed so richly blue, the clouds so purely white, or the water so inviting and such a deep emerald green.

In the middle of the bridge, she stopped just before she stepped on a very small, very flat, very dead fish. Yuck! Even though it was dried out, it was still a smelly, scaly fish.

But then curiosity got the best of her and she picked it up and examined it. Although the scales were dry and the body was thin, the eyes on either side of the fish's head were still shiny and clear, like the star fire glass she'd seen in a museum. And strangely, when sunlight hit the cracked fins, they glittered like the silver and gold of the circle.

Maybe it's not a fish at all. Maybe it's a piece of jewelry, an expensive piece of jewelry that fell off someone's necklace. Or maybe it's a big earring.

Ppeekk cupped it in her hand. Did the dwarf's riddle say something about a fish? *Waves of smoke and fish that sing.* As she recited the poem to herself, she thought she felt the fish tremble a little.

It must have been my hand twitching. She focused on the fish, staring hard. It happened again. Then the fish eye moved in its socket. Or maybe her own eyes blinked and she thought it was the fish.

She stared with wide-open eyes. This was no piece of jewelry at all; the fish eye had moved in its socket.

Ppeekk turned her back to the bridge house so nosy Bridget couldn't see what she was doing. As she continued watching, the pupil in the fish eye darted forward, backward, and then rolled around. Ppeekk's hand felt the tickle of each roll and movement.

These last mornings walking to school have been the strangest mornings of my life. So much has happened in such a short time— strange things. What's going to happen next? Maybe I should throw this fish back into the waterway. Maybe it's not dead after all.

She peered over the railing into the water rippling and flowing below. A school of fish rose to the surface directly below her. The water on their backs glistened in the sunlight. Two pelicans swooped in and perched on a sign attached to a wooden wall near the bank of the waterway that read HIGH VOLTAGE.

The fish and the pelicans seemed to stare at her, like they were waiting for her to do something. If this morning were not strange enough, the watery world seethed with life and energy and motion and beauty. Ppeekk sensed it was directed at her or maybe at what she held in her hand. She heard only the birds squawking, some cars in the distance, and the water lapping against the bank.

She looked down at the fish still cupped in her hand. Its eye peered at her. *The poem mentioned fish that sing, but this dried up fish certainly is not singing. Of course not; that would be impossible.*

Then the tiny crisp mouth of the little fish began to open. Ppeekk was trembling with anticipation. Looking Ppeekk right in the eye, the fish said very distinctly, "Good day, young lady."

CHAPTER SIX

KING OF HIGH VOLTAGE

Ppeekk dropped the fish and jumped back, swiping her hands on her jumper. Her mouth went dry as sand. She glanced around. It must have been the wooden masts of the boats tied up at the marina creaking in the wind or the old bridge groaning under the weight of the passing cars. After all, this was an old, dried-up, dead fish, and everybody knows fish don't talk. She chuckled and straightened her shoulders.

Still, she *had* heard something. Ppeekk eyed the fish while edging toward it, inching along until she stood directly above it. *Hmmm.* Instead of the usual dull color, the fish shimmered a little. Ppeekk eyes widened. It was kind of like the sparkles in the magic circle.

She bent over to observe it and then crouched down, studying it. She poked it with her finger. Its scales were dry and brittle, even a bit dusty. But underneath the scales and dust gleamed a patina of gold. Even the tiny cracked and broken fins glistened in the sunlight.

It *had* to be some kind of light metal, a piece of jewelry. Maybe someone lost it and was offering a reward. When she brushed it with her fingertips, the sharp, crystal-like eye darted and gazed at her.

Fear grabbed Ppeekk's heart, and she would have collapsed with fright if the crispy little fish hadn't spoken again.

"Please, don't be afraid. I won't harm you. I'm in desperate need of your most urgent assistance." Its voice sounded kind and gentle and proper. It reminded Ppeekk of the voice Mom and Dad used when she was ill. Or like the one Grandpa used to say good night when he tucked her in bed when Ppeekk spent the night, only without the regal accent of the fish.

Ppeekk's compassion overcame her fear, and she picked up the fish as if it were something rare and fragile. It weighed next to nothing and felt dry and light in her cupped hands. But she held it at arm's length, far from her face. Just in case. It was still close enough for her to hear the little fish give a sigh of relief. "Aaah, thank you."

Ppeekk cocked an eyebrow. "You're a fish, and a talking one at that!"

"Well, isn't that quite obvious?"

"But . . . but fish can't talk."

The fish squirmed in the hollow of Ppeekk's hand. "As represented by whom?"

Ppeekk brought him closer. "Everybody knows that fish can't talk."

"Everybody? Who is everybody? In my humble opinion, everybody does not exist. Everybody is nobody."

Ppeekk didn't know how to respond to that.

The fish stared at her. "You can hear me, can't you? Only certain special creatures are able to hear and understand others not of their own kind. And you, my dear, are one of the very most special of all."

Her eyes widened. "I am?"

"Indeed, you are. But where are my manners? Allow me to introduce myself. My name is Frederick, Frederick the Ninth, King of High Voltage."

A smile tugged at the edges of Ppeekk's mouth when she gave a short curtsy. "Pleased to meet you, your Highness."

"No need for such formalities, my dear."

"What could be more formal than Frederick the Ninth, King of High Voltage? That's a mouthful. I'm going to call you Fred, just plain Fred."

His eye drooped. "Well, considering I don't have long for this world, I don't suppose it really matters."

"You mean you're dying?"

"I'm afraid so. Didn't I look like a dead fish to you when you first saw me on the bridge, like one of those that wash up on your shore, or get discarded by the fisherman on the bridge?"

She nodded. "I guess so. Well, yes, Fred, you really did look dead. Hey, that rhymes. Maybe I'll call you Dead Fred. Are you okay with that?"

"Under the circumstances, the name seems highly appropriate. And although not quite along the lines of the names of my ancient ancestors, coming from you, it sounds applicable to my resigned situation."

Ppeekk grinned and considered pinching her arm to make sure she wasn't dreaming. Without a doubt, this was the strangest *and* most delightful thing that had ever happened to her. "Then Dead Fred it is!"

"And how shall I address you, young lady?"

"Oh, excuse me. My name is Ppeekk Rose Berry," she said in

her most polite voice. "Pronounced Peekie but spelled double *p*, double *e, double k.*"

"How odd."

"It's a nickname from when I was little. You know, the peek-a-boo game? People hide their faces behind their hands and . . ."

"Not quite possible for us fish, you understand." He wiggled his weakened fins. "No hands."

Ppeekk giggled. "Of course. Anyway, when I was little I used to hide under the covers and just my eyes could be seen. Mom and Dad called me Peeker. When I got older I changed the spelling, and now I've evolved into Ppeekk."

"Why the odd spelling?"

She shrugged. "I just like to be different, unique. Like you, for instance. After all, what could be more unique than a dead fish who talks and claims to be a king?"

"Some people would call your kind of uniqueness by other terms. Weird, for example. But I admire your individuality. And I have to admit that I do think it's rather clever of you—coming up with both your name and my new one."

"You really think so?"

"Without a doubt. The name Dead Fred has a kind of simple rhyme scheme that is appealing on a certain childish level, however moribund. And yours, with all those double consonants, well, it's like something from Eastern Europe or Russia. I once knew a Bulgarian fish that had absolutely no vowels in his name. It drove the authorities mad, just as I suppose your name must frustrate your teachers. Very clever, I say."

"Thank you . . . I think."

"Yes, and my new name—Dead Fred—is quite liberating, too."

"What do you mean?"

"The rulers of High Voltage have been named Frederick for as long as the oldest sea turtle can remember. And that's a long time indeed. What freedom to create a new name!"

The fish sighed again and his eye froze in place, no longer darting around. Ppeekk wondered whether he had finally actually died. "Fred? Dead Fred? Are you still with me?"

The crystalline eye moved, and the corners of the little mouth quivered. "Quite so. Just tired. So terribly tired. I don't belong out here. I don't belong above the surface. It is much too hard for me to live outside."

She placed a hand on her hip. "Where *do* you belong?"

"In the kingdom of High Voltage, in my home and on the throne as ruler. If I am not soon restored to High Voltage, what's left of me shall perish and my creatures and the entire kingdom as well. Without me, High Voltage will cease to exist, and this will leave the starfish and the manatees, the clown fish and the flying fish, and all the other wonderful creatures without a home. If I do not return, High Voltage will be overtaken and destroyed by the fiendish Megalodon and his unrelenting quest for the true and everlasting prize he covets beyond all imagination."

Ppeekk frowned. "But where is this High Voltage? What is a Mega . . . Mega . . . Megalodon?"

"Slow down, young lady. One question at a time. You're standing over High Voltage now."

Ppeekk looked down at the wooden slats.

"No, not the bridge—in the water *below* the bridge. See that wooden rail and the sign attached to it, just above the water? What does it say?"

Still holding the fish in her right hand, Ppeekk clutched the railing with her left hand and leaned out to read the sign protruding from the waterway. Sure enough, the painted letters of the sign spelled out HIGH VOLTAGE. She stretched out her arm and flattened her hand so Dead Fred could slide down into the water.

"AhhEEEEEeeeeee. Don't drop me!"

Ppeekk jerked her hands and arms back toward her body. "For such a little guy, you sure can let out a high-pitched scream. What's the matter, Dead Fred? Don't fish love water? You just said you wanted to go back."

"Yes, but not like that. And not now."

"I'm sorry, Dead Fred. I was just trying to do what I thought you wanted. I wouldn't do anything to hurt you."

"Thank you, my dear. I do trust you. Today you have saved me from an uncertain fate, and for that I shall be eternally grateful. But to put me back into the water at this precise moment would be sure death." He shuddered. "The vicious bloodred remora fish are prowling about High Voltage even as we speak, sent by the evil Megalodon, a beast we've never seen the likes of before.

"I have formulated a plan of attack, but in my current condition I am unable to follow through with it. What I propose is to—"

"Hey, girl," the bridge keeper snapped as she stepped out of the bridge house and stood with her hands on her hips, glaring at Ppeekk.

Ppeekk lowered her voice. "Uh-oh, we're being watched."

"You! Get a move on off this bridge."

Ppeekk bent her head toward the fish. "Hold on, Dead Fred. I'm taking you with me."

She curled the fingers of her right hand gently around her new friend. With her left hand, she grasped her backpack and lunchbox and dashed across the bridge.

The bridge keeper, chewing on a fat and soggy cigar like a cow chewing grass, glared at Ppeekk as she clattered past.

Out of the corner of her eye, Ppeekk glimpsed the old woman's motor-oil stained clothes and mud-caked boots. Like twisted metal wires, her hair stuck out from under a filthy shower cap, and her stubby fingers were stained brown with tobacco juice. Ppeekk's nose picked up a foul-smelling odor coming from inside the hut.

Once Ppeekk cleared the bridge and reached the marina, she released a sigh of relief. "That was close, Dead Fred."

Crrreeaaakk! Ppeekk jumped and twirled around. Two sections of the drawbridge groaned as they separated and rose into the air, looming like tall wooden walls. The old bridge keeper worked the controls, shouting to people in a sailboat passing through the now open waterway.

Ppeekk stopped in the shade and opened her fingers. Her fish friend seemed to be okay, but it was hard to tell. "I have to go to school, Dead Fred. Do you want to stay in my backpack?"

"I've heard of your schools of humans—loud and busy and full of commotion. Not like our schools of fish at all. No, no. Your school won't do for me. I need someplace cool and quiet, where I can conserve my energy and ponder my return as ruler of High Voltage."

Ppeekk twisted a curl of her hair around a slender finger. "Good thinking. Besides, somebody might find you. Some kids poke around in other kids' backpacks. But I don't know where else you can go."

Ppeekk figured it would look weird to anyone passing by to see her talking out of the side of her mouth into her palm. In fact, she was talking to her hand. But if people noticed, they would think she was crazy. That was fine with her. She cupped her hand around Fred and moved across the parking lot toward the church.

While Ppeekk pondered safe hiding places for Dead Fred, someone called her name. She didn't think anyone knew her. Turning, she saw the little girl who lived in the house beside theirs jump out of a car and run across the parking lot toward her.

It was the kid they called Mini Romey, the loudest kid Ppeekk had ever met. The other kids sometimes called her "The Mouth of the South." At home, Ppeekk often heard her squawking over the wooden fence their houses shared. Ppeekk wanted to get away from her, so she dashed toward the church. Thankfully, it was open. But where to hide Dead Fred?

Ppeekk blinked several times to adjust to the darkness. At first she couldn't make out many details besides a few flickering candles and the stained glass windows. As her eyes grew more accustomed, the rows of wooden pews and the altar seemed to materialize. The wooden beams of the high ceiling extended up to a central point. Not a good hiding place—it was all too exposed and too public.

Ppeekk ran down a long narrow hallway past many tall, dark-stained wooden doors with elaborate carvings and brass knobs. Each one she tried was locked. At the end of the passageway, she found the very last door ajar. A small plain door, it opened into a small plain room, very dim, with only one shaded and heavily draped window.

Ppeekk flipped the light switch, lighting one meager bulb. It was the usher's coatroom. A few faded upholstered chairs filled the dingy, musty area. A few oversized wool sweaters and a dozen or so faded maroon sports jackets with name tags hung on a metal coatrack along one wall. They all reeked like dogs that needed a bath. Nobody ever came in here except a few smelly old men.

Then Ppeekk heard Mini Romey calling her name inside the church. That kid had followed her. Now what could she do? She spotted another door in the room. She jerked it open and found a half bathroom with a tiny sink and a rusty old toilet. Behind the toilet, not twelve inches tall, was a little door in the wall. Ppeekk kneeled down and opened it. Behind it were the plumbing pipes and an empty space about the size of a shoebox. Thinking quickly, she spoke to Dead Fred. "You'll be safe in here."

She flattened out a used matchbook on the floor and placed the little fish on it. She brought her arms to her sides and sat back on the floor.

Whack! Ppeekk's heart flip-flopped. Someone had opened the coatroom door. She brushed her finger along Dead Fred's fin, closed the wall space door, jumped up, and ran out.

Mini Romey was waiting in the coatroom. She brushed her dark hair off her forehead and narrowed her eyes. "What are you doing in here?"

CHAPTER SEVEN

BRILLIANT AND ANNOYING NEW FRIENDS

Looking over her shoulder to be sure no audible response from Dead Fred floated toward them, Ppeekk could barely control her annoyance and alarm. This loud, nosy kid was the last thing she needed. She could ruin everything if she started poking around. "None of your business," Ppeekk said.

Mini Romney dug her pudgy hands into her hips. "You're not supposed to be in here. I'm telling on you."

Ppeekk's dark eyes flashed. "Then you're not supposed to be, either, so I guess we'll both be in trouble."

Mini Romney grabbed her backpack and waddled toward the door. "Well, I won't tell, but we'd better go on to school."

Ppeekk closed the washroom door and hoped leaving Dead Fred there was the right thing to do. She moved toward the outer door. Stopping in her tracks, she glanced back. Was noise coming from in there? It almost sounded like someone was practicing the musical scale. Worry rippled up her spine. Oh, no, it was Dead Fred. Singing.

The lyrics floated from his hiding place. "Don't worry about me, Ppeekk. I'll be fine. I'm just going to keep my singing voice in tip-top shape. La, la, la, la, la, la, la."

Then he launched into an official-sounding song, sort of like a national anthem. Ppeekk could make out only a few lines, but she distinctly heard him singing a very solemn tune:

> O BEAUTIFUL FOR SPARKLING SHELLS,
> FOR CORAL REEFS WITH PEARLS,
> FOR SEA TURTLES AND MANATEES
> ABOVE THE WHITE SAND FLOOR!
>
> HIGH VOLTAGE, O, HIGH VOLTAGE,
> THE SUN SHINES DOWN ON THEE.
> AND SHIELD THY SCALES FROM HOWLING GALES,
> FROM BANK TO GRASSY BANK.

O, INTRACOASTAL WATERWAY,
LONG LIVE THY RIPPLING SWELL,
THE CREATURES OF HIGH VOLTAGE
WILL HERE FOREVER DWELL.

HIGH VOLTAGE, O, HIGH VOLTAGE,
THE SUN SHINES DOWN ON THEE.
AND BATHE THY FISH WITH HAPPINESS
FROM BANK TO GRASSY BANK.

Ppeekk didn't know whether to laugh or cry. It was funny to hear this coming from the little fish, but could Mini Romey hear him, too? If so, keeping him a secret would be impossible.

Ppeekk looked at the girl, who just stood there watching her intently. "Do you hear that, Mini Romey?"

Mini Romey grasped the doorknob. "Hear what? All I hear are the horns honking outside and the organ playing church music."

What a relief! But this kid was trouble; that was for sure. Ppeekk noticed the girl's black eyes sparkling with mischief beneath her straight, bowl-cut hair. The oversized school jumper she wore dwarfed her, making her appear even smaller.

Ppeekk breathed a sigh of relief and flicked off the light. "Well, let's go then."

Mini Romey lugged her backpack out of the coatroom into the main part of the church while Ppeekk wheeled hers along and then eased the heavy coatroom door behind her closed.

She stopped for a moment. Everything was happening so quickly and now she had to deal with this little kid. She didn't want to leave Dead Fred, but she had to go to school. Had she left him in a safe enough place? Would he really be all right there in that dark space behind the wall? What if one of the ushers came in to grab a coat and heard him? At least he had finally quieted down. She couldn't hear him singing anymore.

Mini Romey locked eyes with her. "Earth to Ppeekk. Earth to Ppeekk. Come in, Ppeekk."

"What? You know, you're as annoying as a mosquito. Don't you ever stop buzzing around?"

"No, I buzz, buzz, buzz all day." She skipped along the carpeted church hallway. "And sometimes I hop and dance and jump and twirl."

"Hey, Mini Romey, remember you're in church. Keep your voice down."

Mini Romey ignored her and continued her skipping and hopping.

Ppeekk rolled her eyes. "Oh, brother."

They pushed through the church doors and into the bright

morning sunshine. Streams of children and parents struggled out of cars, unloading backpacks, spilling lunchboxes, and meandering toward the school.

The little girl tugged on Ppeekk's blouse. "Come on, Ppeekk, we're going to be late."

Ppeekk cocked her head. "How do you know my name?"

Mini Romey smiled, showing a gap between her two large front teeth. "Everybody knows everybody at St. Vincent's. You know mine, don't you? We're next-door neighbors. And besides, my brother Quatro is in eighth grade, just like you."

"What grade are you in?"

Mini Romey's eyes twinkled. "Guess."

"Second?"

"You think I'm a baby second-grader? No way." She jutted out her chubby chin. "I'm in third grade."

"Why does everyone call you by two names?"

"I'm named after my mom. She's Romey. But because I'm little, they call me Mini Romey. Get it?"

"Yeah, I get it. But what about your brother's name?"

"You can ask him yourself." She waved at a boy while bouncing on the balls of her feet. "There he is, crossing the parking lot. Hey, Quatro! Over here! I've met the new girl, and she's got a secret in the usher's coatroom!"

Parents and children turned to look at Ppeekk and Mini Romey. Some of the students stared and some of the adults smiled, but just as quickly they went back to their own conversations and business.

Ppeekk clenched her teeth and turned abruptly, bending over until her face was level with the little girl's. "Mini Romey, can't you keep quiet? Besides, I'm *not* hiding anything."

Ppeekk's face flushed with embarrassment, annoyance, and a bit of fear. This kid was impossible, maybe even a menace to Dead Fred's well-being. She was going to give everything away. Now somebody, or everybody, was going to know about him. What if he was found out? What if the janitor discovered him and flushed him down the toilet? Ppeekk didn't know what she was going to do.

"Pipe down, Mini Romey." Quatro adjusted his thick glasses as he approached the two girls. "It's not polite to shout like that."

The little girl flipped her palms upward. "But, Quatro, it's true. This is Ppeekk, and she's got a secret in the church."

The boy pushed his glasses up the bridge of his nose and peered at Ppeekk through sea green eyes. "Sorry about my sister."

Ppeekk checked out Mini Romey's brother, Quatro. Where his little sister was round and disheveled, he was long and slim, with spiky black hair and impeccably dressed in a snowy white shirt and neatly creased khakis. His too-long navy clip-on tie was spotless and held in place by a gold tie tack embossed with the St. Vincent insignia. He carried an armload of books, had a guitar slung over one shoulder, and two wooden drumsticks peeked out of his loaded backpack. A musician. Ppeekk smiled approval. She played the piano and sang.

Now the parking lot was almost deserted. If they didn't hurry, they'd be late for flag salute and counted tardy.

Mini Romey skipped ahead of the two older children. "Ppeekk's got a secret, Ppeekk's got a secret."

"Is your sister always like this?"

He smiled at her, displaying a perfect row of teeth. "You mean this annoying? I'm afraid so. The only way to shut her up is to give her what she wants. And ice cream at 7:55 a.m. is out of the question."

Ppeekk sighed. She was going to have to think about this. If she didn't tell Mini Romey *something,* everything might be given away. So she had to reveal at least *part* of the story about the fish on the bridge. And if she told Mini Romey, she would have to tell Quatro, too.

She looked over at Quatro's clear plastic pocket protector holding three identical silver pens and three perfectly sharpened yellow pencils. He seemed smart. No, he seemed more than smart—*intelligent*. In the first days of school, he was already keeping his head in a book and knew all the answers the teachers asked in every single subject. He was definitely one of the top students in her class.

So maybe it wasn't such a bad idea to at least tell Quatro and Mini Romey a little bit about Fred. After all, she didn't know exactly what she was going to do next. Maybe they could help her in some way. With no friends here in this new school and town, she had nobody to confide in. Mom and Dad were too busy with work and their own problems.

Besides, her parents and all the grown-ups she knew would never believe in a talking fish and an underwater world called High Voltage that was filled with beautiful creatures and threatened by evil forces. Adults just didn't think that way. Ppeekk figured Mini Romey would believe her for sure. But could she keep quiet about Dead Fred? Or would she tell the whole world? And Quatro? What would he think?

Mini Romey continued her skipping, clearly without a care in the world, but it was an awkward moment for the two older children. Neither of them knew what to say next. Mini Romey solved that problem for them. "Why are you called Ppeekk? I told you about my name."

Ppeekk told Quatro and Mini Romey the quick version of how she got her nickname. Ppeekk looked at Quatro out of the corner of her eye. "Okay, now it's your turn to tell me how you got your name."

He flashed that perfect smile again, and Ppeekk hoped hers would be like that when she got her braces off.

"When I was a very young child, even before I went to pre-school or kindergarten, the Spanish language fascinated me. I taught myself to speak and read it as I learned English."

Ppeekk relaxed for the first time since she'd put Dead Fred in the coatroom. This Quatro guy was a genius.

Mini Romey interrupted. "Yeah, you know that fence in between our houses? Mom says Quatro kept counting the slats in the fence and saying the numbers in Spanish over and over. *Uno, dos, tres, quatro. Uno, dos, tres, quatro.*"

He frowned at his sister. "So . . . Mother started calling me Quatro, and it just stuck."

Mini Romey twirled. "We saw you this morning, walking on the sidewalk as we were driving to school. Doesn't your mom or dad take you in a car?"

Ppeekk lowered her eyes. "No, I've been walking."

"Walking? Why? Don't you get hot and tired and sweaty?"

Ppeekk couldn't believe how many questions the kid asked. Is this what it was like to have a little sister? All these years Ppeekk had wished for a little sister and now that she had gotten a small taste of it, she wasn't so sure it was such a good idea.

As if Quatro had read her thoughts, he said, "Now you see what it's like to have a younger sibling."

Mini Romey grabbed her brother's arm. "What's a sibling?"

"A sibling means a brother or a sister."

"Oh." The little girl switched her gaze to Ppeekk. "Do you have any siblings?"

"Not yet. Maybe someday."

The corners of Quatro's mouth twitched. "She's lucky she doesn't have to put up with a pesky little sister."

Mini Romey stuck out her tongue. "But she's more lucky she doesn't have a bossy older brother like you."

They arrived at the school porch just in time to hear the bell ringing. As they passed through the double doors, Ppeekk decided to take a risk. "You could walk with me tomorrow morning if you want. To school, I mean."

Mini Romey jumped up and down and threw her arms around Ppeekk's waist so suddenly she almost knocked the older girl off her feet. "Yes, yes, yes! Yes, because we all three of us have funny names. And you'll tell me all your secrets, especially the one about that coatroom in the church, and be my special friend, won't you, Ppeekk? I know you will."

Ppeekk smiled in spite of herself. The girl did have a sort of innocent charm.

"Well, you can walk with me to school, Mini Romey, but you've got to stop saying I've got a secret in the coatroom."

Quatro cleared his throat. "We'll have to ask our parents. If they agree, we would be glad to accompany you on this perambulation to school."

Mini Romey knitted her thick brows. "Quatro, stop using big words I don't understand. It's not polite."

Quatro and Ppeekk looked at each other and smiled. Ppeekk didn't feel so self-conscious about her braces in front of Mini Romey and Quatro.

Mini Romey dashed down the hallway to her classroom and called back over her shoulder. "We'll meet you at the bottom of our driveway. By the rusty gate under the big strangler fig tree."

Ppeekk and Quatro slipped into their classroom and took their seats as the teacher called roll. Quatro opened his math book and notebook and immediately started scribbling. Ppeekk also opened her book, but after everything that had happened that morning, she couldn't focus. She was supposed to be copying the new vocabulary words and the definitions Mrs. Kelly had written on the board. But it was next to impossible to concentrate.

Ppeekk doodled oval shapes with little fins, eyes, and round smiling mouths. It was Dead Fred, of course. She couldn't take her mind off of him. She sketched him over and over on her lined paper as her mind whirled with thoughts and questions: Did the encounter with Dead Fred really happen? If she wasn't dreaming, what was she going to do about him? Who would she tell? Was he okay in the coatroom? Would he still be there when she checked on him next? When would that be? What shape would he be in? After all, he was a fish out of water. And her new friends, if they were friends, would they help or hinder her attempts to save Fred? How was she ever going to get through this day?

PE was the last period of the day, and when Ppeekk made her way back inside, the principal, Sister Mary Clare, was talking to Mrs. Kelly.

The principal adjusted her glasses over an ample nose. "Mrs. Kelly, it is traditional for the school attendance monitor to be an eighth-grader. Do you have a candidate?"

Mrs. Kelly's heart-shaped mouth formed a smile. "Yes, I think I do." Her warm eyes held Ppeekk's. "Ppeekk, would you come forward, please?"

Ppeekk thought about how the whole class would gape at her long, skinny legs or notice the sprinkle of freckles across her nose and cheeks—even more pronounced with the Florida sun. She stood and made her way to the front.

Mrs. Kelly laid her hand on Ppeekk's shoulder. "I thought it might give you an opportunity to become familiar with your new school if you were our attendance monitor. All it would mean is gathering the attendance slips and taking them to the main office. Are you interested?"

Ppeekk forgot about her braces, her freckles, and her long legs. She felt her smile all the way down to her toes. "I would like that very much, Mrs. Kelly."

Before it was time to go home, Ppeekk was excused from class to go around the campus gathering the slips. When she went outside to the kindergarten building, she passed near the church where Dead Fred was hidden. Could she slip in there quickly and check on Fred? Would she get caught? She could always say she went in to say a quick prayer, which she *would* do anyway. Maybe she could pray for Dead Fred and High Voltage. She might even get him back and take him home with her. All she'd have to do is cross the parking lot, dash into the church, then into the coatroom, and grab him.

Ppeekk glanced left and right and then behind her. She studied the classroom windows. No one was in sight. Without thinking, she started across the parking lot. Thank goodness the church was unlocked. She slipped inside the main sanctuary, then on to the coatroom, and into the washroom. As she flung open the small plumbing access door, a melodic verse of Fred's anthem greeted her:

> O BEAUTIFUL FOR SPARKLING SHELLS
> FOR CORAL REEFS WITH PEARLS . . .

Ppeekk scooped up the fish. "Come on, Dead Fred, you're going home with me!"

Chapter Eight

The Strangler Fig Battle

Ppeekk woke, her nostrils flaring to the faint smell of fish. It wasn't a strong odor, but it was unmistakably fishy. She glanced at the alarm clock on her bedside table: 6:03 AM, time for her usual pancakes and bacon—not fish. Still half asleep, she turned her head, cracked open one lid, and stared directly into the eye of a small fish lying right on her pillow.

Whoa! How did a little fish get onto her pillow? Maybe she was still asleep. But the fish stared at her, too. Then it all came rushing back to her—finding him on the bridge, hiding him in the usher's coatroom in the church, and finally stashing him in her backpack and hurrying home with him.

She'd placed him in between her pillow and the pillowcase, right at the edge so he could have a bit of air, as if that made any sense. Somehow he'd wiggled out. Now propped up on his two long side fins, he looked sort of like someone leaning on his elbows. He smiled from gill to gill. "Rise and shine."

It was true, then. It wasn't a dream. He really was a talking fish.

Ppeekk yawned and stretched. "Good morning, Dead Fred. For a small, crispy fish, you sure do smell funny."

"Well, excuse me. I didn't know my aromatic appeal was of such concern to you."

Ppeekk bit her lip. "Oh, sorry."

"I could have commented on your distinctive human aroma, but I have tactfully refrained from doing so."

Irritation gnawed at Ppeekk. "Well, it seems to me you ought to be a little nicer. If it wasn't for me, you'd still be lying out there even more dried-up on the bridge, or worse yet, a seagull could have plucked you up and swallowed you whole."

"True enough. But all manifestations have their purpose."

Ppeekk poked his fin. "What's that supposed to mean?"

"Hadn't you better be preparing for your school of humans?"

"It's just plain old school, not school of humans. And, yes, I should be. But here I am talking to you."

"And a most delightful conversation it is," Dead Fred said sarcastically.

Ppeekk threw back the covers. "Oh, you're impossible, and you're making me late." She reached for Dead Fred. "I'm going to put you in my backpack while I dress."

"As you wish." He sighed and closed his eyes while Ppeekk deposited his stiff little body gently into the front inner pouch of her backpack.

"By the way, what would you like for breakfast?"

He mumbled something that Ppeekk couldn't quite understand. So she reached in and scooped him back out. "What did you say?"

"I said I'm not eating much nowadays. Not since Megalodon began his attacks on High Voltage. Just thinking about all those evil creatures carrying out his cruel deeds and those hideous bloodred remora fish trying to destroy my beautiful kingdom makes me ill."

Ppeekk returned him to the pouch. "You can tell me about it on the way to school."

Then she remembered she was walking to school today with those two kids who lived next door, Mini Romey and Quatro. Well, she'd just take it one thing at a time.

She dashed downstairs to the kitchen. Her mom set the usual large plate of pancakes and bacon on the table in front of Ppeekk.

She noticed that the food on her dad's plate was half-eaten; pacing outside on the deck among strewn vacuum cleaner parts, he babbled on the cell phone. Ppeekk took one bite of everything on her plate, kissed her mom, swallowed her vitamins, grabbed her lunchbox, and ran out the door, hoping to leave her father far behind.

She tried to be as quiet as she could, so her dad wouldn't notice. But there he was, getting into the old Yugo. Maybe she could lose him on the path. She careened down the driveway, dragging her backpack through the crushed shells and sand. She could see Mini Romey and Quatro at the bottom, standing right where they said they'd be, beside the rusty gate and under that huge weird-looking old tree with the weirder name.

A strangler fig tree, they'd called it. She called it completely bizarre. It had dozens of long, thick vinelike roots hanging down from its branches like the tentacles of some gigantic sea beast. They sure didn't have trees like this in Indiana.

As Ppeekk approached, she saw Mini Romey climbing one of the dangling roots. It was as thick and fibrous as a rope, and Mini Romey scaled it hand over hand as easily as a monkey. For all her solid plumpness, the girl was strong and agile and evidently fearless.

After shimmying halfway up, Mini Romey called down to Ppeekk. "Hey, look at me. I'm in the circus. I'm an acrobat."

She extended one arm dramatically and then used her weight to make the root sway like a swing, pumping with her legs and torso. The little girl swung slowly back and forth across the driveway above her brother and Ppeekk.

Ppeekk turned to Quatro. "Why do they call this a strangler fig?"

He touched the tree's rough gray bark, mottled moss green in places. "See these parts that look like thin trunks? They started off as roots like the one Mini Romey's on." He pointed a long, slender finger. "And see that other tree inside? Either a bird drops a strangler seed on the branch of another tree—say a palm tree— or the wind blows a seed onto a branch. The seed sprouts and sends down aerial roots that surround the palm. Those roots attach themselves to the ground and become the trunk of the strangler. Then it grows so big it smothers the palm tree inside."

Ppeekk stared at the fully enveloped, dying palm tree, shuddering at the thought of its slow death. When she stepped away from the strangler trunk, one of the dangling roots brushed against her hair and slapped at her back. She looked at Quatro. "Did you whip at me with one of those roots?"

Quatro straightened his clip-on tie and shook his head. "No."

Ppeekk suddenly felt uneasy, as if the dangling roots around them had come alive and the roots were hands that might strangle them, too. Even the notched and shadowed crannies on the rough surface of the trunk resembled a long, thin face.

Mini Romey kept pumping, getting the ropelike vine to swing in a wider arc. The branches of the strangler fig trembled and creaked, as if the tree were groaning.

Quatro cupped his hands around his mouth. "Okay, Mini Romey. Come on down."

Mini Romey swung even harder. "Wheee! This is so much fun."

Quatro tried to grab the root, but it seemed to recoil and move away from him. "Come on, Mini Romey, we've got to go to school."

The little girl's face blanched white and terror filled her eyes. "Quatro, I'm trying to stop, but it's swinging too fast. Like it's out of control!"

Quatro leaped and jumped, trying to catch hold of Mini Romey, but the root whipped out of his grasp, lashing out at him and cutting his face and hands. "It's got a mind of its own!" The delicate end of the root curled and uncurled as if it were a snake.

Mini Romey hung on for dear life, shrieking the whole time. The louder she screamed, the more violently the root whipped her about. The end of the root rose up and wound itself around one of Mini Romey's legs.

Terror gripped Ppeekk. The root now alternated between spinning like a whirling dervish and cracking like a whip. How was

Mini Romey going to get down? Without warning, all the aerial roots, dozens of them, twirled and snapped like the tentacles of an octopus. They reached out for Quatro and her, too.

Just as Ppeekk was about to help Quatro, two of the roots suddenly changed direction, thrashing about and lashing at her, knocking her down. One root grabbed her backpack with Dead Fred in it right out of her hands. Then the other root wrapped itself around the handle of the backpack and yanked it up toward the branches of the tree.

Ppeekk hung on to her backpack, fighting the pull of the vine root. "Help me, Quatro!"

She and Quatro pulled on the backpack in a tug of war with the root. Quatro took off one of his shoes and hammered the root where it had attached itself to the backpack handle. He pounded until his face turned fiery red and the root lost strength and let go. Ppeekk clutched her backpack to her chest while she and Quatro ran away from the tree.

But Mini Romey continued to swing wildly.

Ppeekk sandwiched her face between her hands. "What are we going to do?"

"Okay, tree, you asked for it." Mini Romey bit down on the root with her two strong front teeth. The root immediately slackened and unwound itself from her legs. She slid down and ran to Quatro and Ppeekk.

Quatro looked at Mini Romey and Ppeekk. "Is everybody all right?"

Mini Romey extended her reddened palms. "Rope burn."

Ppeekk rubbed her sore hands. "Yeah . . . I guess so." She pointed her finger at his cheek. "But, Quatro, your face is cut."

He dabbed at his cheeks with his freshly ironed white handkerchief.

Mini Romey blew on her hands, trying to cool them. "It was like those strangler fig roots were attacking us on purpose."

Quatro folded his handkerchief. "Yes. And it seemed like one of them was trying to get Ppeekk's backpack. Like they were trying to take it away."

Ppeekk hugged her backpack even closer and hoped and prayed that Dead Fred had survived.

Her dad pulled up behind them. "Are you kids okay?"

Ppeekk waded through the weeds and grass at the side of the driveway to get farther away from the tree. "Yes, Dad, we're fine." She assumed her father had not seen a thing and certainly wouldn't believe them if they told him what had just happened.

He opened the car door. "You sure you don't want to ride with me?"

Ppeekk shook her head. "No, Dad, we want to walk. You go on."

Ppeekk, Quatro, and Mini Romey looked at one another and

stopped for a moment to catch their breath. Then they crossed the street, glancing nervously over their shoulders. The aerial roots of the menacing tree continued to tremble and twitch.

CHAPTER NINE

SHARING THE SECRET

The three children crossed the street onto the newly paved path beside the nature preserve. No one said a word. As soon as Ppeekk felt it was safe, she stopped and pretended to tie her shoe. While she kneeled down, she opened the front pouch of her backpack to check on Dead Fred.

She pressed her lips to the pouch. "Dead Fred, are you okay?"

The little fish looked up at her and murmured, "Yes, I am still in one piece. But barely. What took place back there?"

Some of his scales had been knocked off, and his dorsal fin was slightly bent.

Mini Romey jabbed her finger in Ppeekk's direction. "Hey, Ppeekk's talking to her backpack."

"No, I'm not."

"Yes, you are. You've got another secret. You said you'd tell me and you haven't. Now you have another one. You didn't keep your promise. Tell me, tell me!"

Ppeekk zipped the pouch that held Dead Fred. "Listen, something strange is going on around here. That tree, those roots, was that . . . normal?"

"No way. We've never seen a strangler fig do anything like that before, have we, Quatro? The tree and those roots moved all on their own."

Quatro cocked an eyebrow and tapped his lips with his index finger. "I've never known the roots of *Ficus aurea* to move on their own volition. As Mini Romey remarked, it seemed as if the roots were attacking us on purpose. I think they were targeting your backpack."

Silent, Ppeekk stood up and continued walking down the sidewalk.

Quatro followed behind her. "Are you hiding something in your backpack?"

Ppeekk didn't answer. And she didn't intend to. At least not right now.

They were passing the loneliest part of the walk. A few deserted houses lined one side of the street, and the nature preserve bordered the other. Wind-whipped and hurricane-stunted trees grew together so densely the swampy woods seemed not green but greenish black. The branches of the trees interlocked to form a kind of woody cage. If you dared to enter, you might be caught in there forever.

In a few places, sable palms thrust yellowed fronds above the mangroves and the green and silver buttonwood trees, trying to resist the smothering strangler figs. A fog-like mist hovered over it all. Gurgling, throaty birdcalls echoed deep inside the swampy thicket. Branches crackled and broke as if some large animal were thrashing about.

Ppeekk glanced over her shoulder. Her dad coasted behind them in the old car, driving with one hand, holding a coffee cup in the other. Strains of the 1940s big band swing music floated out the window from the cassette tapes he still loved to listen to. For once, she was halfway glad to know he was there.

Quatro pointed out a narrow trail leading into the swampy underbrush. "See that overgrown path? One time Mini Romey went down that path all by herself, and I had to go in and find her."

Mini Romey's eyes widened. "Yeah, I remember that. And I saw a giant man with a white face, white as chalk, and a woman with a scarred face and wild reddish hair, and another lady wearing a little girl's nightshirt. They all sat on a log in a puddle of old sewer-smelling swamp water full of ugly fish and crabs and a bunch of trash."

Quatro looked at his sister. "It really scared Mini Romey. Mom and Dad said it was just some homeless people fishing, but Mini Romey swore up and down they were ghosts, and we couldn't talk her out of it."

Mini Romey shivered. "I'll never go back in there again, that's for sure."

"We've never told anyone else about it before now," Quatro said. "The kids at school would laugh at us if we did."

Ppeekk could see where this was headed. They were confiding in her, so she was supposed to confide in them, too. She had promised to tell them something. Ppeekk narrowed her dark eyes. "How do I know I can trust you two?"

Quatro shrugged. "You don't. It's a chance you have to take. But a calculated chance. I promise to keep your revelations in strictest confidence. And I will personally guarantee that Mini Romey will, too."

Mini Romey's straight black hair bobbed as she vigorously nodded.

They were nearing the glowing circle with her name inside

that she'd drawn in the cement. Ppeekk had dubbed it the Good Luck Circle.

Ppeekk's mouth felt dry. "What if I told you that a little man on a concrete truck blew a smoke ring at me, a smoke ring that sparkled like diamonds and grew larger and larger until it surrounded me?"

"Go on," Quatro said.

Mini Romey faked a cough. "Yucky smoke."

"But it wasn't yucky at all. It smelled sweet and good and didn't bother me. Then when the smoke vanished, I found a strange petrified stick and drew a circle and wrote my name in the wet concrete." She pointed. "It's up ahead."

Mini Romey ran to the circle and stared down at it. By the time Ppeekk and Quatro caught up with her, the little girl's eyes had grown wide with excitement. "It's beautiful. Did you sprinkle all this glitter in the concrete?"

"No. That's one of the strangest things. All I did was draw the circle and write my name."

Mini Romey got down on her knees to look at it more closely. "It looks like it's got silver and gold in it."

Quatro rubbed his chin. "Well, it could be bits of abalone shell mixed in with the concrete aggregate. That would give it a pearlescent effect. But those green flecks? And the blue ones? They almost look like chips of emeralds and sapphires. Now if I could examine them under a microscope . . ."

Just then an elderly jogger approached them on the sidewalk.

Mini Romey looked up. "Hey, lady, come look at this."

Ppeekk gave her a gentle shove. "Hush, Mini Romey."

The woman stopped and smiled.

Quatro hooked his hand through the lady's elbow and guided her toward the circle. "Ma'am, would you look at this sphere on the pavement and tell us what you perceive?"

If looks could kill, Ppeekk's narrow-eyed glare would have demolished Quatro.

The woman ran in place and spoke in gasps. "Just a plain circle and some writing. Kids around here deface public property all the time. I hope you kids didn't do this." Then she continued her jog.

The three children stared at each other, open-mouthed.

"Typical coprolite," Ppeekk said.

Mini Romey frowned. "What's that?"

"Fossilized feces from dinosaurs or our ancient ancestors," Quatro said. "The cavemen, if you will."

"He means very old poop," Ppeekk said.

"Oh. Gross. But why did you call that woman a copro . . . copro . . . what?"

"Coprolite," Ppeekk said. "Because she's ancient and petrified and old-fashioned and . . . and reminds me of dinosaur poop."

"Interesting idea," said Quatro. "But aren't you being a little harsh?"

"No. She's just as boring as all the adults I know, including my mom and dad. It's just work, work, work all the time. Or they just sit and watch the news on television, which always seems to be bad. And everything is doom and gloom and nothing is ever fun."

True, the jogging woman had not seen anything out of the ordinary. Not the glittering bits of platinum and silver and gold, the flecks of azure and sapphire, crimson and vermillion, emerald and jade, or the lustrous chips of pearl and abalone.

Ppeekk whirled and stomped her foot so vehemently her long ponytails swung like two silk scarves around her shoulders. "Now I know it's really true!"

"Know what?" Mini Romey said.

"This circle *is* special. In fact, I think it's a magic circle. And if not magic, at least good luck. That's why I call it my Good Luck Circle."

Quatro crossed his arms. "Please explain yourself."

"Well, the day after I drew the circle and noticed the shimmering, I burst this water balloon in it, getting it all wet; then I walked through it. Actually, I danced through it. At school I took a math test and got an A. And I met you guys the very next day."

"So?"

"Well, you always get straight As, but I never do, especially in math. In fact, I'd never gotten an A on a math test before in my whole life!"

Mini Romey's eyes widened. "Wow!"

Quatro swept his hand through the air. "Mere coincidence."

Ppeekk shook her head. "I don't think so. That same morning, after I'd danced through the circle, I started seeing and finding things."

"What kinds of things?" Mini Romey said.

"Can you keep a big secret?"

The little girl traced a cross on her chest. "Yes, cross my heart and hope to die and stick two needles in my eyes."

Quatro frowned. "Mini Romey, that sort of superstitious non-sense is not necessary. Of course, we promise."

Ppeekk glanced over her shoulder at her father in the idling car and cupped her hands around her mouth like a megaphone. "Dad, we'll be okay from here on."

Her dad waved. "See you tonight, honey." He maneuvered the old car in a wide arc and headed off in the opposite direction.

Ppeekk looked around to make sure no one was watching them. They were almost to the waterway now, at the place where the paved sidewalk ended and the bridge began. Bridget, the bridge keeper, sat hunched over her controls in the bridge house, too far away for her to see what they were doing. Ppeekk bent down and unzipped the pouch that held Dead Fred. She dipped her hand inside and slowly brought it back out.

Ppeekk looked at Quatro and then at Mini Romey. "Promise again."

The brother and sister stood still as statues. "We promise."

Ppeekk opened her fingers one by one, revealing the magnificent talking fish, the magic fish, King Frederick the Ninth, Dead Fred.

Mini Romey scrunched up her nose. "Gross. A dead fish!"

Quatro pinched his chin and twisted his mouth to one side. "Interesting specimen. A golden shiner, I think."

Ppeekk paced back and forth. "It's not just a dead fish. It's a magic fish, a talking fish. And he's my friend."

"Are you reading a lot of fantasy right now?" asked Quatro.

Ppeekk's eyes filled with tears. "It's not fantasy; it's true." She brought the fish up close to her mouth. "Hey, Dead Fred, King Dead Fred, I want you to meet my new friends."

The fish lay flat and seemingly dead on Ppeekk's palm. Then the eye shifted. "How do you do, my fine young humans?"

Ppeekk stuck out her chin. "There, he spoke. He said, 'How do you do?'"

Mini Romey stuck her nose closer to the fish. "He did? I didn't hear anything."

Ppeekk touched her finger to Dead Fred's fin. "Say something else."

"Pleased to make your acquaintance on this sunny day," the fish said.

Mini Romey and Quatro just stared at Ppeekk and the fish.

"Sorry, Ppeekk," Quatro said. "We don't hear it."

Mini Romey turned to go. "Come on, let's go to school."

Ppeekk fought back her disbelief. "Wait, I forgot. I did something else yesterday. I had a water balloon with me and I smashed it in the circle. Maybe that's part of what unleashes the magic."

Ppeekk unzipped the main compartment of her backpack and pulled out a small green water balloon left over from the other day. She smashed it as hard as she could in the middle of the Good Luck Circle. Then she danced through the circle, scuffing up sprays of water and twirling with her arms raised high above her head, swaying and shimmying as if she heard music playing.

She gestured toward Mini Romey and Quatro. "Come on. I've got two more water balloons."

Mini Romey left her backpack in the grass and took the water balloon Ppeekk held out to her. She smashed it into the circle, and then did a kind of Irish jig through the wet circle, her little feet a blur.

"Your turn, Quatro," Mini Romey called to her brother.

He inched toward the circle.

"Come on, Quatro," Ppeekk said. "You can do it."

He took the last water balloon from Ppeekk's backpack and dropped it onto the circle. "This is ridiculous," said Quatro.

It didn't break.

Mini Romey continued her dance, grinning. "Try again, Quatro, and this time throw it like a man."

He picked up the intact water balloon, threw it onto the cement circle like he meant it, and then stepped inside. He lifted his knees one at a time, simultaneously pumping his arms, as if he were exercising. His chest jerked forward, but his head and neck remained rigid, like a machine or a robot trying to dance.

Ppeekk and Mini Romey dropped onto the grass, laughing. Quatro stepped out of the circle, frowning, and crossed his arms on his chest. "I don't see what's so funny. We are not all blessed with the gift of graceful movement."

Stifling a laugh, Ppeekk still held Dead Fred loosely cupped in her right hand. "Sorry, Quatro."

"What did you say?" said Mini Romey.

"I told Quatro I was sorry."

"No, not that. You said something else."

Quatro pressed his finger to his lips. "Sh-h-h. Listen."

The three of them grew quiet. At first all they could hear were seagulls squawking and the water gently lapping against the banks of the waterway. Quatro and Mini Romey thought it was Ppeekk. After all, the sound seemed to be coming from her. But it wasn't like Ppeekk's voice. It was a distinctly regal male voice, and it sounded as if it were far away.

Mini Romey's eyes widened into huge circles. "What's that?"

Ppeekk grinned from ear to ear because she knew it was Dead Fred. She opened her hand wide and held her palm flat so Quatro and Mini Romey could see and hear Dead Fred better.

Dead Fred propped himself up on one fin and lay casually draped across Ppeekk's palm. "Excuse me, what's with all this dancing and falling down? Have a little respect for your sovereign."

Mini Romey, still sitting on the ground, shrieked and threw her arms around her brother's legs. "It talked, Quatro, it really did! I heard it!"

"No, it didn't talk, Mini Romey. I heard something, too, but it's just Ppeekk playing a trick on us. She probably knows ventriloquism. Many of her kind in Indiana can do so. Come on now, Ppeekk, confess."

Ppeekk couldn't contain her laughter. "I swear, Quatro, I don't know any ventriloquism at all."

Quatro turned his back on Ppeekk and stomped across the bridge. "Humph!"

Mini Romey touched her friend's arm. "I believe you, Ppeekk. I heard the fish talk."

Dead Fred puckered his mouth. "Please inform this young lady to whom she is speaking."

"Mini Romey, I'd like to introduce you to King Frederick the Ninth, ruler of High Voltage. But I just call him Dead Fred."

Mini Romey's round nose almost touched Ppeekk's hand. "Wow!"

"Keep your distance, please. The scent of bubble gum is nauseating this early in the morning," Dead Fred said.

Quatro had stopped in the middle of the bridge and was peering down into the water. The two girls hurried to catch up with him. Mini Romey hung her chin over the railing. "What is it, Quatro?"

He pointed at the water below. "Look!"

Ppeekk and Mini Romey stood beside Quatro and gazed out at the waterway. The surface teemed with dozens of different kinds of sea creatures—stingrays and skates, eels and jellyfish and flying fish, even dolphins and manatees—swimming and leaping and splashing in every available inch of the water as far as they could see. Sunlight glimmered off the backs of the sea creatures like a constantly changing light show, a kaleidoscope. The effect mesmerized the three children.

The water was bluer than Ppeekk had ever seen it before. The sky was a pure azure, and rich emerald-green grass and bushes carpeted the banks of the waterway. Everything looked more beautiful than ever before.

Two snowy-haired gentlemen with fishing poles walked up beside the children.

One man shaded his eyes as he scanned the water. "No use trying to catch anything here."

"Yeah, let's find a better spot," said the other.

Quatro flipped his palms upward and stretched them in the direction of the numerous creatures. "But don't you see them?"

The first man scratched his head. "See what?"

Quatro pointed. "All those fish down there."

"Young man, you'd better get on to school. There's never many fish in this part of the waterway."

The old men swung their poles over their stooped shoulders and continued on, leaving Quatro with his mouth hanging open.

Ppeekk looked at her friends. "They don't see what we see."

Dead Fred swept a fragile fin through the air. "Behold my kingdom—the kingdom of High Voltage."

Quatro's eyes widened.

"Now do you believe?" Ppeekk said.

Quatro turned to face Ppeekk, gulped, and nodded his head slowly.

Ppeekk extended her open palm toward Quatro.

"Dead Fred, I'd like you to meet my friend Quatro."

Quatro bowed at the waist, holding his glasses so they didn't slip off his nose. "Pleased to make your acquaintance, your Royal Highness."

Dead Fred tipped his head. "Ah, at last, a worthy companion who knows the value of rank and royalty."

Ppeekk dug her hand into her waist. "Hey, I'm a worthy companion, too."

"Indeed you are, my dear. You have many unique and special qualities. And I will not be able to exist much longer without your intervention. I and all the creatures of High Voltage are depending on you to help us destroy the evil beast Megalodon. You must help us rid High Voltage of him forever before he succeeds in attaining the prize he seeks. Do you recall what I told you about it?"

She shrugged. "Just when you were about to tell me, we were interrupted by the bridge keeper."

Quatro and Mini Romey crowded around Dead Fred.

"Ah, yes, the bridge keeper. Hmm. Well, let me explain. As I said, the evil Megalodon and his cohorts are prowling about High Voltage."

"King Fred," Mini Romey interrupted, "what is Megalodon?"

"Forgive me. I forgot that you do not know. Megalodon came back from extinction not as he was, much like an ordinary shark that lived in the water, but as an amphibious monster. Megalodon must now breathe air as a mammal. He can stay underwater for only so long before he must surface for air. That is one reason he now lives under the bridge."

"What's the other reason?" Ppeekk said.

"His greatest desire is High Voltage and the Eternal Life Circle."

"What is this life circle thing? It must be a special circle. Is it like Ppeekk's Good Luck Circle?" Mini Romey fired questions at Dead Fred.

Dead Fred paused, seeming to order his thoughts. "The Eternal Life Circle is High Voltage's most important and valuable possession. It is the symbol of all that is good in our watery world, giving it and all its creatures their very essence and existence. As I said, Megalodon was once extinct in his prehistoric form, but he has returned as an evil mutation of his original being. He needs the Eternal Life Circle to avoid permanent extinction. The earth has been void of his original form for over fifty million years, and he is determined not to become finally and forever extinct."

"Fifty million years? Wow!" said Ppeekk.

"Like me, his time here is limited unless he is able to possess the Eternal Life Circle. He prowls the waterway looking for a chance to enter High Voltage, find the secret cavern, and steal the Eternal Life Circle. His current genetic makeup is tied to what existed millions of years ago, and the combined DNA of prehistoric times and today's environment is not suited to his survival, no matter how great his strength. If he can possess the circle, he will be able to manipulate its immense powers to reproduce a legion of monster Megalodons, and at the same time become immortal."

"So," Ppeekk said, "Megalodon wants to, no, he *needs* to get the Eternal Life Circle for himself."

Dead Fred bowed his head. "Yes, and if he ever does, High Voltage and all the good creatures of the sea will be helpless to oppose him. He will use the Eternal Life Circle to multiply, and you land-dwellers and all who breathe air on this fair earth will experience the repercussions, because the earth itself is a great circle. If one part suffers, it all does."

Ppeekk frowned and shook her head. "That's wrong. We can't let that happen."

Dead Fred lifted his fin. "And to make things even worse, Megalodon is sending other corrupted creatures against us as well—his loyal barracudas, moray eels, swordfish, sawfish, red crabs, and bloodred remora fish that can suck the life out of any living creature. Including humans."

Quatro began to pace. "This sounds serious."

"You have no idea, young man. Keeping the Eternal Life Circle out of the grasp of Megalodon is crucial—for all of us. That is why I need your help in defeating him. Will you help me?"

The children looked at one another. Ppeekk wanted to help Dead Fred, she wanted to save High Voltage, but could she? After all, she hated water. For some kids, swimming and playing in the water was great fun, but because she had moved around so much, she never learned how to swim that well. And there was so much water here! It scared her. But if she didn't help save High Voltage, well, her world would suffer, too.

Quatro and Ppeekk stood in stoic silence as the significance of Dead Fred's words reverberated in their minds.

Looking around, Quatro broke the silence. "Hey, where's Mini Romey?"

Ppeekk surveyed the bridge. "Has she gone on to school?"

At the same instant, they spotted her. She was on the bank of the waterway below the bridge, perched on a big rock hanging out over the water, gesturing toward all of the fish and sea life in front of her. "Hey, guys, come on down! You can see a lot better from here."

Quatro hung over the rail. "Mini Romey, get off that rock and get back up here on the bridge!"

Ppeekk and Quatro watched as Mini Romey leaned far out over the water to touch a manatee coming to the surface. She teetered on the edge of the rock for a long second.

Ppeekk grabbed her head. "No, Mini Romey!"

But it was too late. The little girl tumbled head over heels into the deep blue water and sank into the mysterious, teeming sea life.

CHAPTER TEN

THE UNDERWATER WORLD
OF HIGH VOLTAGE

Quatro pushed past Ppeekk, sprinting across the bridge and down the great rocky stepping-stones to the water's edge. He flung off his always untied shoes and plunged into the water. Ppeekk, hesitating for only a second, followed him, stopping short at the water's edge. She caught sight of Bridget out of the corner of her eye. The old bridge keeper slept sitting up in her chair, head lolling against the torn window screen.

Ppeekk stood on a large boulder on the grassy bank, staring at the place where Quatro had gone under. The surface of the waterway calmed—the ripples died down, no bubbles, no waves, no nothing. Where had all those fish and other sea creatures gone? Had her friends both drowned?

She paced back and forth, nervously hugging herself. She'd only just met these two, but already she liked them a lot. Quatro's immediate and clearly instinctive effort to rescue his sister amazed her. Her own mom and dad would have done the same for her, but Mini Romey was lucky to have a brother who loved her. It made her wish for about the gazillionth time that she had a brother or sister.

Were her new friends lost forever? Surely they'd come up any moment now. But she didn't even know if they could swim. How long had it been since they'd gone under?

In a burst of bubbles and foam, Quatro's head popped up on the surface of the water, his black hair wet and sleek as a seal. He gasped and spit out water. "Mini Romey is safe, but I can't believe what I witnessed down there—a truly scientific phenomenon, an improbable occurrence in nature." His face lit up with a huge smile, and his dripping eyeglasses hung off the end of his nose. Then he disappeared under the water again.

A moment later, Mini Romey's wet head also bobbed above the surface. "You've got to see this, Ppeekk. You're going to freak out!" She giggled and sputtered. "Come on in. It's amazing!"

Ppeekk still held Dead Fred in her hand. She didn't know what to do. She didn't want to be late for school, but she didn't want to leave her friends in the water alone, either. Should she call for help? If she did, a bunch of coprolites would ruin everything, or worse yet, Bridget would wake up.

Ppeekk thought about the strange things that had been happening to her and all the magical things she had seen and experienced over the past few days—the strangler fig tree; the strange little man and his smoke ring and poem; the Good Luck Circle; Dead Fred, who could not only talk, but was also king of an underwater world. So if Quatro and Mini Romey saw something in the water, maybe it was part of the magic.

She looked down at the fish in her hand. He locked eyes with her. "Ppeekk, even though Megalodon and the remora prowl the water, you and your friends should be safe in High Voltage. You have received a measure of protection from the Good Luck Circle. It is also high tide now, when Megalodon usually avoids our kingdom."

"High Voltage? You mean in the water?" Ppeekk gulped.

"Yes, my underwater kingdom. Now that you have drawn the Good Luck Circle, danced within it, witnessed its power and majesty, and chosen to protect me on land, you are now the most important part of the fight to save High Voltage. Go on. Join your friends. Go see the beauty of High Voltage for yourself and report back to me."

"Don't you want to come, too?"

"Not yet. I am not strong enough. Put me in your backpack and leave me here. Trust me. Trust the inhabitants of High Voltage. Trust the water." He lowered his voice. "Go."

Ppeekk placed him in the inner pouch and turned toward the waterway again. Dead Fred said she'd be protected. Could she trust him? But what would she find down there? She was scared of the water and scared of not knowing what was really down there. But she was an eighth-grader now. Her teachers had told her class how the younger students look up to the older ones. She was an example, they said. So she would have to face her fear; it was the only way to overcome it. Besides, she couldn't let a geeky boy like Quatro and a loud little kid like Mini Romey think she was scared of getting wet in the Intracoastal Waterway.

She looked around at the green banks and the glassy water as if it might be the last time she ever saw them. She slipped out of her shoes just as Quatro had done. Then she took a deep breath and waded in, school uniform and all. *Here goes.*

The stab of the cold water shot up from her bare feet to the top of her head. The muddy floor of the waterway gushed between her toes like mucky Jell-O. She pushed herself to wade farther, up to her knees, then to her waist. Each time she went deeper, she felt another shock of cold. Shivering, she bent her knees and everything except her head was under water.

When she had adjusted to the temperature, she relaxed. She was still unsure about all this, but the water wasn't as bad as she thought. She squinted up into the bright blue sky. A flock of gulls swooped and dived overhead. Several pelicans joined them. They circled and plunged lower and lower, nearer and nearer to the water and to Ppeekk. A few of the birds flew dangerously close to her head. They seemed to be coaxing her under the water. Well, she'd come this far. She should at least go check out whatever Quatro and Mini Romey had seen.

Ppeekk took a great gulp of air, held her breath, and lowered herself completely under the water. She moved her hair from in front of her face and opened her eyes. At first everything was blurry and she couldn't see anything. But as her vision cleared she could make out two shadowy shapes in the distance. Could that be Quatro and Mini Romey? It was deeper down here than Ppeekk had suspected. She aimed her head downward and used her arms in a breaststroke while kicking her legs like a frog.

As she swam deeper, the water began to clear. Light filtered down in golden beams. Some of the rays refracted into rainbows of color like prisms. A silvery school of fish swam by. They moved in unison, rippling like the living body of a great beast. Sparkling bits of sea dust drifted down, while blue and black striped fish darted from rock to rock. A giant sea turtle slowly glided above and ahead of Ppeekk, waving its flippers like heavy wings.

Where were Quatro and Mini Romey? What she thought were their silhouettes moved toward other larger shadows. Were those boulders? Ppeekk swam, pumping her arms and legs as hard as she could, until she feared her lungs would burst.

Then she saw the outlines of Quatro and Mini Romey. But they were wearing something on their heads, something round and clear, like glass or plastic. Mini Romey turned around, saw Ppeekk, and smiled, beckoning her. Quatro turned around, too. When he saw Ppeekk, he swam to her, grabbed hold of her arm, and pulled her toward him. Several huge spiders, fully encased in bubbles, hovered near them in the water.

Quatro guided Ppeekk toward one of the spiders, but she pulled back, twisting, trying to free herself from Quatro's grip. She hated spiders, even more than water, and these were larger than any she had ever seen before—as big as basketballs. Besides that, she was almost out of air.

The spiders' eight black and hairy legs constantly moved, their back legs spinning silk. What were they doing in the water? But Quatro nodded his head from inside what looked to be an air bubble, gesturing that the creatures were safe. Mini Romey even touched one.

Even though he was right beside Ppeekk, Quatro's voice wavered and reverberated in the water, sounding as if he were very far away in a huge echoing chamber. "Giant water spiders. They spin nets out of silk and fill them with air they trap on the surface. That's how they live underwater."

Ppeekk studied the group of spiders. Each spider's air bell pouch, made of the finest, thinnest silk, slowly grew larger as they used their legs to spin and weave. Every few minutes one of them would abandon its air bell, go up to the surface, and then return with a bubble of air.

Quatro inclined his head toward one of the spiders and then motioned for Ppeekk to do the same. Nothing seemed logical or ordinary anymore, so why not give it a try? Her lungs felt near to bursting, and she knew she couldn't hold her breath much longer.

When she put her head near the spider's air bell, the spider slipped out and swam toward the surface. Quatro grabbed the air bell and slipped it over Ppeekk's head. It looked like a diver's helmet. It even stuck to her neck to keep water out.

Ppeekk took one tentative breath, sighed, and then breathed deeply. She reached up to touch the silken air bell. It felt as delicate as a flower petal, yet strong as thick wire mesh. Although it wasn't completely transparent, she could still see Quatro and Mini Romey clearly and in detail.

The three new friends grinned at one another. They gave each other high fives, the weight of the water slowing their motion. Protected inside their bubble helmets, they laughed and celebrated. Now they could *really* explore.

Mini Romey turned somersaults in the water, a tangle of arms and legs tumbling in slow motion. Quatro examined the water spiders and their work. Ppeekk pulled herself through the water with strong strokes and gazed about in wonder, forgetting about school and the world above. Her long hair streamed behind her as she swam, and drifted around her air bell when she stopped. She felt weightless and free, as if she were swimming in a dream.

Irregularly shaped boulders and strange and beautiful forests of coral dotted the white sand floor. A garden of seaweed, sea grasses, and water hyacinths waved in the current while small fish darted in and out of them. High above, the water surface shimmered like thousands of cut glass fragments.

Then the bright surface above them was broken by great hulking shadows. Ppeekk grabbed Mini Romey around the shoulders. Three huge, rounded shadows floated above. Were they boats? They resembled some kind of oversized sea creatures. Ppeekk's heart raced, and her breath came quick and shallow as the adrenaline kicked in and she prepared to flee. Even Quatro's smile faded, replaced by a somber grimace.

Ppeekk's eyes were glued to the slowly moving shadows. Surely sharks were faster than that.

As the children continued to watch, the shadows left the surface and dove down toward them. They were not sharks at all, but something else altogether. The grayish brown creatures had small heads surrounded by thick folds of skin; snouts dotted with bristles; thick necks; two wide front flippers; rotund bodies at least eight feet long; and powerful blunt, short tails. Buried in the gray skin of their faces, their eyes seemed tiny, but the children could tell these creatures were intelligent and kind.

Mini Romey swam toward one of them. "Sea cows!"

"Excuse me," the nearest one said, "but we prefer to be called manatees."

That the manatee spoke shocked the three children into silence.

"Or *Trichechus manatus,* to be precise," Quatro said.

Another manatee approached him. "That degree of scientific accuracy is not necessary, young man. Most of our friends call us by our given names."

Mini Romey stared wide-eyed. Quatro revealed no emotion at all, but Ppeekk soon recovered from the shock of a talking manatee. After dealing with a small talking fish for a few days, she accepted that anything was possible. "Pleased to meet you. My name is Ppeekk, and these are my friends, Mini Romey and Quatro."

The manatees slowly nodded their heads.

"You may call me Mr. Mann," the largest one said.

"I'm Manny," said the smallest.

"And I'm Anna," the medium-sized one said.

Ppeekk cocked her air-belled head to one side. "But why are you here talking to us? And why are all these other sea creatures here?"

"Yes," Quatro said. "Almost as soon as we entered the water, the giant water spiders gave us air bells. Why are you helping us?"

"Because we heard *you* are helping us," Mr. Mann said.

"What have you heard?" Ppeekk suspected Dead Fred was involved in all this. "And who told you?"

"The seagulls told us," Anna said. "They saw you rescue our king, King Frederick the Ninth, on the bridge up above. Isn't that true?"

"Yes, I picked him up and took him home with me. And he's told me a bit about the underwater kingdom he calls High Voltage. But how did the gulls tell you? Can you understand them? It just sounds like screeching and squawking to me."

"That's because you are human and do not speak Gull," Mr. Mann said. "I am fluent in a dozen languages, including Manatee, Dolphin, Sea Turtle, Jellyfish, Starfish, Flying Fish, and Stingray, with a smattering of different fish dialects, and a little Shark thrown in just to get by. But Gull is essential if we want to know what's happening in the world up above."

Quatro nodded. "Fascinating . . ."

Mr. Mann circled the children. "And, of course, we learn English by listening as we cruise the shoreline and hear humans talking while they swim or boat. Our hearing is acute, and humans tend to speak loudly, so we can hear them easily, even without being too close. I've studied your language since I was just a calf at my mother's side."

"The gulls are talking to us right now," Anna said. "They tell us that King Frederick is resting safely and singing in a child's backpack on the bank of the waterway."

Ppeekk chuckled. "That's right. He's in my backpack. He told me to come down here and report back to him. What do you think he means?"

The manatees moved in closer and spoke in hushed tones.

"We are under attack," Mr. Mann said. "The kingdom of High Voltage, part of which you now see around you, is under attack by a ruthless and evil enemy we thought was vanquished long ago. But he has returned. Megalodon has returned to eradicate the plant life, kill all the creatures, poison the waters, and destroy the kingdom of High Voltage."

"Megalodon!" Quatro said. "Dead Fred told us about this prehistoric creature that has returned from extinction."

"Yes, but as a horrible morphed beast that looks very much like Megalodon. We believe it *is* Megalodon, come back as an amphibian, restored by evil forces in the deepest, darkest part of the open ocean."

"He cannot stay underwater for too long. That is why we are safe at higher tide. But when it drops, we must be on constant alert," Mr. Mann said. "Megalodon wants to rule High Voltage and claim its treasure, the Eternal Life Circle, for himself. There is another part of High Voltage, a secret cavern, which is where the Eternal Life Circle stays protected from harm."

Mini Romey gripped Ppeekk's arm. Ppeekk squeezed her hand and looked at Mr. Mann. "But how did Megalodon and these other creatures get from the sea into the waterway?"

"A few inlets open from the waterway to the ocean. The creatures swim from the ocean into the inlet and directly into our waterway. That's why this water is half-salty, half-fresh."

"But don't worry," Anna said. "The gulls will let us know when danger approaches. They patrol the waterway and keep a close eye on everything. Besides, it's high tide right now."

"Amazing!" Quatro said.

Ppeekk thought about all that Dead Fred had told her about his kingdom and the horrible Megalodon. He had asked for her help, but she hadn't answered him. He said it would be dangerous.

But she was just a thirteen-year-old who was afraid of water. How could she help save this underwater world? Dead Fred had said that she was protected by the Good Luck Circle; the denizens of High Voltage would aid them, like the spiders giving them air bells and the gulls warning of approaching danger; and she had two friends.

"But how can we help you?" Ppeekk asked.

"Of that, we are not sure," Mr. Mann said. "We believe our king has a plan, to be revealed in the proper time."

"Excuse us for a moment," Anna said.

The three manatees slowly raised themselves upward, paddling with their large flippers, until they broke the water surface with their snouts. After a moment they drifted back down to the children.

"We mammals must breathe air."

Manny swam downward. "I'm hungry." He dug his nose into the sea grass and nibbled on a frond.

"Would you like a tour of High Voltage?" Anna said.

The three children nodded enthusiastically.

Mr. Mann sidled up beside them. "I can take two of you on my back."

Quatro and Mini Romey straddled Mr. Mann's wide back, and Ppeekk climbed onto Anna's. She lay prone on Anna's back and wrapped her arms around the creature's neck. Only folds of skin were available to hold on to, but the manatee wasn't going very fast. Although not unpleasant, Anna's skin was rough and mottled with splotches of dark green, as well as scars from healed cuts and gouges.

Ppeekk and Anna followed Mr. Mann with his two riders. Mini Romey turned and smiled, waving at Ppeekk, who waved in return.

Mini Romey jabbed her finger toward the sea turtle Ppeekk had seen earlier. It swam right up to them and peered at them out of large, seemingly insightful eyes. Schools of different kinds of fish, more than Ppeekk could identify, swam toward them and gathered around.

A dozen flat stingrays hovered like triangular pancakes with lazily flapping wings. A group of sea snakes slithered in beside the rays and skates, their long sinuous bodies undulating in and around one another. Ppeekk shuddered. Then a group of jellyfish floated in, their tentacles dangling in the current. Small groups of different-sized blue crabs congregated on the sandy bottom. Even a small cluster of seahorses gathered nearby, wrapping their tails around the trailing webs from the children's air helmets.

All three children stared at the animals gathered around them. Truly, this spectacle outdid any aquarium they'd ever visited.

The manatees would occasionally dip down toward the floor to grab a mouthful of sea grass. Every five minutes they'd rise to the surface to take a breath of air. The children lay very low on the backs of their guides when they surfaced their snouts, in order not to be seen by other humans. When the manatees immersed again, the children could sit tall and witness the wonder all around them.

When Manny joined them, Mini Romey slipped off Mr. Mann's back onto Manny's. She wrapped her arms around him, laying her head on his neck and smiling. Quatro flipped over and interlaced his fingers behind his head, stretching out on Mr. Mann's back. With air bells on their heads, the trio could drift and ride with the manatees for hours.

The two larger manatees swam down toward one very large boulder on the waterway floor. When Manny and Mini Romey caught up with them, all three mammals turned and faced one another.

"We would like to show you our most secret and sacred inner sanctum, a place we of High Voltage protect and defend with our lives," said Mr. Mann.

Anna lowered her voice. "It's a place where humans have never gone before, the place where the Eternal Life Circle lies safe within the giant clam and where King Fred used to rule from his throne. But you must promise never to reveal its location."

Ppeekk nodded. "We promise."

"Oh, yes," Mini Romey said, "your secret is safe with us."

Quatro sat up. "Without a doubt, you may place your full trust in our utmost discretion."

Loud squawking interrupted the solemn moment. The manatees moved swiftly upward, swimming faster than the children imagined possible, considering the creatures' huge bodies. Ppeekk gripped Anna to keep her balance and avoid falling off.

"The gulls!" Anna said. "They've seen something. We're not safe. The water level's dropping. You have to go back, and we have to hide."

Mr. Mann elevated his huge head. "Or fight."

Manny shook his tail and flipper vigorously. "Yeah!"

Ppeekk squinted into the distance, thinking she could see something dark and shadowy moving toward them. The water trembled, and a rumble, like that of a freight train, thundered down the length of the waterway toward them. Fear crawled over Ppeekk's skin.

"But what will you do?" said Ppeekk. "Where will you go?"

Anna broke the surface and swam toward the shore. "We have places and ways to hide. Don't worry about us."

When Ppeekk's head and body emerged from the water into the air, the silken air bell on her head collapsed like a wet spider web.

She flicked it off and slid from Anna's back into the shallows. "Thank you, Anna. I wish we could do something to help now. We'll come back."

Quatro and Mini Romey slid off their manatees, too. The three mammals turned and, with a slap of their tails and a wake of bubbles, plunged back into the water before anyone could blink.

The three children hurried out of the water and stood on the bank. What would happen to their new manatee friends and all the other sea creatures in High Voltage? Was Megalodon coming for them, or was it something as harmless as a dense school of fish? They looked at one another in complete silence. Then they peered down. Their clothes and hair were completely dry—as if they'd never been in the water.

Ppeekk clapped her hands to her face. School! They were late. Or maybe they'd missed the school day completely. She shaded her eyes to look at the sun. It was still low in the sky. She noticed Quatro was wearing a watch. Knowing him, it was probably a waterproof watch. "What time is it, Quatro?"

"My watch says seven forty-five." His eyebrows shot upward. "How can that be? It seemed like we were down there a long time. We still have time to make flag salute."

Mini Romey stuffed her chubby feet into her shoes and dashed up the big stone steps. "Well, come on, then."

Ppeekk and Quatro knelt down to check on Dead Fred. Quatro opened the pouch. "He's snoring. Can you believe it?"

Ppeekk shook her head. "After all we've been through. And he wanted me to report back to him. Oh, well, I'll tell him later."

Ppeekk zipped the pouch and started to leave, but at that precise moment a huge flock of gulls swooped and dived over the water where the children and the manatees had been. They were attacking something making a wake as big as a submarine's.

Ppeekk looked more closely, and her jaw dropped. A huge shadow, the outline as large as a school bus, moved through the waterway not twenty feet away from where she stood.

At the same time, the window of the bridge house banged open and Bridget the bridge keeper started yelling. "Is that you again? Haven't I told you not to go down there? You're gonna get yourself hurt, girl, or worse! And you other kids, too."

Ppeekk raced up the stone boulders to the road, just steps behind her friends. The old bridge keeper stood in front of the shack, glaring, as they raced down the street toward school.

CHAPTER ELEVEN

DEAD FRED HOLDS COURT
IN THE TREE HOUSE

Ppeekk and Quatro ran as fast as they could down the sidewalk past the marina. Mini Romey struggled to keep up with the two older kids. "Wait for me!"

While waiting for Mini Romey, Ppeekk and Quatro stopped under the marina awning. Finally, Mini Romey arrived and threw herself down onto the concrete floor, panting. Ppeekk and Quatro plopped down beside her.

"Who was that strange, scary-looking woman in the bridge house?" Mini Romey said.

"More important, what was that enormous silhouette moving under the water?" Quatro said.

Ppeekk flipped her hair over her shoulder. "The woman in the bridge house is Bridget, the bridge keeper. She's ghastly and, oh, so horrible. Avoid her. But that huge thing in the water? I'm not sure. It must have been Megalodon."

"Whatever it was, it was as big as a house and moved as stealthily as a submarine or something," Quatro said.

Ppeekk's head and shoulders drooped. "It all seems like too much. How are we going to keep Megalodon out of High Voltage? How are we going to help Dead Fred become king again?" She twisted a strand of her long brown hair around her fingers and closed her eyes. "Nobody will believe we talked to manatees and singing fish."

Mini Romey sighed. "It was so cool riding on those manatees. Do you think we'll ever get to go back down there again?"

Quatro pushed his glasses up on his nose. "Maybe. But Ppeekk's right. We have to figure out what we can do to help save High Voltage. And I have to admit this situation is perplexing. I think I'm going to have to indulge in some creative thinking."

Ppeekk sat up and looked each of her new friends straight in the eye. "Can I count on you two to keep all this secret? We can't tell anybody about it. Especially not any grown-ups."

Mini Romey's eyebrows formed a V. "Can I tell my hamster? I want to tell him about Manny the manatee."

Quatro rolled his eyes.

The corners of Ppeekk's mouth tipped upward. "Just don't let anybody overhear you."

A car loaded with several girls in Ppeekk's and Quatro's class drove by. Some of the girls stared at the trio.

Ppeekk jumped to her feet. "We'd better go on. I've got to get Dead Fred into the usher's coatroom before flag salute. Can you two come over to my tree house after school?"

Quatro stood and smoothed the creases in his pants. "Sure. Our mom won't care."

As the three friends crossed the school parking lot, another car came to a stop nearby. Several boys from the upper and lower grades tumbled out with sports gear and backpacks. The one known as McFlyo spoke first. "Well, if it's not the Three Musketeers."

"More like the Three Stooges," said a younger boy called GJ, short for George of the Jungle, his hero.

Ppeekk turned to Quatro and Mini Romey. "Ignore them. You two go on. I'll see you after school."

Ppeekk waited a moment and then slipped into the church to put Dead Fred in his safe hiding place in the usher's coatroom.

The rest of the day passed slowly for Ppeekk. She couldn't wait to meet with her new friends in her tree house. Her mind felt focused, sharp, and fast. Her thoughts continually went back to the incredible experience in the waterway—the giant spiders, the air bubble helmets, the talking manatees, the huge beast under the water that threatened the manatees. But she just as quickly shifted gears to answer questions about American history and to work math problems on the board. She felt more alive and extreme than she'd ever felt before.

Still, it was paramount to talk to Dead Fred. And now with Quatro and Mini Romey involved, there was no turning back. They were deeply involved, and they'd already proven helpful. If Mini Romey hadn't fallen into the water and Quatro hadn't jumped in to save her, would she have had the courage to go in alone?

During last period, when Ppeekk made her rounds with the attendance sheets, she slipped into the church coatroom to retrieve Dead Fred. Soon she was outside with her backpack and there was her mom waiting for her in the Yugo. When Ppeekk slid into the front passenger's seat, she got a whiff of strawberries and chocolate. "Mmmmm. Do I smell the special Berry brownies?"

Mrs. Berry grinned. "You sure do."

"My favorite dessert in the whole world. Hope there's enough for me and some friends. Do you mind if I have two friends over today after school?"

"Of course not. I'm glad you're beginning to make friends. But you'll have to get the brownies yourself. I've still got several dozen cream puffs to whip up and a party to cater tonight. Your dad's at home, but he's got calls to make. You can do your homework in the tree house."

Ppeekk slumped in her seat and sighed. Although she was used to her parents working long hours, she didn't like it. She and her mom got home in five minutes. Ppeekk slipped Dead Fred out of her backpack and into her jumper pocket, put several brownie squares on a plate, grabbed a quart of milk, and went outside to wait for Quatro and Mini Romey.

Soon the brother and sister came strolling up the driveway.

Ppeekk went out to meet them and passed the milk jug to Quatro. "Let's go into the tree house."

She led them into the yard and climbed up the tree house ladder with one hand, balancing the plate of brownies in her other. Built high up in the branches of a banyan tree, it was the largest, most elaborate tree house Quatro, Mini Romey, and Ppeekk had ever seen. And now it was all Ppeekk's.

Mini Romey climbed through the tree house trapdoor and onto the platform. "Double whammy wow!"

The tree house had a real door and real glass windows on all four sides under a sturdy roof. Ppeekk opened the door. From three sides, the children could see the housetops of the town of Delray Beach and look down into nearby yards. On the other side, they had a gorgeous view of the Atlantic Ocean—an endless white sand beach with a green fringe of palm trees along low dunes and the two-lane road. It was like a scene from a picture postcard.

"This tree house is bigger than my room at home," said Mini Romey. She opened a door. "You've got a toilet, a bathroom sink, and a small shower." She scurried up a ladder. "And a loft with space for sleeping bags."

Quatro looked from side to side. "You can see everything from up here. And in all directions—the ocean to the east, neighborhoods to the north and south, and west to the nature preserve and the waterway."

Mini Romey leaned over the loft rail and peered down at Ppeekk and Quatro. "What's that good smell?"

"Cedar," said Ppeekk. "The walls are made of it."

Quatro nodded. "It smells great. I feel like I'm deep in a forest."

Mini Romey came down from the loft and began jumping on one of the big stuffed chairs as if it were a mini-trampoline. It creaked and groaned under her weight. "I want to have a sleepover in your tree house, Ppeekk. Can we, please?"

Ppeekk and Quatro ignored her, sitting down at the table and chairs and munching brownies.

"Mini Romey, we've got a very important meeting to conduct here," Quatro said. "This is no time to talk about sleepovers."

Mini Romey plopped down onto the chair. "Oh, yeah, I forgot. That humongous thing in the water. Whatever it was. Well, the manatees will get it. They'll fight it."

She came over to the table, took the largest brownie off the plate, and stuffed half of it into her mouth while grabbing another with her other hand.

Ppeekk smiled and shook her head. They did have important things to think about, and only one person, or rather only one *fish,* could help. She took Dead Fred out of her pocket and laid him on the table.

The little fish twisted and stretched his stiff tail. His cracked and broken top fin drooped. Ppeekk thought he seemed smaller and frailer, but that ever-present smile crossed his face.

Dead Fred lifted the front part of his body up on his two front fins and looked at the children. "Where am I?"

"In my tree house," said Ppeekk.

"Please assist me in getting a look outside."

Carrying him in her hand, Ppeekk crossed to the window overlooking the ocean. She held him up high so he could see.

Dead Fred fluttered in her palm. "Good heavens, put me down. I feel quite faint. Oh, my stars above, I've never been so high, since . . . since a nearly fatal flight with a pelican years ago when I was hardly bigger than a fry. And the ocean is so vast, it was quite overwhelming."

Ppeekk quickly took Dead Fred back to the table. "Well, I must say, I never expected to end up in a tree house with three children," the fish said.

Ppeekk cocked an eyebrow. "And we never expected to be taking care of a talking fish."

"Of course not, of course not. But you must tell me everything. Did you go to High Voltage?"

Ppeekk told Dead Fred all about getting the air bubble helmets from the giant spiders, meeting and riding the manatees, and glimpsing something huge and scary in the water.

Quatro took off his glasses to clean them. "The manatees were just about to take us to a sacred place to see what they called their most guarded and prized treasure, the Eternal Life Circle."

"But there came a loud rumbling in the water," Ppeekk said, "as loud as a train, and then the manatees rushed us back to the bank. We saw something huge and black in the water. Oh, Dead Fred, we barely escaped. I hope the manatees are all right."

Dead Fred's eyes widened. "It must have been Megalodon. No doubt about it. His attacks are increasing in frequency and severity."

Mini Romey slammed her pudgy hand on the table. "Yeah, and the grossest thing is the remora fish they told us about. The manatees said those bloody-looking red fish would suck the life out of me." She shuddered and reached for another brownie.

"The manatees speak the truth," Dead Fred said. "They are among my staunchest allies and my most trusted advisors. But they are no match for Megalodon and his remora. Manatees are gentle creatures."

Mini Romey licked brownie crumbs off her fingers. "Manny said they were going to fight. Mr. Mann said so, too."

"If they do, they are going against their natures. Manatees are not meant to fight. They do so only out of loyalty to me and out of fear for all the creatures of High Voltage. They are no match for Megalodon and his army."

Ppeekk narrowed her eyes. "What is this life circle thing?"

"The Eternal Life Circle is the perfect shape. It has no beginning and no end. It is infinite, just like the life force itself. It exists everywhere in nature as a symbol of the life force—from the sun and the moon to the iris of your eye and the iris of mine."

"Oh . . ."

"Our Eternal Life Circle shines as brightly as a single star and keeps growing in intensity until it glows as brilliantly as a galaxy. It allows High Voltage and its inhabitants to maintain our very existence in perpetuity. Some circles are special. Ours is exceptional, the most special in all the world."

The children watched the little fish closely, listening silently to his long explanation. Even Mini Romey was quiet. The only sounds in the tree house besides the fish's deep and melodious voice were birds calling and twittering and an occasional bee buzzing at the window.

"Those who understand the Eternal Life Circle and defend it and revere it will live forever. Maybe not in the expected usual form, but they will exist in some form and dimension forever."

"Interesting philosophy," said Quatro.

Ppeekk's eyes sparkled. "It sounds wonderful. You know, this all started for me when I drew a circle in the wet concrete. But even before that, a strange little man blew a circle of smoke at me."

"Yes, my dear, you have been chosen as a beneficiary of the Good Luck Circle and, by association, a protector of the Eternal Life Circle itself. It is both an extreme honor and a significant responsibility. Few are chosen. Few appreciate the beauties and transcendent qualities of all that is good and eternal about the circle and about nature and its creatures."

Mini Romey put her face up to Quatro's and stared at his eyes.

He pushed her away gently. "Mini Romey, what are you doing?"

"I want to see the iris in your eye."

"Be quiet, Mini Romey, and sit down." He grabbed a brownie and extended it toward her. "Here, have another one."

Ppeekk's eyes were glued to Dead Fred.

Dead Fred cleared his throat. "The dwarf knew that when he witnessed you walking alone on that dangerous path beside the nature preserve. I authorized him to select someone, and he chose you. I must say he chose well."

"But how did you get to know this strange little man who works for the concrete company?"

"That is not his real job. He was a fisherman when I met him many years ago—many lifetimes ago in your time. He caught me with a net as I was racing to save a school of young fish from getting trapped. But he was sensitive and wise enough to listen to me and believe in me and in the power of the Eternal Life Circle. I rewarded him by taking him down to High Voltage, just as the manatees took you. He has stayed with me as a loyal servant for many, many years."

Ppeekk blinked several times. The honor of being chosen touched her. "Thank you."

Quatro sat up straighter. "Wait a minute. You said dangerous? What do you mean that the path beside the nature preserve is dangerous, Dead Fred?"

"It borders an area where Megalodon and members of his army have been known to morph into fiendish land creatures."

Quatro turned toward Ppeekk. "Ppeekk, remember we told you that Mini Romey saw some weird people in the nature preserve?" He lowered his voice. "Maybe those were morphed Megalodon creatures."

Mini Romey squinted her dark eyes. "I knew they were really, really bad, and so ugly too."

Dead Fred waved his frail fin. "Do not venture into that area."

They looked at one another and nodded.

The fish looked at Ppeekk. "And now you and your two friends have been invited to see the Eternal Life Circle. You must go back into the water and find the manatees and the puffer fish and see the circle for yourselves. That is the only way you will come to understand its powers."

"Wow," said Mini Romey for about the tenth time. "High Voltage is some kind of super-duper special place. It's a thousand times better than Disney World!"

"For many years it has been a special place," Dead Fred said. "Now Megalodon has come back from extinction, and he and the remora are destroying the creatures and the plants of the water-way in Megalodon's effort to gain the Eternal Life Circle, and thus be forever saved from extinction. They are even venturing onto land, poisoning trees and plants of the upper world. Soon they will remove all joy and imagination from human beings, too."

Ppeekk turned her palms upward as if in surrender. "How can Megalodon go on land? I thought he was a kind of shark."

"Millions of years ago he was. But now he is neither fish nor shark nor any kind of animal or creature we have ever known. Since returning from extinction, he has become amphibious and taken the form of something wholly unnatural. He is above all to be feared and defeated. If he gains ownership of the Eternal Life Circle, High Voltage and ultimately the land above the surface will be doomed. Megalodon will reign supreme and terrorize all."

Mini Romey's eyes brimmed. "But I love those manatees. I don't want anything to happen to them."

Ppeekk put her hand on Mini Romey's shoulder. "We all love the manatees. And the water and everything in it. Even the giant spiders."

Dead Fred wiggled. "That is why we—myself and all of High Voltage—need your help to destroy Megalodon. I have a plan to defeat Megalodon, but I can't do it alone. It won't be easy, and you will have to do everything in your power to succeed. Will you help? Even in the face of great danger?"

Ppeekk remembered all that she had experienced in the last few days: the dwarf and his poem, the Good Luck Circle and how it made her feel, finding Dead Fred and visiting his kingdom. She felt a connection with not only this little fish, but also with the gulls and the manatees and, strangely enough, the giant spiders. How could she not help? "Oh, yes," said Ppeekk.

Quatro nodded. "Most certainly."

"My heart rejoices that you have accepted the call to save High Voltage. My deepest thanks." Dead Fred seemed overcome by emotion. After a brief pause his gills opened—in what Ppeekk assumed was like taking a breath—and he continued. "What I propose is to capitalize on one of Megalodon's main weaknesses and use it against him. Recall that Megalodon came back from extinction not as he was, a shark that lived in the water. Megalodon must now breathe air as a mammal. He can stay underwater for only so long before he must surface."

"That's why he lives under the bridge now. When the tide goes out, it's easier for him to get to the surface, and stay out of view," Ppeekk said.

"True, and it keeps him in close proximity to High Voltage, where he can be close to his desired prize, the Eternal Life Circle," Dead Fred said.

Quatro clenched his hand into a fist. "That must be why we saw this large object breaching the surface when we came out of the water. He must have been coming up for air."

Mini Romey scrunched up her nose. "Yeah, kind of like when we go snorkeling at the beach. My breathing tube and mask always get full of gross-tasting, salty seawater."

"My plan is this," Dead Fred said, "since Megalodon must breathe air, if you are cunning enough to lure him into a place where he cannot escape, you can flood it so deeply and completely that he will no longer be able to breathe."

Ppeekk gestured with up-turned palms. "But how in the world are we going to lure a creature that is bigger than a school bus anywhere, let alone into a place we can fill with water?"

Dead Fred's eyes looked kinder than ever. "I have full faith, my dear, that once you visit the Eternal Life Circle, you will summon the ingenuity and the courage to find a way. You must have faith."

Mini Romey peered out the west window. "Hey, I can see the bridge from here. And a lot of seagulls, too."

Ppeekk and Quatro joined her at the window. The sun was casting long, low rays across the green landscape as it approached the horizon. One ray lit up a group of girls and boys doing something on the bridge.

Ppeekk pointed. "I think those girls are from the class below us. Isn't that Little Feet and Frizz?"

"Yep," Mini Romey said. "I recognize her frizzy hair, and she never goes anywhere without Little Feet."

"What about the boys?"

"That must be McFlyo, GJ, Firecracker, and Danimal," Quatro said.

"What are they doing?" Fred said.

Mini Romey smashed her nose against the glass. "It looks like they're throwing things at the seagulls."

"And the gulls are diving at the kids," Ppeekk added.

"This is not a good situation," Dead Fred said. "You must go there and stop this immediately. Those seagulls are crucial to our mission. They must not be harmed."

Quatro looked at Ppeekk. "What should we do?"

"I don't know about you," said Ppeekk, "but I'm heading for the bridge right now. Dead Fred, you'll be safe here in the tree house."

She put the fish in a shoe box and then flung the door open and raced for the ladder.

Quatro grabbed her before she started down. "How are you going to get there? Are you going to tell your mom?"

Ppeekk planted her foot on the first rung. "No time. I'm going to have to sneak out the back way. She'll never know. I'll be back before dinner. You two can go on home, but I've got to see what's going on and stop it."

She raced across the path down the hill. When she glanced back, she saw Quatro and Mini Romey close behind her. "So you're going to come, too?"

Quatro's glasses bounced on the end of his nose as he and Ppeekk and Mini Romey zigzagged through the dense woods in Ppeekk's backyard. "Yes. I can't let you go alone."

Ppeekk smiled. It was nice to have his protection and support.

Quatro tried to stop his sister. "But Mini Romey, you're too little. You can't keep up with us. Go wait for us in the tree house and we'll be right back."

"No way. I wouldn't miss this fun for anything."

CHAPTER TWELVE

FLYING LUNCHBOXES

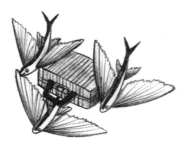

As Ppeekk and Quatro approached the bridge, Mini Romey huffed and puffed at some distance behind them. Ppeekk stopped and perked her ears. An odd sound caught her attention— like the singsong taunt you'd hear from little kids on a playground, or a jeering dare from someone. But it was even more like the strange, distant chanting of many tiny voices.

"Nah, nah, nah, nah, nah." The pitch of the chant rose and fell in a familiar rhythm, over and over again. Who or what could it be?

When they finally made it to the bridge, Ppeekk and Quatro found a group of kids from school leaning over the railing and looking down at the water. Gulls circled in a frenzy above them. Thankfully, Bridget the bridge keeper snored her head off, slumped over the bridge controls.

Ppeekk's footsteps clattered loudly on the wooden bridge as she ran toward the first person she saw and grabbed her arm. It was Frizz, a tall seventh grade girl with frizzy brown hair. "What's going on? What's making that noise?" Ppeekk asked.

Frizz pointed toward the big rocks on the bank, the same T-shaped rock Mini Romey had fallen from when they'd all gone down into the waters of High Voltage. "I don't know, but look over there," the girl said.

Ppeekk scanned the waterway, looking for signs of the manatees. Once again, the water was crowded with all kinds of fish and sea creatures skimming the surface. She could see the triangular forms of stingrays as well as fish of all shapes and sizes. Many fish leaped out of the water in shimmering silver arcs. Even though Ppeekk couldn't spot the manatees, she knew they were down there in the water somewhere, and she hoped they were safe.

Quatro and Mini Romey stood beside Ppeekk by this time, staring at the animals in the water. Ppeekk looked back at their classmates on the bridge. Some of the boys had opened their lunchboxes and were throwing paper juice containers, wet balled-up napkins, and plastic silverware at the gulls. Ppeekk was relieved to see that they weren't throwing rocks—but heavy juice boxes, giant spitballs, and plastic knives were not much better. Lots of people tossed crackers to the gulls, but throwing trash was just wrong. The birds swooped and soared in a disorderly pattern. The kids' actions made a mess in the waterway, and it was dangerous for the fish and the gulls and all the creatures living in the channel. Ppeekk had to do something.

"Nah, nah, nah, nah, nah."

Where *was* that chanting coming from?

"I still can't see who's making the noise," Ppeekk said.

Little Feet, the girl beside Frizz, spoke up. "What noise?"

Then Ppeekk sighted them—the brightest, most colorful fish she'd ever seen. They were not large, only about eight inches long, but black and white stripes encircled their deep orange bodies. They were like Nemo from *Finding Nemo,* only larger and more colorful. Hundreds of them swarmed around the rocks, swimming and circling, leaping out of the water. That's where the odd chanting was coming from. Those fish chanted a playground taunt in unison. "Nah, nah, nah, nah, nah."

Mini Romey burst out laughing so hard that Quatro had to hold on to her so she didn't fall off the bridge. The other possibility was that she might even jump in on purpose to see the funny fish. The other kids looked confused. Ppeekk figured the kids could *see* the colorful fish, but not hear the chanting. The boys on the bridge threw paper and plastic missiles, both at the gulls and at the orange fish.

"Nah, nah, nah, nah, nah."

But Mini Romey and Quatro heard it for sure because as they raced toward the bridge, they'd done a quick dance through the Good Luck Circle.

Ppeekk and Quatro locked eyes. These were no ordinary fish. Surely they had something to do with High Voltage. Just what, Ppeekk was not sure.

Quatro lowered his voice. "Ppeekk, if I'm not mistaken, those orange fish are clown fish."

A grin crossed her face. "How appropriate."

"Yes, but clown fish are not native to Florida. They're usually in the Pacific, or even the Indian Ocean. Those fish are a long way from home."

Ppeekk plugged one of her ears trying to block out Mini Romey's chanting and the other kids' laughing and talking and yelling. "All this has to be connected with High Voltage, don't you think?" Ppeekk said.

One of the boys had poked a handful of plastic knives, blades out, into a giant napkin spitball, making it look like a balled-up white porcupine. He launched it toward the clown fish.

Ppeekk felt heat rise within her and could no longer stand it. "Stop!" Her screaming hushed the children, and the boys stopped throwing things and gaped at her.

McFlyo, one of the largest boys in the eighth grade and a little intimidating with his Zac Efron-meets-Elvis Presley good looks and muscles, stood next to his brother, Danimal, who held a full juice box in each hand. "Why should we?" McFlyo was wearing the same school uniform as all the boys, but he wore the same pants almost every day with indifference and a sophisticated flair. Some kids even called him "Pants Boy."

McFlyo pushed his way through the crowd and marched right up to Ppeekk. Narrowing his blue eyes under a slicked back shock of smooth blond hair, he stared at her, a lethal projectile in one hand.

Three smaller boys came around to flank McFlyo—the reddish-haired Firecracker with his hands in the pockets of his baggy pants, Danimal, and little GJ, even younger and smaller than Mini Romey. Quatro moved to stand beside Ppeekk. Mini Romey stood behind Quatro and looked with wide eyes out from behind her brother.

Ppeekk didn't know exactly what to do or say, but she didn't flinch. She looked McFlyo right in the eye. "Because throwing stuff in the waterway is bad."

Quatro quietly and carefully enunciated each syllable. "And

because littering is detrimental to the environment."

McFlyo exploded in laughter. "Is that right, Mr. Goody Two-shoes? Detrimental to the environment! Why don't you just stick to reading books, with those big glasses of yours?"

Danimal, Firecracker, and GJ laughed with him. "People do lots worse than this all the time, smart boy," McFlyo said. "Are you gonna be a professional nerd when you grow up?"

Frizz shoved the boy. "Lay off it, McFlyo. He's got a point."

Ppeekk's eyebrows shot upward. She never expected Frizz to speak up like that.

"I wrote a paper about it last year," Frizz said. "It *is* bad to throw plastic and other stuff in the water."

"But it's not just bad for the water," said Ppeekk. "It's bad for the fish and the gulls and all the animals that live in the waterway."

McFlyo put his hands on his waist and leaned toward Ppeekk, jutting out his lower lip. "Well, well. The new girl's an animal lover. What's your name again?"

Mini Romey stepped forward. "Her name is Ppeekk, and I'm an animal lover, too. What's wrong with that?"

"Hey!" Little Feet said. "Me, too!"

McFlyo snickered. "Well, let's start a girly animal lovers club, and"—jabbing his thumb toward Quatro—"old four eyes can be the president."

"Yeah," Firecracker said. "We can have an animal lovers' club and a . . . a . . ."

"A firecracker lover's club, one that blows things up," McFlyo bellowed.

"Count me in," GJ said.

Quatro frowned. "But firecrackers can be dangerous."

"Too bad," McFlyo said, "because my friend here isn't called Firecracker for nothin'. He's got a pocketful of M–80s and Black Cats, and we're gonna hide 'em in a piece of bread, light 'em, and send 'em over the side of this bridge to see how many fish and birds we can blow to smithereens!"

Ppeekk heard the clown fish chanting their taunt again. It was almost as if the silly fish *wanted* the kids to throw something at them. But it wouldn't be firecrackers or trash if she could help it. Some of the fish were acting strangely, swimming in circles around one another. She looked more closely. Others actually had comical expressions on their faces. They were indeed clownish— probably the court jesters of High Voltage.

But the other kids didn't understand or know anything about Dead Fred's kingdom. Would they believe her or understand her? No, it would be nearly impossible to convince this crowd, plus with a gang like McFlyo's, who says they wouldn't side with Megalodon?

Ppeekk's hushed but firm voice quieted them all. "It's wrong to do this. It's the wrong thing to do all the way around—for the water, for the animals, and for all of us. When you do the wrong thing, bad things happen. To everybody. When you do the right thing, good things happen."

"Oh, man," McFlyo moaned, "this philosophy's too deep for me." But he wasn't smiling or laughing now, and neither were his sidekicks.

"And it's not just plain good things that happen," Ppeekk said. "Sometimes wonderful, magical things occur when you do the right thing."

Ppeekk leaned on the railing, looking away from the group. She was tired after this outburst, tired in body and mind. The late afternoon sun burned hot and bright, sapping all her energy. She had so much to think about and so much to do. She hadn't even been to see the Eternal Life Circle yet, so how could she save High Voltage? She couldn't even keep kids from throwing stuff into the waterway. Quatro and Mini Romey helped and stuck up for her, but it wasn't working.

"What do you want us to do?" little GJ said.

Mini Romey grabbed his arm. "I know. We could just throw plain old food—without wrappers. No bottles or boxes. Just crackers and cookies and things. We could feed the animals and the fish. Come on, GJ. Can I have a cracker from your lunchbox?"

GJ opened his lunchbox and passed his leftover food to Mini Romey. They began tossing sandwich bits to the gulls and to the group of clown fish below. Frizz and Little Feet joined them, tossing bread crusts and chunks of fruit.

The antics of the clown fish increased. They leaped to catch cookie and cracker crumbs before they hit the water. They twisted and twirled above the water like acrobats.

McFlyo stood on the bottom rung of the metal railing and wound up his arm like a pitcher preparing to throw a fastball. "All right. You dumb fish asked for it. Look out below! Bombs away!" McFlyo let loose and launched his dark green *Incredible Hulk* lunchbox toward the big rocks and the clown fish.

At the same time, four small creatures with shimmering blue bodies and gold wings leaped out of the water, and with their wings and bodies guided the lunchbox over the swarming mass of clown fish, dropping it squarely on top of a large, T-shaped boulder. The T-rock they called it. In unison, the children gasped *oohs* and *aahs* as the silver-blue and golden creatures veered away from the T-Rock and then dived smoothly back into the water.

Ppeekk's voice was barely a squeak. "Flying fish."

Frizz's hair seemed to stand up even more. "They're beautiful."

Ppeekk thought about the words of the dwarf's poem. They were coming true. She had danced in a magic circle, met a singing fish, and now she'd seen glittering wings—the wings of the flying fish.

A group of gulls dropped onto the rocks and pecked at McFlyo's lunchbox until they had it open. The gulls fell upon the food and flew away with half a sandwich, some chips, a cookie, a half-eaten apple, and a banana peel, leaving behind a few crumbs and a small heap of plastic and cellophane wrappers.

Firecracker pointed. "Did you see that? Those were flying fish. Do it again, McFlyo. Here's mine."

McFlyo took Firecracker's lunchbox and repeated his performance. This time the second one sailed even higher and farther, and four more flying fish guided it right next to the T-rock.

When GJ attempted to fling his *Bob the Builder* lunchbox from the bridge, his throw was not as strong as the older boy's. It looked like it was going to land in the middle of the waterway. But six flying fish darted close to the water's surface, right below the lunchbox. The moment GJ's lunchbox started to drop, all six fish spread their side fins and lowered their tail fins, propelling themselves straight up and out of the water. Flapping their fins like wings, the six shimmering fish guided the lunchbox to the T-rock next to the other two. Then they twisted like aerialists and plunged back into the water. By the time Frizz and Little Feet tossed their own lunchboxes, the flying fish had made a series of graceful glides, dipping into the water and rising again, to push and guide the lunchboxes onto the target rock.

The children on the bridge cheered and clapped their hands, jumping up and down. The four girls laughed and hugged one another. The five boys grinned and did chest bumps, with Firecracker whooping and McFlyo whistling a cheer. Even the orange clown fish leaped and twirled, as if they were celebrating with the children.

Mini Romey said what all of them were thinking: "That was amazing!"

"Yeah, Ppeekk," Little Feet said. "You were right. Something unbelievable did happen when we did the right thing by stopping the trash fest, although Mom probably wouldn't think launching our lunchboxes off the bridge was that great of an idea."

McFlyo came up to Ppeekk and Quatro. He twisted his mouth to one side. "I've got to admit it. It was a lot more fun to toss the lunchboxes toward the rocks and watch the flying fish than to throw things at the gulls."

Ppeekk smiled. The kids had stopped throwing trash in the water and trying to hurt the animals. And having met new kids she thought were kinda cool to boot was a big bonus. Hurling the lunchboxes over the water and watching the flying fish guide them to the T-rock was the best game she'd ever played. But now they couldn't just walk away and leave all the litter floating in the waterway. "Quatro and Mini Romey, will you help me pick up all that stuff down there?" Ppeekk said.

"We'll help, too," Little Feet said.

Frizz turned to McFlyo, Danimal, Firecracker, and GJ. "Come on, guys." They set off toward the rocks near the water.

Ppeekk wondered how they were going to retrieve the trash floating on the waterway. Hadn't she seen a long pole with a net on the end outside the bridge house? Maybe they could use one of those to fish the stuff out of the water. She moved cautiously toward the bridge house and peered inside the dusty windows. Bridget was asleep on the floor, still snoring like a five-hundred pound gorilla.

Quatro came up behind her and Ppeekk pressed her index finger to her lips. Together they took the long pole off the side of the bridge house and lowered it over the side. Painstakingly, they picked up every piece of debris on the water. By the time they had finished, Ppeekk's arms ached.

The last piece of paper they pulled out was almost as thick as a piece of cardboard and was colored bright orange with wide black and white stripes. Moving out of Bridget's earshot, Mini Romey took it and flattened it and tried to read it. "I don't understand it, Quatro. Can you read it for me?"

"It says, '*The bearer of this certificate is entitled to one free, unabated twenty-second shopping spree at the Eighth Street 7-Eleven store. Said bearer may grab all the candy, chips, ice cream, Slurpees, or soda he or she can carry out on their person in the stipulated twenty seconds. No bags, backpacks, or other artificial storage devices shall be permitted. Compliments of the Clown Fish.*'"

"Whoa," Mini Romey said.

Ppeekk cocked an eyebrow. "All the candy, ice cream, and soda you can carry? It's got to be a joke. Do you know how much good stuff they have at 7-Eleven?"

Mini Romey rubbed her hands together. "How much do you think we can grab in twenty seconds? I wonder how many Slurpees I can carry by myself."

"It doesn't say anything about not being able to stuff your shirt full of goodies. That's what I'm going to do," Quatro said.

A hoarse voice croaked as a clawlike hand snatched the paper away from Quatro. "I'll take that!"

Ppeekk whipped around to stare at the bridge keeper. "B . . . B . . . Bridget? Where did you come from?"

The smelly old woman crumpled the orange paper and stuffed it into a pocket inside her heavy Army jacket. "It's more for me to be asking you where you've come from, seeing as this here's my bridge."

Mini Romey crossed her arms. "Hey, that's not fair. We found that paper. It's ours."

"You found it using *my* pole on *my* bridge and in *my* waterway, little missy." The old woman spat a brown substance from between cracked lips. "And if I were you, I'd be getting off ol' Bridget's bridge lickety-split."

She yanked the pole out of Ppeekk's hands, and the three children backed away. Ppeekk glanced down at the rocks near the water. The clown fish had disappeared. The kids had gathered what was left of their lunchboxes and trash, and were standing around talking. She saw no sign of the flying fish, and all the gulls were gone. The waterway surface was perfectly calm, unnaturally quiet compared with all the recent activity.

Without warning, the water began to ripple and boil. Then something roared and exploded through the water's surface, drenching Bridget and the three children on the bridge. Ppeekk thought a bomb had been dropped in the water. Bridget's soggy cigar dangled between her lips and went out with a hiss.

Ppeekk's heart thumped furiously in her chest and terror gripped her throat. It was a beast, sharklike but big as a whale, and with a glare more piercing than the devil's. It dropped and rose and lunged again, opening its tremendous gaping mouth, packed with rows of huge daggerlike teeth. The monster was so close to

Ppeekk, Mini Romey, and Quatro they could smell the stench of its breath, like a thousand rotting corpses.

It snapped at them again and again, its snout slamming the bridge with every attempt. Hundreds of bloodred remora fish, embedded all over its slimy skin, flopped and fell off around the trio as the gigantic fiend attacked without mercy.

Mini Romey screamed.

Bridget flailed her arms. "Get out of here!"

Ppeekk couldn't tell whether Bridget was shouting at them or at the beast.

Ppeekk, Quatro, and Mini Romey ran off the bridge in the direction of their homes. Ppeekk could only hope and pray that the others down near the water were also able to escape. She knew she had just come face to face with the fearful enemy Dead Fred had described—the one called Megalodon.

CHAPTER THIRTEEN

A BAND OF NINE

Later that same night, phones buzzed all over Delray Beach, as Ppeekk, Quatro, Mini Romey, and their six new friends called one another not once, but several times. Ppeekk was relieved all the kids had gotten away safely.

"Did you see that huge monster of a fish?" Firecracker asked Danimal in one phone call. "It must have been fifty feet long!"

McFlyo called Quatro. "Was it a shark?"

Quatro gave his explanation a least a dozen times to six different kids. "It was an ancient sea creature that looks a lot like a Megalodon. It used to be considered extinct, but it must have come back in a form similar to what it looked like millions of years ago. Did you see those piercing, devil-like eyes?"

Ppeekk added important information. "Yeah, and I hope you noticed how it had to breach the surface to breathe air."

Little Feet's voice trembled when she phoned Mini Romey and then Frizz and then Ppeekk. "Should we tell our parents?"

Frizz shared her own problems with Ppeekk in another phone call. "I was soaked, and my mom's mad about my lunchbox. I told her a dog bit into it."

"Those flying fish were awesome!" GJ said to McFlyo.

"None of those fish seemed normal. It was like the flying fish were playing with us," McFlyo said to Ppeekk. "There's something going on here, and I want to know what it is."

Ppeekk decided they all needed to get together. She was going to have to tell them something, but what and how much she wasn't sure. One thing she *was* sure of—she didn't want to share Dead Fred with this group yet. After all, how did she know she could really trust them with something so important?

At that moment, Dead Fred was safely hidden in the small shoe box under the chair in the tree house. No one went into the tree house without Ppeekk or her permission. She had taken Quatro and Mini Romey there only once, and she wasn't ready to bring in all those other kids just yet.

Luckily, the next day was Saturday. Ppeekk decided they should meet somewhere safe, away from the bridge, in between her house and school. Even though Dead Fred had warned them about the nature preserve, it would have to do. After all, it *was* a nature preserve. How dangerous could a few butterflies be? They would stay well away from all strangler fig trees.

Frizz helped Ppeekk start a telephone tree. Frizz and GJ called Little Feet, who called McFlyo and Danimal, who then called Firecracker. Of course, Ppeekk called Quatro and Mini Romey. The meeting was set for Saturday evening at 7:00, after soccer games, dance lessons, and dinnertime. They were supposed to meet under the big gumbo-limbo tree near the nature preserve.

Saturday night was always Ppeekk's mom's busiest night of the week. This particular Saturday she had an important party to cater and had been baking all afternoon. After Ppeekk and her parents had a quick dinner of take-out pizza, her mother was still up to her eyebrows in flour. That meant Ppeekk would have to help.

Her mom set her to decorating the tops of miniature cheesecakes, drizzling chocolate over each one. Several batches of cookies were in the oven, as well. Ppeekk enjoyed drizzling the chocolate. It was like making art. And she liked working beside her mother. They munched and laughed as they worked. Her dad was in the other room watching the History Channel. Once in a while, he'd sneak into the kitchen to snatch a cookie.

When Quatro and Mini Romey showed up at the back door, Ppeekk's mom was mixing more cookie dough, and Ppeekk was taking a batch out of the oven.

Mini Romey wiggled her nose like a rabbit and looked at all the baked goods piled on the tables and counters. "What smells so yummy?"

Ppeekk slid fresh cookies onto a cooling rack. "Mom, do you think I could go hang out for a while?"

"Sure, honey. Take some cookies for your friends and go on. Your dad can help me finish."

Ppeekk dropped a dozen cookies into a plastic bag and ran out the screen door. Her parents were so busy and distracted they didn't notice that the three kids first walked slowly toward the tree house, and then suddenly darted off down the driveway toward their rendezvous spot.

It was weird to see Quatro out of his usual school uniform and without his pocketful of pencils and pens. He wore khaki shorts and a new-looking brown T-shirt with Delray Beach Chess Club stamped on the front. Mini Romey had on bright pink short shorts and an orange halter top that was too small for her. Ppeekk was so glad to be in blue jeans and a regular old T-shirt instead of her navy blue jumper.

Mini Romey trotted to keep up with Ppeekk. "Can I have one of those cookies?"

"Wait until we're all together."

Quatro looked at the girls. "And remember to avoid that strangler fig."

"For sure," Mini Romey said.

They walked as far away as they could from the treacherous tree, filing past it on the opposite side of the driveway. It had attacked them once, and they weren't about to risk it again. Ppeekk glanced at the tree with its dangerous roots dangling down like ropes made of brown steel wool. She shuddered, remembering the tips of the roots slowly curling and uncurling.

They left the driveway and crossed the street to the newly paved path alongside the nature preserve. It had been a warm, sunshiny day, but now some clouds and a strong breeze rolled in off the ocean. The fronds of palm trees in the yards of nearby houses waved and rustled.

"Looks like we might have an early cold front approaching," Quatro said. "We might have some popcorn convection, but it's far too early for colder weather."

"What?" Ppeekk said.

Mini Romey gently shoved her brother. "He means a thunder-shower. Wish we had some real popcorn." Her eyes flitted to Ppeekk. "But I'll take a cookie instead."

"Just be patient, Mini Romey."

Frizz and Little Feet already waited for them under the gumbo-limbo tree. It stood out among the palm trees, its shiny light-brown bark and limbs twisted and gnarled as an old person's arms. The branches seemed frozen in place, reaching out and grasping for something. *Maybe this wasn't such a good idea*, Ppeekk thought. *This tree might attack us like the strangler fig did.* She decided they should move deeper inside the preserve to get away from it, just in case.

The group of four boys came from the direction of the bridge, with Firecracker and Danimal on skateboards and the other two on scooters. They looked even tougher in their street clothes. They ditched their scooters and skateboards in some tall grass and joined the others.

Ppeekk pushed the low-hanging branches from in front of her face as she ventured a few steps deeper into the preserve. "Let's go down here a little way."

"No," Mini Romey whined. "I don't like it in there."

"Me neither," Little Feet said.

"We're not going far. We need to be where no adults can see us," Ppeekk said.

"Get over it, Mini Romey. It's still daylight," Quatro said. "And we're quite a large group."

McFlyo wagged his head from side to side. "What's the matter? We got two girly scaredy-cats?"

Ppeekk planted her hand on his chest. "No more name-calling, or you can go home, McFlyo."

He glared at Ppeekk for a moment. Then, following her, he strode into the preserve, trailed by Firecracker, Danimal, and GJ.

"See," Ppeekk called to Mini Romey and Little Feet. "Everybody's going in. Nothing is going to happen if we stick together."

"Except one of those mean strangler fig trees could get us." Mini Romey squeezed Little Feet's hand. "Or one of those spooky, ghosty people I saw in there." She squeezed Little Feet's hand again and told her the story of how she climbed a strangler fig root and it spun her around. She babbled on about seeing ghosts in the swamp.

The two girls, with Frizz beside them, followed Ppeekk and the boys into the nature preserve. Quatro brought up the rear.

Ppeekk stopped in a small clearing at the edge of a swampy area of mangrove trees. Not a strangler fig in sight, but a few gumbo-limbo trees were growing behind the mangroves. GJ poked a stick in between the mangrove roots that grew horizontally just above a swampy area, forming a kind of open woody platform over the inky water.

"This is where I saw those really scary people," Mini Romey said. Everybody except Little Feet ignored her.

"Okay, Berry, I want to know what's going on," McFlyo said.

Quatro's eyes blazed behind his thick lenses. "That kind of attitude will get you nowhere."

Ppeekk threw him an appreciative sideward glance.

"I mean," McFlyo said, "I'd really like to know about that huge shark or whatever it was in the waterway. I'm not taking another step until someone starts talking."

Frizz sat down cross-legged in the tall sea oat grass. "That's better, McFlyo. Please tell us, Ppeekk. We all want to know."

Mini Romey and Little Feet sat down beside Frizz. McFlyo squatted down on his haunches, as did Firecracker, Danimal, and GJ. Quatro and Ppeekk plopped down on the other side of the girls, stretching their legs out in front of them.

"Well," Ppeekk said, "Quatro has told all of you on the phone about Megalodon."

Mini Romey reached out her hand. "Can we have some of those cookies now?"

Ppeekk passed her the bag of cookies. "So, you know that Megalodon is a giant shark that was around in prehistoric times. At least that's what some scientists say. They say it's been extinct for millions of years."

"The word *Megalodon* means 'Big Tooth,'" Quatro added.

Mini Romey opened her mouth wide, bared teeth smeared with melted chocolate, and made a mock roar. Little Feet and GJ giggled, but everyone else ignored her.

"Yeah," Danimal said, "that thing was humongous."

McFlyo plucked a long blade of grass, gnawed on it, and then spat.

"It was, in fact, the largest carnivorous fish the world had ever known," Quatro said.

Ppeekk smiled shyly. "Quatro did a lot of research on it."

"But how did it come back from being extinct? How did it get into the waterway? Why isn't it in the ocean where it used to live?" McFlyo said.

"Great questions," said Ppeekk. "It must have come into the waterway through one of the inlets. That's the only possibility. But the big problem now is what are we going to do about it? What *can* we do?"

All the kids were quiet. Ppeekk hoped they were thinking about the problem of the monster fish while they ate the cookies.

Mini Romey's mouth was caked with chocolate crumbs. "The manatees told us all about Megalodon when I fell in the waterway. We all swam down and met these wonderful manatees and they gave us rides on their backs and . . ."

Firecracker's eyebrows shot upward. "Talking manatees? This kid is nuts."

Mini Romey's face flamed. "I am not. First, we danced in the magic circle, then we met Dead Fred the king of High Voltage, and he—"

"Dead Fred? What kind of a name is that?" GJ said. "I've got a great uncle named Fred, but he's still alive."

McFlyo dug his hands into his waist. "Who is this Dead Fred?"

Oh, no. Mini Romey is going to tell everything. Ppeekk had forgotten that Mini Romey was a motormouth who couldn't keep a secret.

Ppeekk clenched her teeth. "Mini Romey, what are you talking about? That's enough!"

"You mean you believe the kid?" McFlyo said.

"McFlyo, you saw those clown fish in the waterway and how they were acting and playing with us."

"Yes," Quatro added, "and clown fish are not native to Florida."

"So," Ppeekk said, "if clown fish are not supposed to be here and yet they are and we all saw them, doesn't that tell you that maybe, just maybe, things you thought weren't possible, are?"

Everybody was quiet again. Little Feet spoke first. "I believe you, Ppeekk and Mini Romey. I believe it could happen."

"Don't forget the behavior of the flying fish," added Frizz. "We all saw them, too, and they deliberately flew beside our lunchboxes, guiding them to the T-rock. I've never seen fish do anything like that. Have you? But we all saw it yesterday."

Everybody nodded and murmured in agreement. They couldn't deny that they'd all seen the strange antics of the clown fish and the flying fish. But the clearest image in their minds was, of course, Megalodon.

McFlyo nodded. "Yeah, I saw the clown fish and the flying fish. And the big fish, that Megalodon, too."

"But why should we have to do anything about it?" Danimal said. "Let's just report it to our parents or the police."

Ppeekk shook her head. "No. That's the last thing we want to do. Please, if we're patient and put our heads together, we'll figure this out."

The sun set behind the tall palm trees, while the clouds thickened, and the overcast evening darkened even more. A sudden gust of wind blew Ppeekk's hair around her face. As the unusual chill passed through the swamp and sent shivers up her arms, a conviction gripped her with a certainty she had seldom felt before. "We've got to get rid of Megalodon and make sure he stays extinct permanently. That's one thing I know for sure."

Everyone looked shocked, including tough-guy McFlyo. He whistled long and low. "You mean kill it?"

Ppeekk's mouth set in a grim line. "Yes."

"But Ppeekk, we're just a bunch of kids," Frizz said.

Firecracker's eyes danced. "I could blow him up! We could throw big firecrackers at the shark or pack some hollowed-out coconuts with tons of explosives, light 'em, and then toss 'em at the big fishy."

Mini Romey clapped her hands. "I could make a strangler fig lasso and we could catch him around the neck. Those strangler fig branches are strong as ropes!"

GJ jumped up and down. "I could throw a Jell-O cup at him. Remember how mine exploded in the cafeteria yesterday? Bam! Right in his eyes!"

The kids laughed.

Ppeekk lowered her voice and looked around behind her. It seemed like the trees around them bent toward them, straining to listen. "No, you guys. This is serious. I've got a better idea. We're kids, yes. But we can do anything we put our minds to. With all of your help, I'm going to give it the best try I've got."

She glanced at Quatro, who smiled back at her. "I'm with you, Ppeekk."

It was so quiet the only sound was the rustling of the leaves in the heavy breeze.

Ppeekk felt excited and unsure all at the same time, but her conviction was firm. "Okay. Here's how we defeat the beast. We need to lure Megalodon somewhere in the water where he can't get out. We need to trap him."

"But what's the big deal with that?" McFlyo said. "Fish live in the water."

"This Megalodon is different from the others. He's amphibious," Ppeekk said.

Little Feet cocked her head to one side. "Amphibious?"

"That means he lives on both land and water. He has to come up to breathe air. Like a killer whale does."

"Oh . . ."

"But how are you going to trap a monster shark, amphibious or not?" Frizz asked.

"I don't know yet, but I'm working on it. Quatro's going to help. And I'll need all of you to help, too. Can I count on you?"

Quatro had taken a small spiral notebook and a pencil out of his pocket and was busy jotting notes. She should have known he'd be prepared and making plans at the first possible moment.

Murmurs of "Sure" and "Yeah" rose from the group. Only McFlyo hesitated. After a long minute, he shrugged his broad shoulders. "I guess."

Ppeekk looked from person to person. "What I need everyone to do right now is to be quiet about all this. Don't tell anyone at all. Not your parents, not your teachers, not other kids, not anybody."

"But, Ppeekk, we've got to be careful," Frizz said.

"What if that shark thing hurts someone?" Little Feet asked.

Mini Romey closed her eyes and clutched Little Feet's arm.

"He's not after anything human," Ppeekk said. "Hmm . . . except maybe me. I know more about this than I can tell you right now. But I promise, I'll reveal everything if you'll just be patient and give me some time to figure things out."

McFlyo jutted his chin. "Why should we wait? Why don't you tell us now? Maybe this monster fish is more than you can handle."

Ppeekk sat up straight and looked him in the eyes. "You've got to trust me. If you don't want to help or be part of this, you can leave right now and nobody will bother you about it again."

McFlyo looked away from her. "I said 'I guess.' That means I'm in."

Mini Romey rubbed her bare arms. "I'm cold."

Frizz jumped up and pulled Little Feet along with her. "We'd better be getting on home."

Everyone else stood up, too.

Firecracker slapped Ppeekk on the back. "This is wild! Just let me know if you need any explosives."

McFlyo swaggered around the clearing. "I never would have expected this out of you, new girl. Come on guys, let's get out of here."

The four boys followed Frizz and Little Feet out of the nature preserve. The path's misty haze swallowed them. A few raindrops fell, and a roll of thunder rumbled. Mini Romey ran around the clearing while eating the last of the cookies.

Quatro nodded his head toward Mini Romey. "Too much sugar."

"Let's wait here a minute until she simmers down," Ppeekk said. "I want to tell you about another idea I've got."

But before Ppeekk could get out a word, Mini Romey's blood-curdling scream pierced the quiet.

CHAPTER FOURTEEN

THE VOODOO PRIESTESS, AN ALBINO GHOUL, AND A BLOODSPITTER

Mini Romey shrieked again. Her feet were caught between the tangled mangrove roots, and she was standing almost up to her knees in swamp water, slowly sinking. She had been bouncing on the roots just a moment before, but they had broken beneath her.

Quatro shook his head. "Now look what you've done, Mini Romey. Quit playing around."

"My feet are stuck. My shoes won't come out. And I'm sinking in the mud!"

"Well, just slip your feet out of your shoes."

Tears streamed down her cheeks. "I can't, Quatro. I can't move my feet or my shoes or anything."

Quatro and Ppeekk rushed to help her. Quatro stooped down and pulled on one of Mini Romey's legs, but it wouldn't budge. When Ppeekk yanked on Mini Romey's other leg, she braced her foot on the mangrove root shelf, and her foot slipped and crashed through, too.

Her shoe felt cemented in concrete and sucked down as though in quicksand. "Oh, no, not me too."

Mini Romey wailed and shivered. Ppeekk grabbed one of the girl's hands to comfort her, and Mini Romey threw her arms around Ppeekk's neck. Ppeekk glanced down at the mangrove roots and into the black water beneath. She thought she saw a flash of fleshy white. She leaned over to peer closer at the densely matted roots and then stood upright. Movement—something darted around in the muddy water. A fish?

She made out a distinct swirl of white and black, like two colors of paint being mixed together. Then she spotted a flash of rusty red. These weren't the colors or shapes of ordinary fish.

When Ppeekk bent down to put her hands into the water to get her foot out, she hesitated. What kind of fish could they be? Before she made a move, a bloodred remora fish sprang out of the water and attached itself to her leg. Her whole body shuddered in revulsion as the fish sank its suckers deep into her skin and a sharp pain shot up her leg. Feverishly, she tried to pull it off, but the gross creature was so slimy her fingers couldn't get a grip on it.

Now dozens of remoras flailed about in the black water, leaping and slapping against her legs and one another. An awful stench, as rank as three-day-old roadkill, rose up from the water and hovered around them. Mini Romey screamed at the top of her lungs.

The wind picked up speed and rain began to pelt them.

Ppeekk's heart leaped into her throat when she saw two red and swollen eyes materialize in the cloudy water. The bloody globes were set in a fleshy face above a black leering mouth. Straggly black hair floated around it.

Ppeekk fought back the urge to scream. "Pull, Quatro, pull. Get Mini Romey out of here. Now!"

Both Quatro and Ppeekk pulled as hard as they could. Mini Romey sobbed hysterically. The wind increased and the rain turned into hail the size of eyeballs, pounding them. In moments, all three were drenched, bruised, and chilled to the bone.

As the wind intensified, the trees were almost bent to the ground as easily as if they were rubber. Palm tree fronds lashed back and forth like whips. Mangrove branches were wrenched off and flew past the three children. Then three long, twisted branches from a gumbo-limbo tree some yards away reached out toward them. Its gnarled fingerlike branches flexed and extended as if to grab the children. *Now we're going to be attacked by a gumbo-limbo!* Ppeekk braced herself, but the branches passed over her shoulder. They went straight for the water where Mini Romey's feet and one of Ppeekk's were trapped.

Ppeekk gripped the little girl tightly. "Hold on, Mini Romey!" Mini Romey's arms were still wrapped around Ppeekk's neck. The pain in Ppeekk's leg was excruciating. She felt hot and light-headed, as if she might faint.

But the gumbo-limbo branches weren't after the children. Instead, one of the branches plucked at the twist of black and white in the water. Another branch thrust itself at the rusty red swirl and tugged, while yet another poked at the flesh-colored face. The thunder and lightning seemed to be right above them. But even above the booming thunder, Ppeekk, Quatro, and Mini Romey heard a terrible howling rise from the water.

Remora fish leaped all around. They flopped across the surface of the tree roots and out onto the ground, flinging bloody slime. A second remora had attached itself to Ppeekk's other leg. One had latched onto Mini Romey's arm. Quatro raked at them with a stick. Ppeekk felt alternately hot and then cold as her legs continued to burn and throb where the fish sucked at her skin. She fought to stay upright.

Ppeekk thought the gumbo-limbo branches would surely snap. The three creatures in the water seemed to pull back just as strongly as the gumbo-limbo. Showing supernatural strength, its branches were taut with the strenuous effort, jerking at the things in the water and locked in a mighty tug of war.

Slowly, from between the roots of the mangrove tree, the gumbo-limbo hauled out what looked like three wet and ragged pieces of cloth, heavy with foul-smelling swamp water and with a substance, if you could call it that, like smoke or fog. Each of three branches gripped three horrifying creatures writhing spasmodically in the struggle.

Ppeekk stared. Could these things in the swamp water be what Dead Fred had warned them about? Oh, no, what had she done? Why had she brought herself and her friends into the very place Dead Fred had told them not to go? It was all her fault. She felt sick to her stomach. Mini Romey hid her eyes, but Ppeekk and Quatro faced the chaotic scene in front of them with wide-open eyes.

The reddish swirl Ppeekk had first seen in the water had filled out and now pivoted toward them stiffly, as if on an axis. It was a sickly looking woman, no bigger than four feet tall. The wind flapped the layers of tattered wrappings that hung from her hunched back and emaciated body. Odd trinkets of chicken feet and human fingers were wrapped in a necklace around her shriveled neck. Scars on her face wiggled like worms. Her dark red eyes fixed on the children. Through broken and yellowed teeth she leered a hideous smile at them, as if she were possessed by the devil himself.

"What is it, Quatro?" Ppeekk shouted.

"She looks like some kind of mambo, a voodoo priestess."

Ppeekk gulped. "Quatro, these must be the fiendish land creatures Dead Fred warned us about. These are Megalodon's remora fish that have morphed into monsters."

When Quatro looked at Ppeekk she saw in his frightened eyes the truth of her statement.

The creature hunched before them let out a sickening laugh so deep it resonated to their bone marrow. She lunged at them, bony arms outstretched, but the gumbo-limbo shook the evil voodoo priestess and held her upside down while she continued to screech maniacally.

The black and white swirl Ppeekk had seen in the water now looked like a wet white sheet streaked with black. It was stretched out and dangling limply from the tip of a gumbo-limbo branch. As she watched, the thing grew, inflating to nearly ten feet tall, with an even wider width. Two parts on the sides, where the arms would have been, began to protrude like a stiletto knife and spread out with a giant wingspan. The white demon hovered above them like a silver gray ghost.

Its large, distorted face was transparent with leeches attached on the skin around its bluish eyes. Blood dripped from its hollow nostrils. Lesions and splotches of thin white hair covered its oversized head. Ppeekk and Mini Romey cowered and squatted down, trying to make themselves as small as possible.

Ppeekk raised her voice. "Quatro, get away. You could go get help and save yourself."

"And leave you two here alone? No way."

Even in the midst of the terrible situation, Ppeekk felt a wave of relief and warmth that her new acquaintance, who was such a nerd and a geek, was also a loyal brother and a good friend.

The white ghoul tried to speak. Its lips and mouth oozed a milky substance. Something thick and gelatinous dripped off the limp gray tongue hanging out of its mouth.

When the huge white head drifted down toward the children, the gumbo-limbo branch rose up and stretched itself to twice its length and held the white demon aloft. White mucus dripped over the children, covering them with a blanket of white slime.

While the white creature hovered above the swamp, the last monster reared above the children. It rotated its head 360 degrees to shake the remora out of its long brown hair, wet and straggly, covered with fish guts and rotting weeds. It looked like a little girl, yet had no nose and a mouth the size of a dime. Her eyes were overlarge and bloodshot. Hundreds of cockroaches crawled through her small mouth and over her blistered skin as she spat insect-filled blood toward the children.

She thrashed and twisted and jerked against the gumbo-limbo branch's gnarly fingers firmly wrapped around the fiend's waist and throat. The girl-monster roared long and low, as deep as a grizzly bear, then screeched like a banshee. Mini Romey covered her ears. Ppeekk went cold and numb. Even Quatro shivered and appeared to be in a state of shock, staring motionless at the blood-spitting creature.

They watched in horrified fascination as the tree branches thrashed the three howling monsters against the trees and slammed them to the ground. Ppeekk thought the creatures would be shredded into a thousand pieces and could never survive. But the bizarre fiends fought back fiercely. The voodoo priestess tried to swipe at the children again, but the gumbo-limbo kept all three beasts firmly clutched.

In one last mighty effort, the gumbo-limbo branches reared back, one at a time, and then snapped forward, loosening their grips on the creatures like archers releasing arrows, flinging the creatures far across the swamp toward the waterway. Bits of cockroaches, leeches, remoras, and bloodied cloth were scattered like confetti in the branches of surrounding trees and on the ground.

The children scrambled to knock the remora fish off their skin and clothes before they could sink their suckers in. As soon as they hit the ground, the fish lengthened and slithered away like snakes.

Mini Romey's and Ppeekk's feet popped out of the muddy glop with a sucking sound. The little girl collapsed into Quatro's arms. Ppeekk reached down and yanked the remora fish from her legs and Mini Romey's arm. The area where the suckers had implanted themselves was bloodied and swollen. She reached into the water and tried to fish out Mini Romey's shoes as well as her own. But it was no use. They were nowhere to be found. The three of them grabbed one other's hands. Quatro practically carried his sister. "We've got to get out of here," he said.

Ppeekk limped along beside them, bending down to support Mini Romey's injured leg. The three exhausted children turned their backs on the clearing and the mangrove swamp and started down the path, but Ppeekk couldn't resist one last backward glance. The gumbo-limbo's branches sagged. Some branches were twisted and broken, covered with debris from the battle. Others hung off the tree at awkward angles with white innards exposed. Its shiny brown bark was scratched and muddied. Hundreds of torn leaves lay scattered about on the mangrove roots and the grass of the clearing. The trees looked as ragged and bare as if a hurricane or tornado had just passed through.

"Thank you, gumbo-limbo," Ppeekk silently mouthed to the tree. Rain poured down her face. She blinked hard to keep the water out of her eyes, but she was certain the gumbo-limbo tree bowed forward at the middle, while also tipping its top in a nod. The trunk slowly swayed a few times and then doubled gently backward in a limbo dance step as the last of the remora fish flopped out of the water, turned into snakes, and then slithered deeper into the swamp.

Ppeekk knew that if Megalodon had morphed three remora fish into those monsters and sent them against her and her friends, then his power was formidable, much greater than her own. But she also believed in the powerful magic in Dead Fred and the Eternal Life Circle. Surely this good and powerful magic must also be in the gumbo-limbo tree. But would it be enough?

CHAPTER FIFTEEN

INFECTION SETS IN

Ppeekk, Quatro, and Mini Romey limped home in a silence broken only by Mini Romey's whimpering. At the entrance to Ppeekk's driveway, Quatro, grim faced, uttered a quick "'Bye" and then Ppeekk trudged on by herself, not even trying to avoid the strangler fig. When one of its branches swung near, she flicked swamp mud on it and it drew away from her.

She stopped once to try to wipe some of the mud off her arms, but that only made it worse. She looked as if she'd been in some kind of slime-wrestling contest, and in a way, she had. She felt weak in the knees and light-headed.

The Yugo was gone; that meant Mom was delivering desserts. Maybe Ppeekk could sneak in without Dad noticing. She stopped outside the garage at the water spigot and rinsed some of the dirt and glop off her hands, arms, and face. She even got most of it off her bare and swollen feet and around the sores that were forming where the suckers had latched on. But her jeans and shirt were torn and dirty and probably ruined.

She tiptoed up to the house. The sun had set, and soft blue shadows slanted from the trees, the house, and the deck. The area around the house showed no signs of the storm that had raged in the swamp just a short while ago. Ppeekk glanced over at her tree house where Dead Fred was stashed. It too was completely unscathed. Dead Fred would just have to stay there for the night. She didn't have the strength to climb the ladder and fetch him. He'd be fine until tomorrow. All Ppeekk wanted was to go upstairs and soak in a tub with lots of hot water, soap, and shampoo.

Strains of music from one of Dad's big band CDs drifted outside. She hoped it would mask any sounds she might make while sneaking into the house. She got the back door open and was slowly limping upstairs on the balls of her bare feet when her father strode into the hall. Maybe he wouldn't notice the state of her clothes in the dim light.

"Ppeekk?" Then getting a full view of her, his face contorted with anger. "What have you been doing? What happened to your clothes? Where are your shoes?"

"Dad, I—"

"Look at the mud you're tracking into the house."

"But—"

"You're too old to be playing in the mud. You've ruined those jeans and your shoes, too, no doubt. Well, it's all coming out of your allowance. Now go on upstairs and take a bath." He turned and stormed away.

Fine. That's what I wanted to do anyway. He wouldn't have cared if she'd been hurt. She could have had a broken bone or something, and all he would have cared about was the house and her clothes and money and other stupid things. He wouldn't even listen to her.

The effort of climbing the stairs exhausted her. It took all her strength to bathe. After cleaning up, she inspected her legs, twisting around to see the backs. It surprised her that the bruises and wounds were much smaller than she had imagined. She had been certain she would have huge sores where the remora fish had attached themselves. But all that remained were tiny red puncture holes, as if something small and sharp, like staples or needles, had penetrated her skin. How had the fish had been able to latch on through her jeans? Studying the puncture marks made her feel weak and sick. She fell into bed and slept throughout the night and well into the next morning.

"Good morning, Ppeekk." Her mom flung open the curtains, letting the sunlight stream into the room.

Ppeekk groaned and rolled away from the brightness.

"Are you going to sleep away the whole day?" Mom sat on the edge of Ppeekk's bed and pulled the cover off her face.

"I don't feel so good. I think I have a cold or something."

Her mom placed a cool hand on Ppeekk's brow. Without a word she left the room. Ppeekk heard her rummaging in the hall closet. She returned with a thermometer.

"Open up."

Ppeekk opened her mouth just enough for her mom to slide the thermometer under her tongue. After a few moments, Mom pulled it out. "Looks like you've caught some sort of bug."

Ppeekk's eyes flew open, thinking one of the horrid cockroaches or leeches had stuck to her.

"You've got a slight fever. You'd better stay in bed so you will be well for school tomorrow." She tucked the covers snuggly around Ppeekk and closed the curtains before the leaving the room.

Ppeekk lay in bed listless, doing nothing, all that long Sunday.

She didn't think about anything, and she couldn't sleep. She felt like a zombie. The world seemed flat and gray and dull. Her mom brought trays of food and treats up to her, but she only picked at it. Even brownies and cheesecake couldn't tempt her to eat, and she wasn't interested in reading or watching TV.

What was happening to her? Had the remora fish given her some horrible disease or infected her with something? She remembered that Dead Fred had warned her about something, but what was it? Maybe she was turning into a coprolite like her dad. Maybe his dullness was rubbing off on her.

At 5:00, Quatro telephoned, and Ppeekk made an effort to talk to him. "Quatro, something's happened to me. I feel really blah and dull. I haven't even changed out of my pajamas all day."

"Mini Romey's the same. She doesn't want to play or eat or even talk. And you know something's wrong when she won't do those things."

"Yeah, well, that's a stupid little kid for you."

"Ppeekk, this doesn't sound like you. I mean, I don't mind if you insult her. She's a real pain in the you-know-what, but you don't usually say things like that. You must have a fever or something."

Ppeekk's voice took on a hard edge. "Now you know the real me."

"Ppeekk, I do know the real you, and this is not it."

"Oh, Quatro, I don't know what's wrong. I've got to get a grip."

She pulled herself out of bed, still holding the phone, and shook her arms and legs as if trying to shake the fogginess out. "Mom thinks I've got a head cold. But I've got to go to school tomorrow. And I've got to talk to Dead Fred—soon."

"You can do it, Ppeekk. I'll meet you tomorrow morning at the bottom of your driveway at the usual time."

Ppeekk set her alarm clock and fell back into a restless sleep filled with strange and frightening dreams. Images of Quatro and Mini Romey and herself fighting the horrible creatures in the swamp drifted in and out of her mind. Once she woke in the middle of the night certain that a huge, sharklike beast was bearing down upon her.

When she went downstairs early the next morning, neither of her parents was awake yet. Outside, Ppeekk walked through the dew-soaked grass and climbed up the tree house ladder to retrieve Dead Fred. Everything took a tremendous effort, but she told herself she could do it—it was mind over matter. She could and would conquer the lethargy of mind and body that had come over her.

Dead Fred was sleeping, but he woke up immediately, irritated. "It's about time you came for me. Whatever can you mean by neglecting me for so long?"

"It's a complicated story. Can it wait for a bit? And I have to put you in my pocket for a little while. Okay?"

"If you must."

Her mom looked pleased that Ppeekk was up and dressed, ready for school, and had an appetite again. But it was all a front. Ppeekk had to force herself to take a few bites of pancakes. Her dad wasn't talking to her. Still, he followed in the car as she trudged down the driveway and out to the street to meet her friends.

Both Quatro and Mini Romey waited for her, Mini Romey looking decidedly pale and vacant eyed. The little girl's shirttail hung out of the waist of her skort, which was buttoned crookedly.

"We convinced Mom that Mini Romey just had a twenty-four-hour stomach bug," Quatro said. "She decided Mini Romey might as well go to school as lie around the house all day."

Mini Romey's eyes were glassy, and her expression was blank. She didn't look at Ppeekk or Quatro or say anything at all. Instead of smiling and chattering and bouncing around as she usually did, Mini Romey just stared straight ahead and walked as if in a trance.

Ppeekk felt spaced out and distant, but at least she could talk and look at people and make a little conversation. Mini Romey's condition seemed worse than Ppeekk's. Even so, Ppeekk knew she'd lost something important. The landscape around her seemed dull and colorless and static. She didn't feel like anything was ever going to be fun and exciting again.

The three children traipsed along the paved path. The only sound was the wheels of their backpacks whirring. Ppeekk felt like her heart was frozen and the world had dimmed. When they passed by the swamp in the nature preserve where they'd been attacked on Saturday, Mini Romey crossed to be on the far side of the swamp. She whimpered and cowered, clinging to Quatro.

I've got to pull myself together. I can't let this happen to me or to the others, Ppeekk thought. But she wasn't sure she had the strength to do anything about it.

Quatro stopped and pulled Ppeekk around by the shoulders to face him. "What about Dead Fred? Look at me, Ppeekk. Where's Dead Fred? Have you got him?"

Ppeekk shook her head. "What? Dead Fred?"

A muffled song floated on the air. Dead Fred was singing the High Voltage national anthem. Quatro's eyes widened and he pointed. "In your jumper pocket, Ppeekk. He's in your pocket."

Ppeekk slowly reached into her pocket and pulled out the little golden fish. She peered at him with a puzzled face, as if trying to figure out who or what he was.

Dead Fred raised his head. "Quatro, we've got to get Ppeekk and Mini Romey to the Good Luck Circle. Pronto." Dead Fred swiveled on Ppeekk's palm and used his brittle and cracked front fins to pull himself up Ppeekk's arm past her wrist and elbow to the top of her shoulder, where he perched himself just under the drape of her long hair. He propped himself up facing forward. "Onward!"

Quatro guided Ppeekk by her elbow, with Mini Romey holding on to his shirt. The three children passed the nature preserve and tramped down the paved walk toward the bridge.

When they reached the Good Luck Circle, the silver shimmering patch glittered in the morning sunlight.

"Quatro," Dead Fred said, "have you got any water?"

"I don't think so. Wait." He rummaged through his backpack. "Yes, I've got a water bottle in my lunchbox."

"That will have to do. Throw your water bottle in the Good Luck Circle and dance inside it. Then put Mini Romey and Ppeekk in the circle. Let's just hope they will make a few dance moves, too. If they don't, I don't think my magic can help them."

Quatro opened the top of his water bottle and slammed it to the ground inside the glittering Good Luck Circle while the two girls stood beside him like statues. Quatro stepped inside the dampened circle. This time his arms moved more fluidly and naturally. He bent his knees in rhythm with the movement of his arms and swiveled his torso on an imaginary downbeat to music in his head.

He stepped out of the circle, picked up the water bottle, and threw it inside the Good Luck Circle again, splashing water everywhere.

He led his sister into the circle. "Come on, Mini Romey."

The little girl stood stone-faced and silent.

He shook her gently. "Dance, Mini Romey."

Nothing.

"Move, you silly girl or I'll give you a pinch."

Nothing.

Quatro wanted to shake her. In desperation, he tickled her just where he knew it was most effective, in her armpit. The girl twitched and jumped, and Quatro did it again. This time Mini Romey yelled out and whirled around and looked at him. "Hey! What are you doing?"

"Shake your arms and jump."

"You're crazy."

He tickled her again and she swiped at him. He danced around her, tickling her while she spun inside the Good Luck Circle, swatting at him with her arms.

She jumped, twirling and giggling. "Cut it out, Quatro. Leave me alone." Her eyes became animated, and her face radiated life. "Hey, I'm in the Good Luck Circle. Hurrah!"

She danced an Irish jig and jumped out. Mini Romey was back! Now it was time for Ppeekk.

Quatro carefully picked up what was left of the cracked water bottle and tossed it one last time into the circle, which was now very wet and shiny and sparkling with a rainbow of crystalline colors. Quatro and Mini Romey led Ppeekk into the circle.

"Ppeekk, you're in the Good Luck Circle," Mini Romey said.

Ppeekk just stood there.

They took Ppeekk's arms and swung them back and forth. Ppeekk began to nod her head. The brother and sister swung Ppeekk's arms harder. Ppeekk's head nodded faster. Mini Romey bent down and lifted one of Ppeekk's feet and moved it up and down a few times. Ppeekk's foot started tapping. Then Ppeekk's knee started lifting. Mini Romey moved to Ppeekk's other side and repeated everything.

Quatro took Ppeekk by the shoulders and swiveled her torso from side to side. Ppeekk started moving her shoulders; Dead Fred dangled from her long hair as if from ropes. "My word, what a ride!"

By this time, Ppeekk had cracked a smile and looked directly at her friends. She was dancing on her own, her steps increasing in intensity, dancing as if her life depended on it.

She danced out of the Good Luck Circle, breathless. Ppeekk smiled at Quatro and Mini Romey and then hugged them. "Thanks," she said to her friends. She felt fully alive again. The air smelled fresh and salty and ripe with the fishy diesel odor that surrounded the marina. The sky was a deep blue bowl filled with fluffy white clouds like giant marshmallows. Her friends' faces were bright and lively. She heard the water lapping against the bridge pilings and the gulls calling. The world was beautiful again, and she was part of it.

"And what about me?" Dead Fred said. "I deserve a bit of thanks, too."

"Where are you?"

Dead Fred laughed. "Tangled in your hair."

Mini Romey loosened him gently and put him in Ppeekk's hand.

"Of course I thank you, Dead Fred," Ppeekk said. "But for what, I'm not exactly sure."

"Ah, my dear, you've been the victim of Megalodon and his evil remora fish that had morphed into land creatures. I can tell because before you danced in the circle you were, for all intents and purposes, devoid of the most important feeling that makes life worth living—joy."

"Yep," said Quatro. "These two looked a lot like the zombies I saw in a scary movie on the Sci-Fi channel."

"I feel like I've been sleepwalking for days," Ppeekk said.

"I feel like I've just been plain old asleep," Mini Romey said.

Quatro paced, rubbing his chin. "But why wasn't I affected?"

"The remora fish must not have latched on to you," Dead Fred said. "Did any of them bite into your skin?"

"No. They got only my sister and Ppeekk."

"How many times was Mini Romey bitten?" Ppeekk said.

"It's weird. She hardly has any visible marks at all."

"I'll bet she does. I have these little puncture marks on my skin in three places."

Mini Romey bent down and unrolled her kneesocks and found at least six patches of puncture marks.

"What does it mean, Dead Fred?" Ppeekk said.

"All the remora fish in this area have been infected with the evil essence of Megalodon. They attach themselves to his skin with their needlelike suckers and siphon out the evil poison he stores in his body. He encourages them to do this. Then he orders them to imbed their suckers into other creatures and infect them. In this way, he spreads his negative influence over all living beings, both in the waterway and on land. He hopes they will then turn on and destroy one another, making his pursuit of the Eternal Life Circle that much easier."

"I didn't want to go into that swamp," Mini Romey said. "But they made me. And we saw horrible monsters. I know I'll have nightmares forever."

Ppeekk lowered her eyes. Her actions had caused this near tragedy for herself and her friends. She'd feel scars of her failure for a long time.

"Who made you?" Dead Fred said.

"Ppeekk and all those other big kids."

"Mini Romey, you have much to learn. No one can make you do anything against your will unless you agree to it. You did not have to follow the others. You could have stayed on the paved path or gone home. Isn't that true? So, in fact, you chose to follow the others into the swamp. Do not blame others for your own choices and actions."

Mini Romey hung her head and backed away.

Dead Fred turned toward Quatro and Ppeekk. "As for you two older children, you have done wrong, as you well know. As an older brother and an intelligent and logical person, Quatro, you should have considered more carefully your own welfare and that of your younger sister."

Quatro bowed his head. "You are right, Dead Fred."

Dead Fred turned in Ppeekk's palm and faced her. He looked smaller and duller than she remembered. His gold scales faded more each day. But his voice carried great authority. "You, Ppeekk Rose Berry, have put yourself, your friends and, even by association, myself and thus all of High Voltage in grave danger."

Ppeekk said nothing. She knew it was true. She wanted to look away, but she needed to face the truth of Dead Fred's judgment. So she met the fish's gaze, trying to control her welling tears.

"You knowingly disobeyed me when I told you to avoid the swamp, Ppeekk."

"But I didn't disobey on purpose. I didn't remember. I didn't think."

"That is correct. You did not take the time to consider. You must always think carefully before you act. Think and consider and listen to your head. And to your heart. When you have done wrong, make no excuses. Accept your responsibility and learn."

Ppeekk bit her lip, but said nothing. She knew his advice was wise and true.

His voice softened. "But you have already been well punished for your rashness. You nearly paid the ultimate price for your act of indiscretion. Those monsters were manifestations of Megalodon's power. You have seen how he can transform himself. Did you note how red the remoras were? When they absorb Megalodon's blood, he can create horrifying, otherworldly manifestations of himself. All three of you could have been killed."

For the first time, this sobering realization appeared to hit the children. Even Mini Romey was quiet and had quit fidgeting.

"But the gumbo-limbo tree saved us," Quatro said.

Dead Fred nodded. "Ah, yes, the good gumbo-limbos. Their roots sink deep into the soil and burrow down into the earth under the waters of High Voltage. They send those roots into the earthen walls of the cavern of the Eternal Life Circle, where the roots drink deeply. The purified water of the cavern is a powerful healing force and a mighty agent for the good and the beautiful. Those trees that drink our water also dance, as you might have seen."

"Wow," Mini Romey said.

"Thank goodness for the gumbo-limbo trees. Instead of being killed, two of you were infected with only a small dose of Megalodon's evil. And you are also fortunate to have a small Good Luck Circle right here to draw the poison out of you. You can thank yourself, Ppeekk, for creating it."

"But the circle was made with *your* magic," Ppeekk said.

"Yes, with my magic. But also because of your initiative in picking up the petrified twig, your curiosity about the dwarf, and your imagination that prompted you to draw a circle in the wet concrete. Never underestimate your own power, influence, and role. You are an important part of the plan. Your imagination and self-assurance, your hope and your laughter, your love and your dancing are important to all of us."

Ppeekk and Fred exchanged smiles. She felt relieved that he both understood and forgave her. And it was so funny to see the corners of his little mouth turn upward that all three of the children broke out laughing.

"The fact that you drew a circle and then wrote your name in it marked you as an important part in attempting to save High Voltage." Dead Fred's voice lost some of its strength. "You must understand that the circle is an ancient symbol of wholeness. By dancing in the Good Luck Circle, the three of you have restored your basic vitality."

"Yes, that's right," said Quatro. "All cultures around the world use circles as important symbols."

By now the sun was well up in the sky, and a few cars passed on the bridge. A small motorboat cast off from the marina pier, and Bridget trudged up to her post in the bridge house.

"And now that you are all three together and Ppeekk and Mini Romey are almost back to normal, it is time for you to take the next step," Dead Fred said. "You must go back to High Voltage to see and touch the Eternal Life Circle for yourselves."

"You mean today?" Mini Romey said.

"We will," Quatro said. "Right after school."

Dead Fred counseled with great authority. "I mean now. No time is better than the present. This is not a moment for procrastination. We live in the present, and we must act in the present. When you know what you must do, it is better to do it immediately. To hesitate is to be lost."

The three friends looked at one another and gulped.

Dead Fred's voice lilted. "Mini Romey, put me in Ppeekk's

backpack and go to the water. The manatees are waiting for you."

"Why don't you come with us? You could protect us."

"Now is not the time."

Ppeekk strode off, her head high. "Then let's go."

The brother and sister followed her across the bridge and down the giant stone steps. Leaving their backpacks and shoes in the grass, with Dead Fred safely hidden in Ppeekk's pack, they clambered onto the T-rock at the water's edge.

Bridget stuck her head out of the bridge house. "Hey, you kids, again." She waved her arm through the air. "Get out of there."

But Ppeekk had already dived into the water as gracefully and noiselessly as a dolphin. Quatro jumped off the rock right behind her and immediately sank out of sight, followed by Mini Romey, laughing and whooping wildly as she cannonballed into the water with a mighty splash.

PA'UA AND THE ETERNAL
LIFE CIRCLE

Ppeekk swam down toward the floor of the waterway, where Quatro was already pulling a silken air bell over his head. At least a dozen giant water spiders worked furiously. While half of them spun and wove the translucent silk with their eight long legs in a blur of motion, the others swam back and forth between the surface and the workers, delivering air bubbles to fill the bells.

Quatro helped Ppeekk fit one of them over her head and then they both helped Mini Romey. The spiders' beady black eyes watched Ppeekk. In the extreme close-up of the angle, the air bell magnified and distorted Ppeekk's view of the busy, twitching spiders and made them appear even more frightening. Although she knew they wouldn't hurt her, she still felt a little nervous around them and kept a respectful distance.

The three children looked around and spotted the three manatees, Mr. Mann, Anna, and Manny, gliding toward them through the water. This time a convoy of fish and other strange sea creatures surrounded them. Besides several schools of fish, both plain and exotic, they were joined by stingrays, jellyfish, and puffer fish. Mini Romey smiled and paddled toward them, but when she got a closer look, she stopped short and swam back to Ppeekk and Quatro.

Quatro leaned toward the girls. "I'm not sure, but those might be puffer fish. Some puffers are extremely toxic, even deadly."

Ppeekk swam out to meet them. "Well, if they're with the manatees, they won't be dangerous to us."

Mr. Mann greeted the children in his deeply resonant voice. "Welcome, humans."

Anna and little Manny nodded their large gray heads in greeting. They looked so soft and cuddly, Ppeekk thought they resembled big sad dogs.

"We understand from the gulls that you continue to care for and guard our king," Anna said warmly. "For this we thank you."

Ppeekk nodded.

"We also understand that you have been threatened by our enemies on land," Mr. Mann said. "The gulls witnessed the savage attack and have told us everything. Megalodon is increasing in power. He is sending more and new enemies against us. The remora fish are everywhere and anywhere. They may pop up at anytime and morph themselves. You may have noticed that even the water here is darker."

Ppeekk *had* noticed that the normally clear greenish blue water had become somewhat murky with brown sediment.

"Yeah," Manny piped up, "that's why we've got reinforcements."

"The gulls have sent out calls for all good sea creatures to come to our aid," Mr. Mann said. "Marine animals from oceans all over the world are joining us."

"Are we going to be safe around these creatures?" Quatro said.

"Yes. Luckily, many species are friendly to us. Puffer fish are dangerous only to those who threaten them. And these jellyfish and stingrays will not harm you."

Mini Romey stretched out her hand toward one of the small, plain fish. "These don't look dangerous."

But before she came within a few feet of it, all the fish in that group instantly puffed up to the size of birthday balloons. In a chain reaction, another school of fish not only puffed themselves up, but spikes also popped out all over their rounded bodies.

"Whoa," Mini Romey said. "I guess we won't be playing soccer with these balls."

Anna turned to Ppeekk. "What news do you bring from our king?"

"Dead Fred, I mean, King Frederick has asked me and my friends to help you protect the Eternal Life Circle."

Mr. Mann indicated they should follow him. "Excellent. Come. We will take you to it."

To shield the kids from harm, two manatees swam ahead and one behind. They swam faster than Ppeekk expected. They could step up the pace when they wanted to, pumping their heavy tails up and down. The motley crew of fish and other animals followed in their wake. The electric eels undulated through the water like snakes slithering on land. Ppeekk shuddered. She did *not* like snakes of any kind, friendly or not.

Quatro pointed. "Those *are* puffers and porcupine fish. I was right. Those guys can be bad news if they want. The others, too."

Ppeekk swam as fast as she could to keep up. "Let's just wait and see. I trust the manatees completely."

Quatro looked over his shoulder and saw Mini Romey and Manny playing with some archerfish at the surface. Quatro swam up and pulled on her ankle. "Come on, Mini Romey," he said, exasperated.

She turned to follow with Manny right beside her. "Quatro, you should see what those archerfish can do. They can spit water at least three feet," Mini Romey said.

"We're going to need more than water-spitting fish to fight Megalodon," Quatro muttered.

The group neared an underwater, human-built wooden structure extending several feet above the surface to keep boats away from the shallower water near the banks. A faded sign that read "DANGER. HIGH VOLTAGE" stood on top of the wooden wall. Ppeekk knew it referred to Dead Fred's kingdom. Huge black cables the size of a fireman's hose lay on the channel floor, probably carrying many volts of electricity from the town to the barrier island.

Seaweed and other grasses filled the murky water behind the wall. The manatees stopped at the side edge of the barrier and dismissed all the sea creatures except for pairs of puffer fish, porcupine fish, stingrays, jellyfish, and small, ordinary-looking fish. The others darted off and disappeared like sparks of silver fire flashing and then extinguishing.

Manny bragged, nodding toward the remaining fish, "These guys will stay on guard while we go inside."

The two puffer fish and the two porcupine fish swam to the left and took up positions where they could observe the north end of the waterway. The stingrays and jellyfish did the same thing on the southern flank. Only the two plain fish, plus several electric eels, stayed with the manatees.

"Follow me," Mr. Mann said.

The children swam behind the bulky bodies of the manatees into a shallow area behind the wooden wall. In the muddy side wall of the waterway, a thick growth of seaweed and grass hid a rusty iron crisscrossed grate, crusted over with barnacles and looking like it had been undisturbed for centuries.

Ppeekk tried to look through the grate, but it was as black as midnight. She and Quatro and Mini Romey watched as the eels slithered effortlessly through small gaps between the crisscrosses. Then Mr. Mann, with the full force of his weight, rolled aside a large piece of coral with his oversized fin, exposing a gold lock plate with a large starfish-shaped keyhole. "Go get one of those archerfish for us, will you, Manny?" While they waited, Manny swam to the surface for the archerfish while Anna swam down to scoop up several starfish skimming the sandy bottom.

After the archerfish spurted several sprays of water into the lock to clean it out, they were ready to open the grate.

"Now, all of you pay close attention here and memorize the combination," Mr. Mann said.

As he spoke, a pink starfish nimbly placed itself into the lock with all five of its arms spread wide.

"Two turns to the right, followed by thirteen turns to the left, then back to zero, and then nine final turns to the right. Got that?"

Ppeekk repeated the words silently, and she knew Quatro was doing the same. As Mr. Mann finished, the starfish swirled out of the lock. *Creeeaaakkk!* The grate opened with a harsh metallic clank.

Mr. Mann and Manny entered first.

Anna turned to the kids. "You're next."

Ppeekk's breath came fast and shallow as she swam behind the manatees into the black hole of the unknown. When her eyes adjusted, she discovered she was in an arched tunnel tall enough for a kid to stand up in and big enough to accommodate the width of the adult manatees. She stretched her arms out and touched the earthen walls of the tunnel. Then she jerked her hands away when her fingers brushed something slimy.

Ppeekk jumped when she heard another metallic creak and clank. She glanced over her shoulder in time to see the grate slam shut, like a prison door. Looking around at the water-filled tunnel, her stomach clenched and panic gripped her. She felt dizzy and claustrophobic, but there was no going back now. Fighting the impulse to flee with all the will she could muster, Ppeekk continued to swim with Mini Romey and Quatro behind her and Anna bringing up the rear.

Two faint lights flickered ahead. The greenish lights elongated and shone like glow sticks. *Those must be the electric eels*, Ppeekk thought. The other lights were blue and darted up and down in the tunnel. The manatees and the children swam on in the faint glow emitted by the strange fish. Ppeekk fixed her eyes on those almost imperceptible, but reassuring, lights.

At last they came to a crossroads in the tunnel where it split into two passageways. Mr. Mann turned into a smaller tunnel that curved sharply downward.

Ppeekk swam alongside Anna. "Where does that other tunnel lead?"

"It loops around and comes back to the main tunnel. It doesn't go anywhere."

Threadlike roots jutting from the earthen tunnel's walls swayed back and forth in the moving current. There was movement in those mud walls, too, as if tiny sea creatures were burrowing behind them. The water began to clear and brighten.

Then suddenly the bottom of the tunnel dropped completely away, the tops and sides opened up, and light flooded Ppeekk's face. They were in an enormous underwater cavern with an air-space at its ceiling just large enough to accommodate their bobbing heads. Ppeekk's stomach dropped, too, when she looked down to the bottom of the cavern far below and discovered she was swimming in much deeper water.

When Mini Romey came out of the tunnel, she crashed into Ppeekk and spiraled off. Then Quatro bumped into Ppeekk, too, tumbling her in the water. Her air bubble flattened against her face, and she couldn't see a thing for a moment. Then Anna was beside her and offering her back to mount. As Ppeekk fixed her air bubble, her eyes adjusted to the change in brightness. She saw Mini Romey on Manny's back and Quatro on Mr. Mann's.

The underwater cavern was at least as large as the cafeteria room at school, but it shone with the gilded glory of an ornate royal palace. The cavern's water was as warm as a bath and sparkled crystal clear. Thousands of tiny lights hung suspended in the water, blinking on and off like blue and white fireflies. The walls and ceiling glowed with burnished gold. Outcroppings of rocks and coral like elaborate candelabra bedecked with phosphorescent shells shining like jewels were set into the walls and hung from the ceiling. The floor below was polished platinum shot through with blue and green, like the brilliance of the Good Luck Circle magnified a million times.

Fish of all colors, shapes, and sizes rippled through the dazzling scene. Angelfish, butterfly fish, parrotfish, tiny clown fish, some huge silver and blue fish the size of the kids themselves, white and gold and green fish, elaborately finned lionfish, flat zebra fish. Lobsters and horseshoe crabs promenaded on the cavern floor beside hermit crabs dragging their shells behind them. Here, all the shells Ppeekk loved to collect on the beach were inhabited by their natural owners, each slowly gliding through the water and peering out at her.

Stingrays and manta rays cruised like stealth aircraft through the underwater cavern's "sky," while jellyfish trailed shimmering gauzelike streamers. Hundreds of eels slithered like illuminated ribbons. Even the starfish pulsed and glimmered like real stars, both above and below.

Ppeekk clung to Anna while she took in the dizzying splendor. The manatees circled near the top of the cavern to give the children a better view. Then they began to slowly spiral downward. Sea grasses and rockweed and sea lettuce and Irish moss drifted like green clouds. Giant sea turtles flapped their flippers lazily and munched on masses of kelp and seaweed forests.

The manatees stopped in a field of sea grass where a group of the giant spiders had gathered to repair and enlarge a number of air bells. They looked up at the children and manatees as if they were waiting for them.

"You may exchange your air bells here," Anna said.

When the spiders replaced Ppeekk's old air bell for a new one, they moved in a blur. The touch of their eight wiry legs sent chills over Ppeekk's body, but she was grateful for the new air. In turn, the spiders did the same for Quatro and Mini Romey.

Mini Romey giggled as one spider adjusted her air bell. "That tickled."

The spiders' long, thin legs scissored as they swam away.

"We will introduce you to Pa'ua," Mr. Mann said, "and then we must leave you. The eels and the lantern fish will stay to guide you."

A pale light moved up and down the eels' undulating bodies. The lantern fish swam in place nearby, watching and waiting, their blue spots and lines shining softly.

"Did you say 'Papa'? You mean your dad's down here?" Mini Romey said.

Mr. Mann and Anna smiled.

"No, silly," Manny said. "He said 'Pa'ua.' That's the giant clam's name. Go and meet him."

Ppeekk and Quatro exchanged worried looks. What would this giant clam be like, and would they be safe without the manatees? But it looked as if it had all been decided. Mini Romey and Manny had already taken off.

The group moved through the scintillating water as the vision of a giant white shell emerged.

Quatro tapped Ppeekk on the shoulder. "Ppeekk, this is beyond belief. These fish are not native to Florida; they're from the South

Pacific and the Indian Ocean. And these green plants need sunshine, which is nonexistent down here. This is impossible."

But before Ppeekk could think about what this might mean, Mr. Mann and Anna bent down and spoke something to the giant clam. Then the three manatees swam off with a wave of their flippers. The eels and the lantern fish hovered near the children, some ten feet away from the clam.

The giant clam slowly opened the two sections of its coarsely fluted shell. Slowly, inch by inch it opened, and out of the shell a fleshy thing emerged, like two huge purple lips, flapping in the water. Aquamarine dots and patches of pale pink streaked and spotted the lips. Tiny fish and other minute sea creatures swam in and out of the clam's mouth.

Its voice boomed with authority from the depths of its body. "So, you are the children who have saved the king of High Voltage."

The three kids huddled together, staring at the clam. Each part of its scalloped shell measured more than eight feet long and at least as wide. The more it opened, the larger it loomed. It had looked white from a distance, but up close it was pale ivory. Although pitted and scarred, probably from age and battles, both large and small creamy pearls, arranged in elaborate patterns, encrusted it. The whole shell glowed with an inner luminosity.

Ppeekk's mouth felt dry as sand. "Well, we haven't saved him completely just yet. We're taking care of him and guarding him."

"How is our beloved sovereign King Frederick?"

Her voice caught in her throat. "Not very well. He's growing weaker, losing scales, and fading and cracking a little bit more every day. But we love him and want to save him."

"Yeah," Mini Romey said, "and we call him 'Dead Fred.'"

The clam's voice tightened. "You do, do you? We cannot let it come to that. We must work to prevent his demise."

"That's why we're here," Ppeekk said. "The important thing is to thwart Megalodon's plan to steal the Eternal Life Circle. If it falls into his control, all in High Voltage would perish and King Frederick would be lost with them. But how can we stop such a force?"

The giant lips rippled the water when he spoke. "One thing at a time, young lady. I wish to know to whom I am speaking."

"I am Ppeekk." She gestured toward her friends. "The small, talkative one is Mini Romey, and her brother's name is Quatro."

Mini Romey giggled. "The manatees called you 'Papa' or something like that."

The clam's tone softened. "The islanders of the South Pacific gave me the name of Pa'ua. But you may call me Papa Clam if you like."

Quatro cleared his throat and gestured at the cavern and the sea creatures in it. "But, sir, how did you and all these others get here? You're not native to Florida."

"Some questions cannot be explained in the logic of your world. You can only accept and believe what your eyes and your senses tell you is true."

"But how do you survive down here without any sunlight?"

"Do you not know of the word *bioluminescence*?" Papa Clam said.

Quatro's eyes lit up. "Oh, yes. It's the kind of cold light that many sea creatures are able to manufacture."

"Look around you here in the cavern and you will see it. We possess as much energy to create light as flows through the humans' electric cables. The light from these animals allows me to live here. It allows the plants to grow. It's embedded in the very walls and suspended in the water in millions of microscopic creatures. And in your new companions."

The lantern fish showed off, swimming a circle around them, their electric blue spots and lines flashing on and off. The glowing green eels floated down and draped themselves on the rough outer edges of the clam, their long bodies perfectly aligned with the scallops of the shell.

"All the lights in the water remind me of different colored fireflies," Mini Romey said.

Quatro looked pleased to have understood at least one part of this scientific puzzle. "That's another kind of bioluminescence," he said.

"It's the most beautiful place I've ever seen in my life," Ppeekk said. "But it's missing one very important element. Dead Fred belongs here. We are in High Voltage, aren't we? Isn't this his throne room?"

"Yes. You understand that much. But this is what you must also understand. Many years ago, when I was a tiny clam, a wooden boat heavy with fishermen tore its net under the weight of a mighty catch. A single grommet from that net, like a large gold ring, drifted down through the water and balanced on the edge of my shell. I could have knocked it off, and it would have lain useless on the ocean floor, covered by years of sand and silt, or been snatched up by any passing fish. But I took a risk and swallowed it."

The clam coughed and cleared his throat. "Over time I covered it with many layers of the white shell material I fabricate, and so I created something new. I maintained the ringlike shape and enlarged it. As a spider spins her webs, so I have fashioned an object both beautiful and useful, my own creation made of my own self. This is my offering to the world—my wheel of life, my pearl of wisdom: the Eternal Life Circle."

The giant clam opened wider, his lips parting as he extended a huge, dark purple tongue. Like an offering, the Eternal Life Circle Dead Fred had told them of lay on Papa Clam's fleshy tongue. It

resembled a shiny wheel with a golden nimbus of light surrounding it, more dazzling than all the light of all the creatures in
the cavern put together. The three children put their hands up to
shield their eyes from its blinding light.

"Do you have the courage to touch the Eternal Life Circle and
take some of its magic into yourselves?" the clam said. "Do you
dare take this chance?"

Ppeekk and Quatro locked eyes.

"I believe you possess the valor to accept this challenge," the
clam said. "If so, you will gain the power to manifest something
everlasting for yourselves and others that comes from the depths
of your inner souls—your own Eternal Life Circles. Experience it,
and you will be one step closer to your own true selves. Only thus,
as your true selves purified by the circle, can you save High Voltage and its king."

"I'm scared," Mini Romey said.

"We've got to do it whether we're scared or not." Ppeekk's eyes
shone. "Think about what we've been through in the last few
days: The Good Luck Circle and how the world is a much more
exciting and fun place after we dance in it; the encounter with
the strangler fig tree; the battle in the swamp and experiencing
Megalodon's evil power; the gumbo-limbo trees saving us; swimming with all these wonderful underwater creatures. I can't forget

Dead Fred's words when he told me that because I chose to protect him and draw the Good Luck Circle, I'm linked with High Voltage and its creatures—its very destiny and survival. He said I am an important part of the plan. And now you are too. We have no choice but to do what we were called to do."

Mini Romey pointed at the clam's heavy shell. "But what if that shell clamps down on my hand?"

"Maybe we should do it one at a time," Quatro said. "That way it won't get all three of us at once."

Mini Romey's voice quivered. "This is almost as scary as in the swamp."

"It's not going to hurt us," Ppeekk said. "This is a gift, not a danger. I'm sure of it. Dead Fred told us about the Eternal Life Circle and how important it is. The manatees wouldn't have brought us here if we were in any danger."

Ppeekk broke away from her friends and swam over to the giant clam. The light temporarily blinded her, so she stretched out her hands in front of her. She felt the cold, spongy tongue with its rough goose-bump texture. She fumbled about until she grabbed hold of the circle. At first it was cold to her touch, but as she gripped it, gentle warmth traveled down her legs and back up to her head. The heat reminded her of sipping hot cocoa in the oven-warmed kitchen while Mom baked cookies, or of sitting before a roaring fire next to the Christmas tree on a snowy day in Indiana.

Those were special moments in her life, and this moment in the cavern was one of them, too. The touch of the Eternal Life Circle sent power surging through her body. It filled her soul with the power and courage to love and to create.

Quatro and Mini Romey paddled beside her, hands outstretched toward the circle, waiting their turn. Contentment radiating on her face, Ppeekk moved aside and let her friends grasp it.

As the three children's shoulders touched, they were well aware that an invisible bond stronger than any ordinary friendship now connected them. They bowed down, each on one knee, on the sandy floor.

"You now possess a great gift," the clam said. "You may reach deep down within yourselves to create the new and the good out of what you have been given. Golden rings will come into your lives. They will balance for a moment on the edge of choice, and you will have to make a decision to accept them or not."

He paused, and his voice lowered. "We all have pearls inside, but they are different for each of us. Whether they are beautiful on the outside is of no importance. They may be covered with layers of beauty but be dark and ugly at the core. Work hard for the good and trust yourselves. Put your hearts and souls into everything you do, and your inner selves will be beautiful. You will create your own Eternal Life Circles."

With a rush of bubbles, the giant shell began to close. "Rise now and go. Work hard to see that King Frederick is restored to his rightful place. Unlike me, you have freedom of movement. I have been attached to this rock for hundreds of years, and here I must stay throughout the rest of my days. So it is that we all have our different lots in life, our own roles to play. This is mine."

The reverence with which Dead Fred had spoken of the giant clam, the Eternal Life Circle, and the magnificence of High Voltage now resonated with Ppeekk. She had a renewed respect and compassion for the tough little fish who wielded great power and magic as well as humility. She would have been happy to spend her whole life in this beautiful cavern, but she knew she had work to do. She took a breath. The air within her air bubble seemed thinner.

"Ouch!" A pinch burned Ppeekk's leg. She looked down. One of Megalodon's remora fish had latched on to her.

At that same moment, Mini Romey cried out and slapped at her arm. Another remora fish was biting her. Quatro struggled with several bloodred suckers trying to attach to his legs.

Suddenly a jet of water like that gushing out of a fire hydrant shot out of the giant clam. It blasted all over the children, nearly blowing off their air helmets. Remora fish swirled in the dizzy whirlpool caused by the giant clam's forceful blast and Ppeekk was shot straight up several feet, but the children were finally freed of the thirsty parasites.

Many cavern creatures encircled the floundering children. Three jellyfish glided through the water and snatched up the remora, entangling them with their stinging tentacles.

"Those were Portuguese Man o' War jellyfish!" Quatro said.

"That was so cool how Papa Clam knocked those bad fish off us with his water hoses," Mini Romey said.

Ppeekk flipped her palms upward. "But where did they come from? How did those remora fish get inside here? Here in the throne room of High Voltage?"

"This is a very grave situation," the giant clam said. "Very grave indeed. These evil fish have never before invaded our cavern. You must leave at once. The lantern fish and eels will guide you. Follow them to the safety of your outside world. I must close my shell to protect the circle. And I must rest and think. Use the powers I have given you." The heavy shell slowly shut, its mighty thud reverberating throughout the cavern.

Ppeekk, Quatro, and Mini Romey turned to their small guides and pushed off hard, swimming upward with all their strength. They followed the lantern fish and the eels' wavering blue and green lights through the cavern.

Ppeekk trembled. Her second encounter with the evil red fish was nearly disastrous. She feared other unknown challenges that might be waiting for them. If remora fish could penetrate this secret underwater cavern, what else could they do? What other creatures might be hiding in the shadows, ready to ambush them in the mazelike tunnels above?

Chapter Seventeen

High Voltage Invaded!

Ppeekk swam upward through the glistening water with broad strokes. It was difficult to keep track of the glowing green eels and the blue lights of the lantern fish in the brilliance of the cavern. Even in the face of imminent danger, she wasn't ready to leave this beautiful place. Turning her head from side to side, she tried to take it all in and remember it, blinking her eyes as if taking quick snapshots.

She glanced back. The giant clam was now closed and silent, but a sliver of bright inner light leaked from its fluted edges—light from the Eternal Life Circle. It was hard to believe that just a few minutes ago he had told his story, shared his wisdom, and she had touched the circle. Her spirit had opened and soared.

Swimming as quickly as she could, Ppeekk struggled to keep the lantern fish fixed in her line of sight. A knot of pain throbbed in her leg where a remora fish had bitten her. And now that those enemy fish had invaded the secret cavern, Ppeekk knew there was no turning back. She had to do something, and do it now, so Dead Fred could return and take his rightful place.

She glanced down at Quatro and Mini Romey swimming below her. Quatro was doing fine, but Mini Romey, as usual, was falling behind. Besides that, the little girl seemed distracted by the sea creatures.

Still a long way from exiting, as they neared the top of the underwater cavern and the opening to the tunnels, Ppeekk spied a pod of young bottlenose dolphins playing near the warm waters of a thermal vent. She swam toward them to rest and to give Mini Romey time to catch up. The lantern fish and the eels circled back to join her. The gray dolphins chattered and squeaked and clicked, while the lantern fish and eels swam among them. When Quatro joined Ppeekk, they looked at each other uncertainly. The giant clam had told them to leave at once, but Mini Romey was only halfway up the length of the cavern.

In an instant, one dolphin propelled itself downward and

circled around Mini Romey. It tilted its soft, flexible dorsal fin toward her. Mini Romey grabbed on to the fin on the dolphin's back and away they flew through the water. In a flash she was floating beside Ppeekk and Quatro, grinning from ear to ear.

"Ppeekk, do you think the other dolphins would take us?" Quatro said.

"Let's find out."

She swam over to the pod. "Thank you for helping our friend."

The dolphins clustered near her, whistling and clicking.

"Would it be possible for two of you to give rides to me and my other friend?"

With their bright black eyes and wide upturned mouths that seemed to smile, the dolphins squeaked and trilled, nodding their large heads.

Ppeekk and Quatro watched as the dolphins bobbed around them. Two dolphins swam behind Ppeekk and Quatro and came up from underneath, nudging them playfully. They tilted their fins just as the other one had done for Mini Romey.

Ppeekk and Quatro grasped the dolphins' top fins and leaned against the creatures' smooth bodies. They were only about half as big as the manatees. Then following the eels and the lantern fish, the children and dolphins plowed smoothly and quickly through the water into the tunnels.

When Ppeekk's eyes adjusted to the dim light, she could make out the lantern fish and the eels swimming up ahead. But the dolphins were faster and more agile than the manatees, and they soon caught up. Ppeekk kept her body as closely aligned to her dolphin as possible, feeling the tail fin brush against her feet when they turned a corner. The dolphins glided through the tunnels effortlessly and gracefully, taking the curves without slowing down or jolting their passengers.

The water-filled tunnels slanted gradually upward. The farther they swam from the lights of the cavern the darker the tunnels became. Pebbles and clumps of earth dropped and filtered down from the dirt ceiling. Ppeekk was sure she saw remora fish hiding in crevices and stone niches in the tunnel walls. But she told herself she had to be imagining things. When trailing roots wavered in the water and brushed her head and legs, all the nerve endings in her body stood at attention.

Then they were swimming in almost total darkness. All Ppeekk could see were dark shadows in the tunnel blackness. The water rushed past her head, and bubbles streamed from her dolphin's mouth. Well above the tunnels, something large moved, creating a rumble she both heard and felt.

They turned right and then left and then right again, passing the entrance to the looping tunnel, and then the dolphins picked up even more speed. Ppeekk felt the water rushing past her as she steadied her air helmet several times.

Without warning, her dolphin veered sharply, and Ppeekk's legs scraped against the side of the tunnel. The mammal accelerated to an unbelievable speed, and Ppeekk soon learned why. A gang of barracuda fish pursued them, darting out of the side tunnels and closing in, snapping at them with their sharp, gleaming teeth.

Ppeekk could just make out a blurry square of light at the end of the tunnel with the faint blue lights of the lantern fish bobbing near it. By the time they made it to the metal grate and the entrance into the waterway, the electric eels and starfish had opened it.

As she and her dolphin swished past the grate and into the small space behind the wooden wall, a horde of red crabs attacked her, pinching her arms and legs, and pulling and ripping her clothes. *These must be Megalodon's army of red crabs that Dead Fred had warned her about,* Ppeekk thought, and there were hundreds of them. She tried to fight them off, kicking them and picking at them with one hand while with the other hand she clutched the dolphin's fin. Ppeekk struggled to stay on while the dolphin twisted its body from side to side and up and down like a bucking bronco. Then the dolphin zipped out of the murky backwash of the shallows and into the main waterway where darkness and horror engulfed them.

With a thunderous roar and a horrible stench that seeped into Ppeekk's air helmet, Megalodon filled the space of the waterway around them. Moving toward them, the cavern of its mouth slowly opened to the height of an upright adult. Its sharp yellow teeth surrounded the small dolphin and the girl, ready to chomp down. Ppeekk could see down into the gullet of the enormous monster. A tattered piece of fabric hung from an upper incisor, and a canvas shoe was tangled in its lower teeth. Ppeekk shuddered to think about how that cloth and shoe had gotten there.

In an astonishing maneuver, the dolphin pointed his snout straight down and dashed underneath the hulking enemy's body. With the monster facing one direction, the dolphin swam in the opposite. The beast clamped its teeth on nothing, and the dolphin was out of reach before Megalodon could turn around. But the force of Megalodon's jaws snapping shut whooshed the water around them into an intense vortex, purging bits of a prior victim's flesh from between its razor sharp teeth and knocking Ppeekk off the dolphin.

Ppeekk tumbled head over heels, completely losing her bearings. She plummeted through Megalodon's cold surge with no sense of control or direction. Her air bell was ripped off her head and she feared she was drowning.

Then the dolphin swooped up beside her. Ppeekk grabbed its fin and hung on for dear life. He blasted through the water like a missile shot from a submarine. As they skipped across the surface of the waterway, Ppeekk coughed and spewed water from her lungs.

Compared to Megalodon, the red crabs now seemed like a very small problem indeed. A few still hung on to Ppeekk's socks, but with the force of the rushing water she easily shook them off. She turned to catch a glimpse of Quatro and Mini Romey racing on their dolphins behind her.

As the other two dolphins approached, Megalodon swiveled around. But instead of pursuing them, he paused underneath the bridge and then awkwardly thrust his whole body up onto the sandy beach directly below it. The shock waves of Megalodon's maneuver caused reverberations and tremors to ripple through the water. The beast lay there like a beached whale, huffing and blowing.

Ppeekk gulped the fresh air hungrily and turned her face to the sunshine as the dolphin slowed and came to a stop. When Quatro and Mini Romey approached on their dolphins, bobbing in the water, she leaned over to hug them both. The dolphins clicked and nodded and blew through their blowholes while everyone laughed. The lantern fish and the eels had turned off their lights, but floated nearby.

Then one dolphin squeaked loudly, and all three became agitated.

Ppeekk looked over her shoulder. "I don't know what's about to happen, but grab on to your dolphins!"

The dolphins sped off once again, a large school of fish following them. But were they friends or foes? Ppeekk held her breath and ducked under the water to get a better look. She wished she hadn't looked at all.

A school of barracudas, along with a group of larger fish she didn't recognize, pursued them. More of Megalodon's evil army. They were thirty yards back and closing fast. The dolphins zipped down the waterway. Where were they going? With Megalodon guarding the bridge area, how would they get back? Was Dead Fred safe in her backpack on the bank, or had Megalodon snapped him up?

Quatro and Mini Romey on their dolphins were right beside Ppeekk on hers. Thick shrubs and tall grasses shaded this part of the waterway, keeping it out of sight from anyone crossing the bridge. *Most people are at work or in school anyway. But will I even make it to school today?*

Then the bushes on the right-hand side gave way to dirt banks opening up to a sandy channel perpendicular to the waterway. Only a few feet deep at low tide, this was one of the few ocean inlets between the waterway and the ocean where seawater flowed in and out of the brackish channel. The dolphins squeaked in rapid, high-pitched cries, tilted the children off their backs near the shore, and then flashed like gray torpedoes through the inlet and into the open sea. The children scrambled on their hands and knees up the sandy shore to a patch of prickly dune grass.

Mini Romey pointed at the shallow water of the inlet. "Look!"

Dozens of barracudas thrashed about in obvious anger and frustration. Hundreds of remora fish milled about. Moray eels stuck their hideous heads above the water and hissed at the children, venom dripping from their fangs. Farther down the waterway proper, large swordfish reared back and raised their sharp weapon-like snouts to the sky, while sawfish ripped and shredded the water, slicing imaginary enemies to pieces. Megalodon had sent his servants to do the hard work, the dirty work. Or maybe he just didn't think Ppeekk and her friends were worth his personal effort. After all, it was the Eternal Life Circle he wanted, not *them*.

Then a string of large red crabs, each at least six inches wide and looking like they'd been dredged up from the scum of the sea, ascended the sloping shore, marching twenty abreast, their claws clicking and snapping like castanets. The children stood up in alarm. They couldn't go back into the waterway. The only way out now was on the beach.

The crabs advanced in military formation, hoisting their pinchers. The largest crab, its shell faded, scratched and scarred, no doubt from many years of battle, crawled forward. The glossy black beady eyes swiveled wildly on the ends of long stalks. Then it spoke in a raspy squeal. "Our master, Megalodon, sends no greetings. You are not worthy of his notice. However, he requests . . . no, *demands* that you cease trespassing in his waters immediately. You must never approach the metal grate again, or else you will be met with a swift demise. What is contained behind the grate, through to its very core, is the ultimate property of Megalodon. Our master shall not be denied."

The children held their ground confidently against the much smaller crabs, but having shed their shoes what seemed ages ago, they were fully aware of their bare feet and that their toes were only inches from the snapping pinchers.

"*His* waters?" Ppeekk said. "By what authority does he claim ownership of the waterway?"

Mini Romey alternated one foot on top of the other. "Yeah."

The crab clicked its claws sharply. Mini Romey jumped. "By the most ancient of authorities, no creature, neither marine nor terrestrial, defies the right of Megalodon to reclaim all that is his, including the Eternal Life Circle protected by Pa'ua, which you are attempting to prevent our master from possessing."

Ppeekk stood tall. "The Eternal Life Circle does not belong to Megalodon. It belongs to King Frederick and the animals of High Voltage."

The crab erupted in a throaty laugh. "This Frederick of yours is king of nothing. A mere sliver of a fish having no power Megalodon cannot overcome. Our remora fish, barracuda, moray eels, sawfish, and swordfish are excellent spies and worthy combatants. They report that your king has fled High Voltage in fear."

On an impulse, Quatro grabbed a piece of driftwood and threw it at the giant crab, breaking off its right claw. "That's not true. Dead Fred is not afraid of you."

Ppeekk stuck out an arm to prevent Quatro from crushing the menacing crabs. She shot a glance at him. "Shhh, Quatro."

"Ha! This Dead Fred, as you call him, is an apt name. For that is what he and the rest of you will be when Megalodon and his followers finish with you!"

At this, all the crabs raised their front set of legs and danced in small circles, as if already victorious. It reminded Ppeekk of football players doing their funny high-stepping dances after making a touchdown, and she wanted to laugh but didn't dare. The clicking of their claws drowned out the muffled sound of distant waves crashing on the beach.

The children stepped backward. The one-clawed leader and a dozen of his comrades advanced with pinchers opening and closing.

Ppeekk reached down, grabbed a handful of heavy green seaweed and sea grass, and heaved it toward the crabs. The lump of wet sea growth spun for a moment high in the air, like a slab of pizza dough, before it landed and trapped the advancing crabs.

Ppeekk raced down the grassy dune. "Come on, Quatro. Mini Romey, let's get out of here!"

While the army of crabs struggled to free themselves, Quatro and Mini Romey stumbled awkwardly behind Ppeekk across the deep sand at the top of the beach. They followed her, wading through the shallow inlet to firmer, wetter sand. Here they could run like the wind, and run they did. Even Mini Romey did her best to keep close. Their clothes flapped in the wind, and their hair streamed behind them as they splashed though the breaking surf, scattering small sea birds down the beach before them.

Ppeekk peered out at the blue Atlantic where the water glittered and sparkled. She spotted dolphins, maybe even *their* dolphins, leaping out of the water. The wet sand below their feet reflected crystal prisms of color. Above, a flock of gulls squawked and swooped and circled, following them.

Ppeekk breathed in the salty air and rejoiced in the freedom of this run on the beach. The buildings and the houses in the distance looked like Monopoly playing pieces, but Ppeekk knew her house was near. She paused to rest a moment at the point where they would go back to the "real" world. Mini Romey caught up, panting and gasping for breath. Ppeekk pointed. "My house is right up there. I think we can sneak through my yard and down the street to the bridge, where we can get our shoes and backpacks. What time is it?"

Quatro shook his head. "Amazing! We've still got time to make it to school. Time stands still when we're in High Voltage."

They trudged up the beach, crossed a road, and tiptoed through Ppeekk's yard, avoiding the kitchen window where Ppeekk's mom was working. Then they hurried to the bridge, Mini Romey grimacing and complaining all the way about rocks and pebbles stabbing her feet.

When they arrived at the bridge, Quatro found a discarded soda can and went down to the water's edge to fill it. He raced back up the bank and poured what he had collected into the Good Luck Circle. Each of them did a quick dance in the circle. After finishing the ritual, they stepped out and their school uniforms looked as if they had been recently washed and pressed.

Quatro grinned, gesturing in the direction of the big bad crabs and then toward their now perfect clothes. "Who says Dead Fred and the Good Luck Circle don't have power?"

"We're all ready for school," Mini Romey said. "Except for our shoes."

Bridget was busy dealing with some grown-ups and only shot a warning glance at the children as they went down to the grassy area beside the water. It was now high tide and Megalodon had vanished. Only a muddy imprint showed where he had recently lain. They grabbed their shoes and laced them up. They also retrieved their backpacks, shaking off a few red crabs that had latched on to the pouches. When Ppeekk checked on Dead Fred, she sucked in her breath. He stared at her with lifeless eyes.

CHAPTER EIGHTEEN

THE CALM BEFORE THE "CAT 5"

Mini Romey grabbed Ppeekk's arm and pointed at the water. It teemed with Megalodon's minions—remoras and barracudas and moray eels—and the water was no longer blue-green and sparkling, but murky and black as swamp water. As they climbed the stone steps, more red crabs tried to crawl up the bank toward them. How would they ever get back to High Voltage now?

It occurred to Ppeekk that life was sort of like the ocean—a series of calm, gentle waves fun to play in, followed by a crashing, pounding breaker that tumbled and scraped you on the rocky sea floor. Every time something fun happened, something bad seemed

THE CALM BEFORE THE "CAT 5"

to follow. Those dolphins had been the gentle waves, as well as saving graces, for her and her friends. Megalodon and the remoras, red crabs, and barracudas were the raging rip currents.

After the last harrowing encounter, two days passed before Ppeekk felt back to normal again. She and Quatro and Mini Romey had made it to school the day they'd ridden the dolphins, but Ppeekk had been exhausted by the swim out of the underwater cavern and through the maze of tunnels, not to mention being chased by the barracudas. Their confrontation with the red crab army had emptied her emotions, and she *had* been bitten by a blood-infused remora fish, just as Quatro and Mini Romey had. And even though they had all danced through the Good Luck Circle, Ppeekk still felt zombiefied, like she was just going through the motions at school and home in a daze.

When she thought about the conflict with Megalodon and how close she had come to being his breakfast, a shiver of fear coursed through her. Each one of his teeth had been as long as her hand, poised to slash and rip. But she also remembered how exhilarating it had been in the secret cavern with the giant clam, to touch and feel all that is good about the Eternal Life Circle.

She'd woken up the next morning to her parents arguing about the weather, her mom insisting they were in for a bad storm, and her dad protesting that the weathermen always exaggerated. She hadn't known it at the time, but that argument set the tone for the whole day.

Now she was walking to school with Mini Romey and Quatro, the three of them wheeling their backpacks along the paved path under an ominous sky. Unusual for Florida, it had been cloudy the past few days. The children felt overcast and down, Ppeekk more so than the others because Dead Fred was now so weak he could barely talk. He could utter only a few words before having to rest. Ppeekk worried and was beginning to become desperate. They had to do something, anything, to save Dead Fred and High Voltage.

"Those dolphins were so cool," Mini Romey said. "I've gone swimming with dolphins before, once on vacation, but we did it in a penned area and didn't get to ride very far or very long. The ride we had the other day was radical!"

Quatro raised his eyebrows. "Mini Romey, don't forget we could have been killed—on several different occasions and by many different species."

"But we *weren't* killed. The dolphins saved us, and then Ppeekk threw that seaweed on the crabs. Nothing can get us."

"What I don't understand," said Quatro slowly, "is why Megalodon didn't pursue us. Why send the little guys after us when he could do the job himself? Did you see him throw his weight up on the bank? His size and girth is on a scale greater than one of those double-decker buses they have in England."

"I think he makes his army of slaves do the grunt work. Remember, we're not the main prize he's after. He's saving his energy for far more important stuff—like getting his fins on the one thing he covets more than anything—the Eternal Life Circle," Ppeekk said. "Or maybe he just needed to rest and take a breather."

"Yeah," Quatro said, "it's incredible how that huge beast can exist both under the water and in the air."

Ppeekk looked at Quatro. "Megalodon's amphibious . . . right?"

"That's right."

"What does am . . . am . . . phibious mean, Quatro?" Mini Romey said.

"It means when he existed millions of years ago, he only lived in the water and took in oxygen through his gills. Now he has adapted to be able to live on both land and in the water, but he must breathe air through lungs like we do and like the manatees and the dolphins do."

"Are the manatees and dolphins amphibious?" asked Mini Romey.

Ppeekk could explain this one. "No, manatees and dolphins are mammals like us."

"It's only fish that have to breathe under water," Quatro said.

Mini Romey grinned. "Except Dead Fred. Because he's magical!"

Ppeekk was starting to have serious doubts about how much longer Dead Fred's magic could hold up. The last time all three of them had danced through the Good Luck Circle, it seemed to lose some of its brilliance. This morning she carried Dead Fred in her jumper pocket so she could keep a close eye on him.

They had passed the nature preserve and stood only a few yards away from the main intersection. Ppeekk felt hopeless and helpless and at her wit's end. Before going any farther, she decided to try to talk to him again. Carefully and gently, she lifted him out of her pocket and held him on the flat of her palm. Quatro and Mini Romey crowded close to see and to help shelter him from the sun and passing cars.

Ppeekk pressed her lips close to his frail body. "Dead Fred, can you talk to us? We have no idea what to do. Megalodon is getting stronger and bolder. He nearly killed us, and the size and sheer strength of his army seems unbeatable. What should we do? What's the next step?"

The fish sputtered in a weak voice they had to strain to hear. "Destroy . . . the . . . beast."

"We are willing to try, but how? He's so big and all those teeth . . ."

"Protect . . . Eternal . . . Life . . . Circle. He must breathe air . . . trap him . . . underwater . . . drown . . . low tide best."

"Yes," Ppeekk said. "Go on."

"High tide . . . dangerous to him." The fish coughed. "Lure him . . . looping tunnel."

"What else?" Quatro said. "Anything else?"

The three children bent down and put their ears right up against the little fish.

Dead Fred sighed. "Big storm coming. Dangerous . . . dangerous to all."

Dead Fred stilled; his little mouth gaped.

Mini Romey's hands flew to her cheeks. "Oh, no! He's dead!"

"No," said Ppeekk. "But he will be soon if we don't do something to save High Voltage."

Ppeekk gently tucked the little fish back into her pocket. "Dead Fred mentioned the looping tunnel. You know, the little side tunnel that doesn't go anywhere, the one that loops around and comes back to the main tunnel? Anna told me about it, but I'd forgotten until Dead Fred mentioned it. We could get Megalodon in there and trap him."

A honk startled the three of them out of their thoughts. They looked up as a sleek new car stopped and Frizz and Little Feet hopped out.

"We thought we'd walk to school with you," Little Feet said.

"If you don't mind," Frizz added.

Frizz's Mom called good-bye, waved, and drove off. Little Feet fell into step with Mini Romey, while Frizz joined Ppeekk and Quatro. Little Feet jabbed her thumb over her shoulder. "Who's that man in the little old-fashioned car? Is he following us?"

"Oh, that's Ppeekk's dad," Mini Romey said. "He putters behind us till we get to the bridge."

Just then the gang of four—McFlyo, Danimal, Firecracker, and GJ—raced up the sidewalk toward them.

GJ bent over to catch his breath. "We want to walk, too."

McFlyo hit Quatro squarely on the shoulder. "I figured, if you can't beat 'em, join 'em."

Danimal punched Quatro, then his other three pals. "You said it."

Quatro rubbed his shoulder. "Cut it out."

McFlyo picked up a rock and threw it at the stop sign. "Just trying to make a man out of you. Hey, who's that strange dude in the little box on wheels?"

Ppeekk's face flushed red. "It's my dad. He'll be gone in a minute."

Sure enough, when the group reached the bridge, he backed up, turned around, and sputtered away.

Firecracker whistled. "Smokin' little car!"

Ppeekk stopped on the sidewalk before they reached the Good Luck Circle and the bridge. She narrowed her eyes, barely making out Bridget's bulky form in the bridge house. "Listen you guys, we've got more important stuff to talk about than my dad and his car. You remember that gigantic fish we saw last week under the bridge?"

"Yeah, what a beast!" McFlyo said.

Frizz tried to smooth down her hair. "What did you call it? Megalodon or something like that?"

"That's right. Megalodon. Well, it's gotten worse than ever. The water's turning black and other evil fish are swimming in the waterway. Megalodon himself almost killed me and Quatro and Mini Romey."

As they approached the dimming Good Luck Circle, Mini Romey ran ahead and then whirled around facing the group. "Hey, you guys, here's the Good—"

Ppeekk dashed forward and grabbed her by the back of her jumper just in time to muffle the rest of what the little girl was going to say. Tugging Mini Romey back to the group, Ppeekk kept her voice low and urgent. "Mini Romey, the Good Luck Circle has got to be our secret for now. We need to keep it a secret between you and me and Quatro. Okay?"

Mini Romey nodded with big eyes and then skipped ahead again. Ppeekk and Quatro exchanged glances as they brushed over the surface of the circle in the concrete, hoping the others wouldn't notice it.

The group of kids walked up on the bridge and peered into the water. It was as black as strong tea, but no sign of Megalodon.

Danimal jutted out his chin. "I ain't scared of that big fish."

Mini Romey stretched her arms out on either side of her. "You would be if you were this close to him."

"I told you guys I was going to come up with a plan," Ppeekk said. "And walking to school this morning, I did. We were talking about how Megalodon has to come out of the water for air just like manatees and dolphins."

"Is that right?" McFlyo said. "What's your point, professor?"

Ppeekk's eyes twinkled. "My point is that if he's underwater and he can't get air, he will drown."

"Pretty basic logic." McFlyo jabbed his thumb toward his buddy. "Even Danimal here can follow that." Danimal spit toward McFlyo.

Ppeekk turned away from McFlyo and toward the rest of the group. "Well, if we could lure him into one of the underwater tunnels and cause him to become lost and disoriented, we could trap him there and he couldn't get out . . ."

Mini Romey clapped her hands and threw her head back in laughter. "And that would be the end of Megalodon!"

"What tunnels?" Little Feet said.

"We found these secret tunnels under the waterway," Ppeekk said.

"Awesome," Firecracker said.

"Cool," said Danimal.

McFlyo leaned on the bridge railing. "I'll have to see those tunnels before I believe it."

"But, Ppeekk," Quatro said, "how in the world are we going to do that? Megalodon is as big as a semi. We can't possibly get anything big enough and heavy enough at the ends of an underwater tunnel to hold him. It simply can't be done."

"Why not? We've got the looping tunnel and we've got rocks and boulders at the metal grate and at the mouth of the cavern. If you guys can close up the front of the metal grate after I come out, we would be sure to trap the beast. I'll ask the manatees to pile boulders in front of the entrance to the secret cavern, blocking Megalodon's access to the Eternal Life Circle. Dead Fred thinks we can do it, and so do I. We've *got* to do it."

Quatro cocked his head. "Now wait a minute. I'm not committing myself to anything yet. What exactly do you plan to do? This harebrained idea needs specifics. You've got to set it up and then you've got to maneuver Megalodon where you want him. What do you plan to use for bait?"

"Megalodon wants the Eternal Life Circle, doesn't he?"

"Yes . . ." Quatro said.

"And because we're trying to keep him away from the Eternal

Life Circle, he knows he has to go through us to get at it. So he would love nothing more than to sink his teeth into us, too, wouldn't he?"

Quatro glared at her in obvious irritation.

Ppeekk stood straight and still, hands on her hips. "Well, you're looking at the bait."

Quatro crossed his arms and narrowed his eyes. "No way. You can't put yourself in that kind of danger. We've had two close encounters with this beast. The third time might be a charm for Megalodon and fatal for us."

"I'm not talking about us. I'm talking about *me*. I can't just let the Eternal Life Circle fall into evil hands and allow High Voltage to be destroyed. I can't let Dead Fred continue to waste away. You heard Dead Fred explain my role in saving his kingdom. I've got to do something and do it soon."

Quatro's tone softened. "Ppeekk, Megalodon sees you as no more than a gnat on his back. He would devour you in a millisecond. Besides, I don't advise any water activities in the next week. Look at those cumulonimbus clouds in the distance. That's a squall line if I ever saw one. Don't you watch the news? A tropical storm is brewing in the Atlantic."

"I don't care. Dead Fred is dying. And I'll be mostly underwater and wet anyway. What can a little rain matter?"

He waved his arms at the sky and grew red in the face. "A hurricane is not just a little rain. Steve Weagle from channel five is predicting it's going to turn into Hurricane Lars, and it's headed this way, right for the east coast of Florida."

McFlyo stuck out his chest. "Me and my folks, we ride out hurricanes all the time in our house. Nothing to worry about. When it's all over, you just step out your door and swim to town."

"I ain't scared of a hurricane," Danimal said.

"Okay, Danimal, we get it," Quatro said. "You're not scared of anything."

"Is this hurricane for sure?" Ppeekk said.

"Well, the weather is never one hundred percent predictable, and they're also saying it could veer off course and head north—"

"There! You see! We might not even have a hurricane at all!"

"But it's stupid to take that kind of chance. Two years ago we were hit with three hurricanes that weren't supposed to make landfall. Ppeekk, I'm beginning to think you're just as odd as your weird dad."

Quatro stalked off ahead of them to walk to school by himself.

Her friend's public insult turned Ppeekk's face red. She swallowed her disappointment and hurt feelings and looked away.

"What's the matter with him?" Frizz said.

"Yeah, what's his problem?" McFlyo said.

"Quatro knows everything about the weather," Mini Romey said. "He follows it on channel five and on the Weather Channel and reads books about it. He's never wrong about storms and things. I swear he's going to be a weatherman when he grows up."

The group walked on together in silence for a few minutes.

"If Quatro's not going to help with your plan, Ppeekk, I guess I'd better not either," Mini Romey said. "And you know what? Quatro's right. Your dad is kind of weird. Come on, Little Feet, let's go."

Frizz laid her hand on Ppeekk's shoulder. "Ppeekk, I've got to go to my grandmother's tomorrow. Sorry I can't help."

Frizz, Little Feet, and Mini Romey hurried across the parking lot toward school.

McFlyo bowed low and laughed. "The gang of four at your service."

Danimal rubbed his hands together. "Yeah, we can do it. We ain't—"

Ppeekk raised a hand. "I know, I know. You're not afraid of a fish. And you're not afraid of a hurricane."

"You got that right," Firecracker said.

McFlyo's eyes met Ppeekk's. "I gotta hand it to you. You got a lot of nerve for a girl."

Ppeekk brought her face close to McFlyo's; they almost butted noses. "Listen, McFlyo, and the rest of you tough guys, too. I'm not doing this for fun or for the thrill of it. This is important, you understand. And when something's important, it doesn't matter who or what you are. You just do it. I once read a quote by a great author: 'If you're going to have regrets in your life, and you will, regret what you do, not what you don't do.'"

McFlyo's phony grin faded. "You're a little too deep, but we're with you."

Then it was Ppeekk's turn to smile, but it was a smile mixed with sadness. She had people to help her, but they weren't her best friends. Or rather, they weren't the kind of friends she thought Quatro and Mini Romey had been. Now all she had to help her save Dead Fred and High Voltage were these four boys who considered themselves meaner and tougher than they actually were. But she'd do anything and take any help she could get.

She looked at the boys one by one. "Okay, tomorrow morning is the day. The tide will never be lower and it will never be higher than tomorrow's. And I bet this storm everyone's talking about will make the water levels even more extreme."

"Yeah," Firecracker said, "it's gonna be better than the Fourth of July."

The boys laughed.

Ppeekk's brows knitted. "Get serious. Meet me here at the bridge in the morning, at eight o'clock sharp. This is our one shot. We've got to do it then."

A sudden gust of wind blasted across the bridge and walloped Ppeekk in the chest. She gasped as it took her breath. Her long hair whirled up and around her head like an inside-out umbrella. She pushed her hair behind her ears and looked up as the gray sky darkened to purple. A thick bank of clouds rolled in from the sea, blanketing the eastern horizon. Gripping the rail of the bridge, Ppeekk said a silent prayer. Down below, the dark water of the waterway turned black and the wind pumped waves across it, churning and boiling it like an evil brew in a witch's cauldron. Was Quatro right? Was a storm coming? And if so, what kind of fury would it unleash?

CHAPTER NINETEEN

LEAP OF FAITH

Ppeekk woke to the old wooden shutters banging and slam-ming outside her window. She threw on her clothes and made her way down to the beach to see how big the waves were. The wind blew fiercely, kicking up light debris and pelting her with sand. She walked backward to protect her face from what felt like sandblasting, occasionally reaching down to try to cover her exposed ankles.

Even before she reached the beach, she could hear the roar of the surf, much louder than usual. Emerging over the dunes that blocked her view of the sea, she stopped to stare open-mouthed.

The ocean was awash in foam, and the waves were at least ten feet high. They crashed with such force she felt small tremors under her bare feet. Last night, TV weatherman Steve Weagle had forecast eight- to ten-foot swells, and he was right. Out over the horizon, the lowering clouds loomed darker than ever and so close she felt she could reach up and touch them.

She tried to recall something Quatro had explained about high tides and low barometric pressure and hurricanes and how if they all combined it was a worst-case scenario. But this wasn't going to be a *real* hurricane. Her dad said rarely anything had come of the numerous hurricane scares in the past. They usually lost strength or drifted northeast, back out to sea. Ppeekk counted on that happening again. It had to. It was time to get rid of Megalodon once and for all. Now. Today. Before Dead Fred's name stopped being an endearment and became reality.

It was nearing low tide, even though it didn't look like it out on the beach. Dead Fred had told them to trap Megalodon at low tide, and that was what Ppeekk planned to do. Dead Fred had also told them that the best time to act was in the present, and he was right. He'd told them to think before they acted. And that was true, too. But if she thought as much as Quatro did, she might never get anything done. Ppeekk wished she had Dead Fred's help and advice right now, but he was too far gone, lying in a stiff stupor in the tree house.

Why did she like that little fish so much? Was it because, in a strange way, he had been her first friend here in Florida? He had joked with her and laughed with her and been honest with her. He had given her the confidence to do things she never thought she could do. He had needed her as much as she needed him.

But it was more than that. She just plain liked him. Maybe that's how friendship worked. You just liked someone and you didn't really know why. It just was. That's how it had happened with Quatro and Mini Romey, too. She liked and accepted them, with all their good points and their faults, and they did the same for her. But all that was over. They weren't her friends anymore. In spite of everything they'd been through together, with Dead Fred and the manatees and the giant clam and the dolphins, as well as Megalodon and the remora, they'd abandoned her when it came to something really important. They'd shown that clearly yesterday on the bridge. Still, she felt very much alone and wished they were around now.

Ppeekk trudged back up the beach to her house with the wind clawing at the back of her nylon jacket. A few sudden gusts pushed her so hard she lost her balance and had to steady herself with one hand on the ground in front of her. In spite of the weather, she was prepared for anything and had dressed for action with a one-piece swimsuit under her nylon shorts and water shoes on her feet. She also had a shoulder-strap backpack filled with rope, a small crow bar, and a grappling hook she'd taken from the garage last night. She'd stuck in a small waterproof tarp, a towel, rubber flippers for her feet, an energy bar, and a water bottle.

Late last night, when she'd been preparing and sneaking around the house and the garage, her parents had been watching the weather report on local channel 5 with that weatherman and reporter they both liked so much. Ppeekk had watched, too, as Steve Weagle and Chandra Bill talked about storm surges and evacuation routes.

Mom had been very nervous and wanted to pack and load the car to drive inland. But Dad was easygoing and calm. He had put his arm around his wife's shoulders. "Come on, honey. This house has been standing right here on this ground for over seventy-five years. It's been through plenty of storms and even hurricanes, including the great hurricanes of 1942 and 2005. They built these places to last back in the thirties, and this house has a solid foundation. It's not going anywhere, and neither am I. If you're really worried, we'll close what few shutters we have and I'll nail some plywood over the other windows in the morning."

Ppeekk had slept restlessly, but had been determined to get up before her father. Now she walked down the driveway right past the strangler fig, staring it down, daring it to bother her. It didn't. She walked past the swampy nature preserve, which looked more dismal than ever beneath the blustery, overcast sky. She sighed and wished it were just a normal school day and Quatro and Mini Romey were with her. Lights were on in the neighborhood houses she passed, and people moved about in their yards, preparing for the storm, picking up loose toys and stowing lawn furniture. By the time she reached the main road, cars were rushing past, loaded down with boxes and luggage strapped to the tops, headed for what they thought was higher ground and safety.

Ppeekk thought people were silly to make such a big deal out of a storm. Still, the wind blew relentlessly, so she decided to do what she had to do as quickly as she could so she could get herself back home safely. She hoped the manatees would be easy to find in High Voltage and that McFlyo and his gang would arrive on time.

She reached the Good Luck Circle at the end of the sidewalk. Even in the dimness of the overcast morning, the circle still shimmered and sparkled with the promise she hoped lay ahead. She drizzled some water from her water bottle and did a quick dance step in it. Rays of colored light, as if from a prism, shot out of the circle as she walked onto the bridge, confident and smiling. Today she needed all the power of the Good Luck Circle to radiate through her. This was going to be it—do or die.

Ppeekk looked around for McFlyo and his gang, but found no trace of them. She had planned for them to move boulders in front of the main tunnel entrance after she came out and before Megalodon could follow her. If those guys didn't show up, it would throw off all her plans.

Before that, though, she had to contend with Bridget. To get to High Voltage, Ppeekk had to get past her massive figure standing like a menacing troll in the bridge house. Would Bridget even notice Ppeekk if she scooted past? Ppeekk practically ran and made it almost across the bridge, when the old woman suddenly stuck out an arm and grabbed her by the shoulder. "Oh, no, you don't." Brown drool dribbled from her bottom lip while she blew cigar smoke into Ppeekk's face. "There'll be no swimming in the waterway today, especially with the hurricane coming. You and those friends of yours think you got your own private swimming hole down there, don't you?"

"I'm not going into the waterway." Ppeekk felt funny telling a lie, but it was for a most important cause. "We were told to evacuate the island, and I'm meeting my parents at my school."

The old woman shook her head. "No can do. You turn right around, young missy, and go back home."

Bridget twirled Ppeekk around and shoved her between the shoulder blades, pushing her several feet. Ppeekk stumbled, caught herself, and then turned and walked backward all the way to the Good Luck Circle, keeping her eyes on the old woman and racking her brain for a way, any way, to get past her.

After stepping inside the circle one more time, and raking her feet there as if she were a bull readying for a charge, Ppeekk decided she'd make a dash for it. But the old woman had been watching her, and when Ppeekk started to run across the bridge, Bridget wheeled around and stepped into her bridge house, moving more quickly than Ppeekk thought possible for someone as slow as Bridget.

The first thing Ppeekk heard was the awful creaking and groaning of rusty metal levers and gears. The crazy old woman was raising the drawbridge even though no boats needed passage through the waterway. The rickety wooden floor of the bridge began to rise under her feet. Even while Ppeekk scrambled, she slid backward. Then slowly, she climbed upward, digging her fingers into the wood to get a handhold on the angled floor. Bridget howled with a sick cackle, enjoying every second of Ppeekk's struggle.

As the slope of the bridge increased, Ppeekk's muscles ached and she could hardly keep her grasp as the incline was nearing vertical. When her arms were about to give out, she let pure instinct take over. In a sudden burst of strength and speed, she clambered up the wooden floor, splinters tearing into her palms.

Still wearing her backpack, she steadied herself in the blasting wind and crouched on the narrow edge of the top of the drawbridge, which continued to slowly rise. A flock of seagulls appeared from nowhere and flew in a tremendous outward-spiraling circle above her, like a white funnel cloud of birds, squawking and calling, urging her on. She lifted her gaze for a moment to the dark clouds in the sky. Like metal walls, gray sheets of rain rushed toward her as the first drops slapped against her face.

Balancing precariously on the edge, she slowly stood to her full height. Dizzy, Ppeekk wavered with arms flailing. She managed to spare a glance at Bridget far below. The old woman's mouth dropped open when she saw Ppeekk on the very top of the fully opened drawbridge. Then Ppeekk, teetering on the edge, made the sign of the cross, tilted her head back, crossed her arms over her chest like a parachutist, and took the ultimate leap of faith.

CHAPTER TWENTY

SECURING THE CAVERN

As she plunged through the air, time seemed to expand. Colors and images—purple sky, green trees, gray streets, little cars rushing like ants, her school, the pointed spire of the church—blurred and burned into her mind. For a second, she felt she was flying like one of the gulls circling above her. When she hit the water, it was like being ripped from a deep sleep.

With air bubbles tickling the length of her body, Ppeekk sank down to the bottom of the waterway like a heavy stone. In an instant, all the good creatures of High Voltage surrounded her. The giant water spiders scurried to her with an air bell and secured it on her head. Ppeekk looked around, and by the lights of the lantern fish and the eels, she could make out puffer fish, porcupine fish, sea turtles, and dolphins. Ppeekk managed to get the rubber flippers out of her backpack and onto her feet before the three manatees swam up and nudged her from behind.

Mr. Mann nodded. "We've been expecting you."

"There's no time to lose," Anna said. "What can we do to help?"

Ppeekk gasped to catch her breath. "I need you to swim with me into the tunnels and use your strength to move boulders to block the entrance to the secret cavern."

Manny swam in a quick circle. "We can do that easy."

"The most important thing is to secure the entrance to the Eternal Life Circle. Once that's complete, I'm going to lure Megalodon into the tunnels at low tide. It's a real maze in there. I'll swim into the main section of the tunnels, getting Megalodon to chase after me, and then I'll dart back out through the looping tunnel. He'll see me and follow, and then when I come out, we'll lock the grate, pile boulders against it, and Megalodon will be trapped inside and drown."

"I'm not so sure about this," Anna said. "You're talking about putting your life in jeopardy, and doing so with the most evil beast known to marinekind."

"Do you realize the risk you are undertaking?" Mr. Mann said.

"It'll work," Ppeekk said. "It's got to. Dead Fred can no longer speak. We've got to make High Voltage safe enough for him to return."

All the animals hovered, listening. One young dolphin, not much larger than Ppeekk, came forward and offered his fin to her. It was the same dolphin she'd ridden before.

"That's Flash. He's the fastest dolphin in the pod," Manny said. "He's offering to go on the mission with you."

Ppeekk looked into Flash's eyes and smiled. "I knew there was something special about you. You really gave me the ride of my life. You must be one of the fastest dolphins in the entire ocean. Well, we'll sure need all your speed again today. I'm counting on you."

The dolphin nodded and clicked and stayed close to her.

Mr. Mann gestured toward the secret cavern. "We'll take care of blocking the entrance to the secret cavern. That must be done properly to protect Pa'ua and the Eternal Life Circle. There's no need for you to help with that. Stay here and conserve your strength and wait for our return."

Ppeekk inserted a starfish into the locking mechanism and opened the grate with the special combination to allow Mr. Mann and Anna to swim into the tunnels. The puffer fish and porcupine fish stood sentry duty, keeping a lookout for Megalodon and his remoras and barracudas.

Manny was in a talkative mood, but Ppeekk had a hard time following his chatter. He reminded her of Mini Romey. Plus, she was worried about the weather and how she was going to lure Megalodon into the tunnels. She glanced up nervously toward the surface of the waterway where the normally smooth channel was whipped into a frenzy of waves.

Ppeekk swam up to the surface and removed her air bell to evaluate the situation. The wind screamed and moaned as it raced past her exposed head and shoulders. She bobbed in the waves as if she were a bath toy. The rain fell in heavy sheets moving in from the ocean and obscuring her view of the bridge and bridge house. With some effort, she swam to the bank opposite the bridge house and hoisted herself onto the soggy shore.

Someone in a yellow hooded slicker made his way through the bankside underbrush. The spindly legs, untied shoes, and tidy appearance looked familiar. He stooped down beside her and peered at her from behind fogged-up glasses. Quatro!

She could barely hear his voice as lightning ripped through the sky and thunder echoed from cloud to cloud. "Ppeekk, I'm sorry. I didn't mean what I said about your dad. He's no weirder than any of the rest of us. He's been calling our house, frantically looking for you. He's really worried about you."

Ppeekk jerked away from him and moved toward the water.

He grabbed at her. "Ppeekk, this isn't worth it. McFlyo and those guys aren't coming. Everybody's hunkered down in their houses or evacuating. My parents have no idea I'm out here."

Ppeekk was glad the rain hid the tears streaming down her face. "I don't need those guys to help me. I don't need you or anybody."

Quatro took off his glasses and tried to clear the haze with his fingers. "You may not need us, but we need you. Mini Romey and I want to be your friends."

Ppeekk saw the sincerity in his eyes. She knew she should forgive him. "You *are* my friend, Quatro. And I want to be yours. But this is something I have to do."

"Are you sure you know what you're doing? Are the manatees helping?"

She nodded.

"Well, just remember it's low tide now, and if you're going to trap Megalodon, he'll be more likely to go into the tunnels now because he thinks he can come up for air more easily. So this is actually the best, in fact, the *only* time to do it." He smiled. "That is, if you don't get blown or washed away first."

The edges of Ppeekk's mouth tipped upward. The wind was now alternately screaming in a high-pitched whistle and moaning in low, eerie tones. An aluminum lawn chair flew through the air, landing ten feet away in the water.

Ppeekk's eyes widened. "Don't tell my dad where I am or what I'm doing, Quatro."

"Just do it quickly and get back home safely."

Ppeekk squeezed his hand, and he squeezed back. She clambered down the bank and pushed herself under the churning water. As her eyes adjusted to the dimness, she felt the tap from behind. Her heart jumped into her throat. She paddled backward as quickly as she could, and then sighed in relief. It was only Anna and Manny.

"Dad's almost got the entrance to the secret cavern blocked," Manny said.

The giant water spiders quickly equipped Ppeekk with a new air helmet.

Anna looked worried. "He's working as fast as he can. I hope he finishes soon."

"Good luck, Ppeekk," Manny said. "Wish I could go with you."

"The electric eels and the starfish and some of the smaller fish will help you," Anna said. "They'll be hiding in crevices near the grate ready to close and lock it behind you when you come out. Good luck, my dear!"

Manny spun in a circle again. "Hey, Flash is here!"

The two manatees swam away, disappearing into the murky water. Mr. Mann was still deep inside the tunnels, moving boulders across the entrance to the secret cavern. She wrapped her arms around the dolphin and held on. She peered into the dimness that seemed to be dredged up from the depths of the sea, wishing Mr. Mann would hurry up and come out. She and the dolphin swam back and forth in front of the tunnel entrance, as though pacing, first under the water and then on the surface, on high alert for the beast. Megalodon could appear from anywhere during the gloom of the storm, and without warning.

When Ppeekk and the dolphin slipped under the surface, she saw stingrays burrowing under the sand, small fish darting into rocky crevices, and electric eels hiding themselves in the sea grass. Not only were the manatees gone, but no other fish or creatures could be found. Everything became eerily quiet and still in the waterway. Her dolphin stopped swimming and began to click in rapid staccato.

From out of nowhere an ice-cold current coiled around Ppeekk's body and chilled her to the bone. As she strained to see through the watery murk, two eyes gradually materialized out of the darkness. Not the small sparkling eyes of the manatees. Not the bright shining eyes of the puffer fish or the lantern fish. Not even the cold, glittering eyes of the barracudas. But two huge lidless eyes, cruel and red-rimmed, set well away from each other on a wide blank face. The black eyeballs rolled in their shallow sockets and then fixed on her, possessed with single-minded intensity.

It was Megalodon in all his ferocious, hulking monstrosity.

CHAPTER TWENTY-ONE

RIDING THE BEAST

Megalodon's thick gray hide was shriveled and puckered with scars. Dozens of remora fish clung to him, absorbing his evil essence. Bubbles as large as Ppeekk's fists streamed from the monster's nostrils. In a horrifying, mirthless grin, he bared rows of razor-sharp teeth trailing shreds of red-stained cloth. His whole body appeared tense and poised to strike, his powerful tail flexing like the muscles of a panther about to leap. The two of them—girl and beast—were face to face.

This was what she'd been waiting for. This was the moment for action. But Ppeekk froze with fear. What if Megalodon followed them into the tunnels and ignored Ppeekk and broke through to the secret cavern only to capture the Eternal Life Circle? Had Mr. Mann had time to secure the secret cavern? Either way, she was going to have to risk it. She had to get Megalodon to follow her into the looping tunnel!

Megalodon opened his mouth. As the hinged jaws swung up and out, revealing the black depth of the orifice, a strong suction tugged at Ppeekk and the dolphin. She felt caught in a whirlpool of rushing water, as if being flushed into the bowels of the beast.

With adrenaline coursing through her body, Ppeekk tore the backpack off her shoulders and slung it forward, right into Megalodon's mouth. As the beast chomped down on it, the surrounding water was forced outward, hurling Ppeekk and the dolphin in a rushing current. His teeth crunched down on the iron crow bar and the metal grappling hook in her pack. She hoped it would put him out of commission for a few minutes.

Megalodon bellowed in pain and rage. The sound echoed with a dull roar under the water. The beast thrashed and writhed, making more waves in the already roiling water. Ppeekk used all her strength to hold on to the dolphin.

Trembling and screaming inside, she tried to steady herself. Flash seemed frozen in place. She leaned close to him. "Go!" Ppeekk shouted.

The dolphin snapped out of his apparent state of shock. With Ppeekk holding on, Flash dived down and straight through the opened tunnel entrance. It was darker than ever in the tunnels. She could never have found the looping tunnel by herself. She crossed her fingers and hoped the dolphin could make it. He clicked and chattered, finding the way by echolocation. Ppeekk held on to his fin and encouraged him with her voice. She stroked and patted his smooth head and skin. Behind them, the beast snorted as he pursued them. The movement of his massive body through the tunnels forced the water to rush forward, giving Ppeekk and the dolphin extra propulsion.

After winding through an interminable maze of tunnels, the dolphin suddenly reared back and stopped, knocking Ppeekk's head on the earthen ceiling. This was the crucial crossroads, the entrance to the looping tunnel. How would she get Megalodon to follow? She glanced ahead and saw a faint glimmering coming from the entrance to the secret cavern. It must be the light of the Eternal Life Circle. Would Megalodon notice? Would he go to the cavern and the Eternal Life Circle instead of chasing her into the looping tunnel? Her thoughts whirled. She must *make* him follow her! She had only one chance. It was now or never.

Ppeekk felt like a little kid playing tag with a big bully, trying to get him to chase her so she could trip him up. Inside her head she heard the clown fishs' taunts: *Nah, nah, nah, nah, nah.* She remembered how she had chanted challenges when she was young: *You can't catch me.* She waited with Flash until she could feel and hear the beast bearing down upon them.

Then Ppeekk shouted through her air helmet as loudly and obnoxiously as she could, wiggling her body like a worm on a hook: "Nah, nah, nah, nah, nah! You can't catch me, you big minnow!"

Before she knew what was happening, the beast was upon them, snapping his powerful jaws. Two teeth snared one of Ppeekk's rubber flippers and the monster yanked. The rubber strap cut into her foot, and for a moment she feared he might tear her whole foot off. She bent and twisted her ankle, trying to loosen the flipper strap.

Then she felt it snap off her heel like a stretched rubber band. It smacked the beast in the snout. Ppeekk looked back and saw that Megalodon seemed confused, unable to understand what had struck him. He stopped and shook his head and then bellowed as if he had been mortally wounded. Ppeekk remembered Quatro saying something about his nose being a sensitive spot.

Ppeekk gulped as she realized how close she had come to being eaten alive. This was not a child's game of tag. This was a most serious and deadly encounter. The stakes were high, both for her and for Dead Fred, with the prize being High Voltage and the magical Eternal Life Circle. And the danger was now even more threatening. Megalodon was mad!

Flash and the girl veered into the mouth of the narrow looping tunnel, with the beast at their heels. She could feel the rush of the current pushing behind them. Megalodon barely fit in the earthen tunnel. He collided repeatedly against the sides, scraping remora against the walls like squished bugs. The three of them sped through, winding and weaving back and forth as if on Disneyland's Big Thunder Mountain. The speed and curves dizzied Ppeekk. Once, Flash did a barrel roll as they flew through the water, and Ppeekk felt like she was on an underwater roller coaster.

Then a hot rush of fear clutched at her throat and chest. Filaments of slimy things brushed against her arms and legs, and the tunnel stretched longer than she remembered. Would it ever end? She had not expected Megalodon to be so fast or close behind. Wouldn't he have to breathe soon? She perspired inside her air bubble, and her hair stuck to her damp face. Her temples throbbed, and she felt light-headed. Maybe they were lost. What if her bubble ran out of air? And if they did come to the end of the tunnel and found their way out, would they be able to close and lock the grate in time to trap Megalodon inside?

Although she couldn't see the beast, she could feel and hear him struggling through the narrow tunnel, crashing with large dull thuds, causing the dirt walls to partially cave in behind them.

Flash made constant high-pitched squeaks. Then the narrow looping tunnel spit them out into the primary tunnel again. The main opening was in the distance, a little light visible through the faraway grate. Could they make it? Would they make it?

When Ppeekk and Flash blasted out of the tunnel into the open waterway, the starfish and electric eels slammed the grate shut, turned the spindle, and locked it. They were all only a few yards beyond the promised safety of the locked entrance when Megalodon loomed once again in the meager light at the end of the tunnel. With eyes wide and wild, he barreled toward them, picking up speed like a launched rocket.

But instead of being trapped, he crashed through the cross-hatched metal grate as if it were made of paper. Megalodon exploded into the waterway, enraged, scattering electric eels and fish, to swim to the surface for air. While the beast gulped air, Flash did the same, and then the dolphin bolted away so quickly he snapped Ppeekk's head back. But Megalodon was soon pursuing them again. And gaining. Megalodon suddenly lunged and crashed into Flash with the full force of his weight, knocking Ppeekk off, her air helmet thrown from her head.

In a panic, Ppeekk clawed her way upward. She struggled through the churning water and broke the surface, gasping for air and coughing up brackish water. The foaming waves tossed her up and down. She twisted her head from side to side. Where was Flash? Even though she was now on the surface, she couldn't see a thing and her breath came in ragged gasps. Torrents of rain and hail pounded her like nails. No water spiders were in sight to make her another air bubble, and the wind whipped waves into her face, one after the other.

Ppeekk was in the middle of a hurricane. *It must be a full-fledged category 5,* she thought, *just as Quatro and the weatherman predicted.* And even though she had become a decent swimmer in the past few days and she was familiar with the waterway, she might as well have been floundering in the open ocean. She couldn't see the banks or even the bridge. She couldn't see anything at all except wildly thrashing water. The wind howled, and the sky crackled with thunder and lightning.

The water level had risen at least six feet. Ppeekk remembered Quatro talking about a storm surge during a hurricane—a giant flood that swept houses and cars and even whole villages and towns out of existence. Ppeekk coughed and gasped and sputtered, taking in more water than air. She felt paralyzed and was filled with thoughts of her own death. Her plan had failed, and she was drowning in a hurricane. Quatro had been right after all. If only she had listened. If only . . .

Something crashed into her from below, the impact so great she was tossed up and out of the water like a rag doll twenty feet through the air. Her heart panicked. Megalodon had found her.

When she hit the water it felt like landing on concrete. The impact made the skin on her face, arms, and legs burn as if she'd been scraped on the ground. Megalodon played with her as if she were a toy, tossing her like a beach ball. Her sides ached and her ribs throbbed. She wondered if they were broken. Desperately, she tried to swim away.

She knew something was moving below her again. Reluctantly, she reached down in a futile effort to protect herself. As the beast rushed upward with his large mouth gaping to swallow her, a sudden swell washed Ppeekk to the side, bouncing her off Megalodon's head behind his eyes and flinging her to the top of the beast's back. Megalodon's dorsal fin scratched her arms. Ignoring the sandpaper roughness and her pain, Ppeekk wrapped all ten fingers around the fin and gripped tightly, holding on for dear life.

When the beast figured out what had happened, he bucked violently, trying to shake her off. Ppeekk's hands began to bleed from trying to hang on to the abrasive fin. She knew, with a kind of insane glee, she could ride Megalodon just as she had ridden the dolphins and the manatees. Her actions didn't make a lot of sense, but at least she wasn't being devoured by Megalodon's stinking maw of a mouth.

All right. I can do this. I can survive. I'm in control. She sat upright on the monster's back and straddled him with her legs, clutching his fin. The enraged beast bellowed as he surged and drove his massive body above the surface of the churning water.

No one could hear Ppeekk over the raging storm except maybe the beast. "Yee-haw!"

Megalodon did not give up easily. He dove and surfaced numerous times. He thrashed his head and bent his thick neck backward. He twisted and snapped his huge jaws at her over and over again, like a dog trying to scratch the itch in the middle of its back. He thrashed his tail toward her. It came closer to her than she liked, slapping like a huge fly swatter just inches from her feet.

They moved down the waterway and Ppeekk caught a brief glimpse of the bridge as they passed underneath and then beyond it. The lazy waterway she'd grown to love, the beautiful world of High Voltage, was now like raging, white-water rapids. But at least Dead Fred was secure in the tree house. Or was it even still standing? She didn't know whether the creatures of High Voltage were safe or being swept out to sea.

Without warning, Megalodon leapt from the waterway, and a clump of low hanging mangrove trees scraped Ppeekk off his back. She was tossed into the raging torrent, completely unable to swim in any direction against the powerful current. When part of a big cypress tree trunk almost crashed into her, she grabbed on to it to keep her head above water. Looking over her shoulder, she saw that Megalodon was being pushed by the water right behind her. Were they both being swept out to sea?

Ppeekk felt terror like she'd never known, but her fear helped her mind to focus. She thought of the ones she loved—Dead Fred, her mother, even her father. Would she ever see them again?

CHAPTER TWENTY-TWO

EYE OF THE STORM

Edward Berry awoke to a nightmare situation on that Saturday in late August. The weather report called for a major hurricane, and he rushed around, trying to nail sheets of plywood on the windows.

When Mrs. Berry dissolved into a sobbing mess because she couldn't find Ppeekk, he had promised to find her. He looked all over the house and even climbed into the tree house. He'd found a bunch of candy wrappers, a few brightly colored sketches of a brilliant circle with kids dancing inside it, a drawing of a big shark, and a small box containing a tiny shiner fish, dead and dried out, eyes perfectly preserved in a strange way. Why would his daughter collect such things? By then he was operating in full panic mode.

He slapped on his brown felt fedora, clambered into the Yugo, and gunned the engine. It was raining so hard he could barely see the road in front of him. Although he could have walked, he chose to drive next door, thinking that the neighbor kids were covering for Ppeekk. He banged on the neighbor's front door shutter. By the time they'd answered his pounding on the door, he was soaked, and water dripped all over the floor from his black trench coat.

"Where is she? Where's Ppeekk?" Mr. Berry nearly shouted at Mini Romey cowering behind her mother.

"Ppeekk went to the bridge," Mini Romey mumbled, hiding her face in her mother's skirt. "T-t-to check on the dolphins."

Mr. Berry's stomach clenched. Why would his daughter go into the waterway in this weather? What possessed her to take such a risk? Or was this little neighbor girl deluded?

Quatro appeared at the door. His father grabbed his shoulder. "Where's the Berry girl? Is she down at the old drawbridge?"

Quatro's voice trembled. "Yes. I've just seen her there."

White-faced, Mr. Berry tore out of the house toward his car. The wind whipped his fedora from his head, and what was left of his hair was soon sopping wet and dripping down his collar. The wind howled at the Yugo as it swerved through the flooded streets, spraying water in wide arcs from all four wheels. He was cold and wet, but it didn't matter. He thought about the mornings he'd driven these same streets behind Ppeekk and her friends while they talked and laughed. He'd followed them, trying to ignore them, making a sales call or drinking coffee or listening to the radio, sometimes all three at once.

But what had they talked about? Or laughed about? He couldn't begin to imagine. He didn't know what interested his daughter, what she liked and disliked, or what made her happy or sad. A hard lump formed in his throat. Had he lost the chance to know his own daughter? Why had he neglected the girl who meant the world to him, the daughter he loved with all his heart?

He slammed on the brakes, skidding off the road and landing in the drainage ditch. Pinned closed by the gale force wind, he kicked open the door and jumped out of the car at the entrance to the bridge. Rain sluiced down the sloping sidewalk, rushing over the curb in miniature waterfalls. This was where Ppeekk and the kids often stopped and played before crossing over the waterway.

In spite of the near-blinding rain, something on the sidewalk caught his attention. Right before the bridge began, whatever it was shimmered and sparkled. *Must be a refraction of raindrops on pavement. But that couldn't be because the sun wasn't shining. It must be some kind of watery optical illusion.* The rain pummeled his bare head. He had to find Ppeekk, but the strange patch of light in the middle of the storm drew his eyes like a magnet.

As Edward fought to stay upright, he stared at the glowing circle shining from the depths of the concrete. How was this possible in the pelting darkness of the storm? Then his mind flashed back to Ppeekk's drawing of the circle he had seen in the tree house. Without thinking, he stepped inside the circle, his mind suddenly flying back to his childhood. He remembered a happy time when he had played in the rain, running and sliding through the wet grass, trying to catch raindrops on his tongue, getting wet and not minding, twirling and slipping and falling down and laughing and getting up again.

He smiled in spite of himself and shuffled in his soggy shoes. His shoulders loosened, and he moved his arms and elbows, gently bending his knees. He lifted his face to the sky and let the rain fall down on him with abandon. He opened his mouth and drank the rain as he had so many years ago. And then he did something completely unexpected: He laughed, as he had as a boy. And then he danced some more.

Mr. Berry ran onto the bridge, knowing he had what he needed to find his daughter. He rushed up to the bridge house. *How unfortunate that the bridge keeper is so ugly and disgusting. All this time I thought she was an old man.* But his thoughts were quickly followed by a rush of compassion.

He stepped into the bridge house and shook the old woman's cold and clammy hand, pumping it vigorously. "I'm looking for my daughter, a girl about thirteen years old, all legs, with long brown hair."

She mumbled through a soggy unlit cigar dangling from her mouth. "Oh, yeah. That fool of a girl climbed on the drawbridge as I was raising it. Now, mister, that's against the law. Then she jumped into the waterway. If she's not already drowned, she's a goin' to jail."

He stared at the woman and then he shook her hard by the shoulders. "Well, call the coast guard!" he shouted. "What are you waiting for?"

He flung himself back into the storm, pausing in the middle of the bridge where the two sections came together. Leaning on the rail with both hands, he stretched his torso out, peering at the raging flood beneath him. The waterway was so swollen with rainfall and storm surge that it had risen nearly eight feet. Howling gusts tore at his clothes, and a thunderclap shook the wooden bridge. Lightning ripped like a knife through the clouds while the rain poured down. "Ppeekk! Ppeekk!"

He called his daughter's name over and over, praying she would hear and answer. But all that responded was the shrieking wind and the torrential rain and water rushing like a freight train.

A sound caught his attention, a sound not caused by the storm. It was a high-pitched human sound, like someone singing or yelling. Or yodeling. *Ppeekk.* "Ppeekk! Ppeekk! Ppeekk!" He grew hoarse from trying to yell over the raging storm.

Then he saw something as large as a whale flash by. He blinked and rubbed his rain-soaked eyes. He recognized the remnants of a backpack bobbing on the water in the wake of what looked like a giant shark. It was Ppeekk's backpack.

Ppeekk didn't know if she was going to survive either the storm or the beast. Still hanging on to the cypress log rushing through the water, she was determined to do her best to keep this monster Megalodon away from High Voltage. Her body had become numb from the cold water, but she experienced a strange kind of freedom and power. She shouted it to the winds until her throat ached. When she paused for a moment, she thought she heard someone calling her name. *I must be hearing things,* she thought.

She glanced over at a figure where the banks should be. It looked like a man waving his arms, but it had to be a tree with branches buffeted by wind. Still, she continued to stare. The silhouette seemed to run along the banks parallel with her, following her. At first it looked like Bridget with heavy clothes flapping around her. Ppeekk squinted through the gray curtains of rain. Dozens of remora leaped through the drenched atmosphere, and the figure blurred, transforming into what looked like the albino ghoul she had seen in the swamp.

Exhausted, water running down her forehead and into her eyes, she couldn't tell if what she saw was real or an illusion. The albino ghoul rose up into a huge amorphous cloud and faded away, obscured by rain and mist. When the curtains of rain parted again, she saw the purple-gray face and figure of the voodoo priestess, whipping itself in jerky, distorted movements with the gusting wind. Ppeekk was so tired it occurred to her she was probably hallucinating.

This second image contorted and disappeared, replaced by the bloodspitter heaving torrents of bloodred remora fish. Then that apparition shrank, shrouded in mist like rings of smoke, and this time Ppeekk saw the dwarf from the concrete truck, the little smiling man. He ran beside her on the bank of the waterway—running and waving and smiling while shaking his pipe.

In a flash of lightning, Ppeekk saw it wasn't the dwarf at all. And it wasn't the ghoul, the bloodspitter, or the voodoo priestess.

It was her father running on the bank, waving at her, shouting. Her hands nearly slipped off the tree trunk she clung to.

When Ppeekk's father saw his daughter struggling to hang on to the log and spotted what looked like a giant shark fighting the current and following her, he didn't think; he acted. He knew he had to save his daughter. He threw himself into the raging water and swam toward her. But he couldn't have foreseen how cold and strong the currents were.

If Ppeekk was surprised to see her father on the bank, she was shocked to see him jump into the water. Was he trying to rescue her? He had never been a good swimmer. Now he floundered, sinking and rising and then sinking again, just like a drowning person in those old cartoons. He was always showing up when she didn't need him, complicating her life. But here he was, trying to save her. She wasn't a good swimmer, but he was worse. She couldn't just watch as he drowned.

The wind and the rains washed him down the waterway toward the inlet and the open sea. She knew she had to let go of the log and swim out into the flooded channel to help her father. So Ppeekk struggled through the water toward him. By then, it was only a couple of yards, but it took every ounce of her strength. When she reached him, they grasped each other's arms and both sank. Bobbing back up, Ppeekk struck out for the shore, pulling her father along by his trench coat's sleeve. The current threw her against the bank, but she was too weak to pull herself out of the water. She was at the limit of her strength. She feared she couldn't save herself, much less her dad.

Ppeekk wept as she scratched and clawed at the shoreline. With her young life flashing before her eyes, she saw her father as a pain and a nuisance, but also as the one who'd taught her to ride a bike and catch a ball, who'd danced with her to the "Butterfly Kisses" song at their annual father-daughter dance at her old school. When she was little, he'd tucked her in at night and read her stories. The father she usually disdained, the man who irritated her and angered her, who didn't seem to have any time for her . . . now he was helpless in the storm trying to save her, and she was unable to help him. Ppeekk trembled as the fear of losing him and the emotion of loving him washed over her.

Panting, she rested for a moment, one hand struggling to find a handhold on the slippery bank and the other grasping her father. Her face and arms were scratched and bleeding. Her ribs ached, as did every muscle in her body. She knew it was only a matter of time before Megalodon found them helpless in the channel.

The giant clam's words echoed in her memory: "Gold rings will balance on the edge of choice" and "Use the power I have given you." She drew strength from her inner self. She wouldn't give up.

Through the pelting rain and the wind-whipped water, something brushed Ppeekk's head. A long branch from a gumbo-limbo tree on the bank dangled in the water right beside her. Slowly, like a flexible cord, the branch wrapped itself around Ppeekk's arm and tugged. She moved her hand up and grabbed on to her dad's arm more firmly. Inch by inch, the tree branch pulled her and her father out of the water.

They lay sprawled in the mud, gasping for breath, her dad only half-conscious. Ppeekk dragged at him as she crawled up the muddy bank. When she reached the gumbo-limbo tree, she released him and leaned against the trunk as the hurricane winds continued to scream and howl.

Ppeekk couldn't guess how long they sheltered here. Her father, though unconscious, was still breathing. She lost track of time and must've fallen into a deep sleep. The quiet woke her. And the light. The rain had stopped, and the wind had died down. In fact, sunshine filtered through the branches on them.

Ppeekk raised her weary head and looked up. Like a round window into heaven, a massive circular opening in the clouds hung in the ethereal blue sky. All around the hole, dark purple storm clouds raged. They stretched from the edges of the window down to the ground, but these storm clouds were miles away from where Ppeekk and her father huddled, wet and dirty and exhausted.

Ppeekk glanced over at the waterway. Although the wind had calmed, the water was still churning out of control and Megalodon's huge bulk floundered there. Obviously fatigued, he still fought the storm surge and the flood tide sweeping toward the ocean. It looked like he was trying to swim against the current, back to the area of High Voltage. Or maybe he was simply trying to save himself and not be swept out to sea. Ppeekk could do nothing more to save High Voltage. She had to stay with her father.

She sat up, wincing with pain. A yellow slicker approached. Was it Quatro again? What was he doing here?

Quatro offered his hand. "It's the eye of the storm. We've got just a short period of time to get you home before the other side of the hurricane hits. Sometimes that's the worst part. Those walls of clouds are headed this way. Come on!"

"Can you help me with Dad?"

Ppeekk and Quatro stooped down to help Mr. Berry stand. They supported him, one under each of his arms, and started walking.

Ppeekk cast a glance back at Megalodon and saw that the raging waters around him had intensified. How could that be? Was he caught up in some kind of rip current? She stopped and took her Dad's arm off her shoulder and leaned him against her body. She peered down the waterway. Dozens of High Voltage creatures swam faster and faster circles around Megalodon, stirring the waters with their bodies. All the fastest swimmers of High Voltage were there, mostly dolphins, but also fish of all kinds as well as stingrays and eels. As the animals picked up speed, their movement made a shallow circular indentation in the water. A low wall of water rose up around the beast. The animals swam with lightning speed, and the water rose higher and higher.

Ppeekk nodded toward the channel. "Quatro, look!" Suddenly, all the High Voltage creatures dived and disappeared. But the circular movement continued, a watery vortex rising all around Megalodon. The beast swam frantically, throwing himself against all sides of the wall of water. But he couldn't break through. He lost strength and crashed off the walls like a steel marble in a pinball game.

Then the wall of water rose up so high Ppeekk and Quatro could no longer see the beast trapped inside. The spinning, whirling vortex had sucked up several tons of water and began to move faster and faster. It spun and sloshed against the bank, hovering over the channel.

Quatro's eyes widened. "Wait. It's a waterspout!"

The waterspout lifted the evil shark in its slippery hands and seemed to play with Megalodon as he had played with Ppeekk earlier. They could see the beast's enraged thrashing as the whirling water lifted him thirty feet into the air. Ppeekk had heard of tornadoes lifting cars into the air and tossing them like toys. Now she was seeing what a waterspout could do.

Then, just like tornadoes on land, the waterspout moved faster down the waterway. The impending return of the storm pushed it at an ever-increasing speed toward the inlet and the sea. The kids strained to see the waterspout towering high and flinging its top edge outward in all directions. Megalodon spun around at the top of the vortex, and then with an incredible centrifugal force, the waterspout flung the beast toward the ocean. With remora fish falling away from his limp body, Megalodon made a massive splash far out in the ocean, the impact nearly splitting him in two. He disappeared from view, releasing the last of his air bubbles as he slowly sank. Ppeekk and Quatro watched for a long minute.

Megalodon was dead.

CHAPTER TWENTY-THREE

RISK OR REGRET

It was the first Friday of the month of September, and Ppeekk prepared to walk to school with a brand-new backpack for the first time since the hurricane had struck. School had been closed for four days due to catastrophic damage to the structures. She would have to attend classes in the building with the least damage—the church. She wore the same navy blue jumper and white blouse she'd worn on the first day of school almost three weeks ago. She had the same lunchbox, too, but she was not the same girl.

Everyone said it was a miracle that she and her dad had survived such a brutal and destructive hurricane. When they had finally trudged home with Quatro, they saw the magnitude of the disaster—roofs of houses ripped off, shards of shattered glass, trees stripped bare of leaves, street signs bent in two, power lines strewn across the streets.

But their little house, while battered, still stood intact on a small rise above the beach. Hurricanes were odd like that. Sometimes it destroyed one house and spared the other right beside it. The neighbors said Ppeekk's house had survived because it was surrounded by trees and dense foliage.

Even the tree house seemed to be all there, minus two broken windows and a few missing shingles, which was a great relief because that's where Dead Fred had been the whole time.

Ppeekk had wanted to put Dead Fred into the waters of High Voltage immediately, but going to the bridge had been impossible. It was lucky that school was canceled because she had slept for two days straight after the ordeal, and then she was so sore she could barely move. Her mother kept a close eye on her and would not allow her to go beyond the yard while work crews repaired power lines. She could only climb into the tree house and sit with Dead Fred.

That was the worst—Dead Fred could no longer respond. His eyes and face were blank and lifeless. No matter what or how Ppeekk spoke to him, he didn't answer. Ppeekk feared he had truly died, and she blamed herself for not helping him sooner. She still didn't know if the waters of High Voltage were safe for him, or if the animals of High Voltage had hung on and survived or had been washed out to sea.

Ppeekk felt completely alone, with Dead Fred unable to talk and Quatro and Mini Romey confined to their houses as well. She couldn't talk to anyone about High Voltage or its wise king or Megalodon or what had happened in the hurricane. No one else would believe her. No one else would have believed anything she'd seen or experienced, the huge waterspout tossing Megalodon into the ocean included. Now that the monster shark was consigned to a watery grave in the open sea, maybe High Voltage could recover. She just hoped it wasn't too late for Dead Fred.

She had placed Dead Fred in her jumper pocket, intending to put him back into the water on the way to school. But that was not how she had meant it to be, nor what she had imagined. She had always thought releasing Dead Fred into the waterway would be a beautiful, thrilling ritual at a more special moment than just on the way to school. She had envisioned it as a time of great celebration and rejoicing. In Dead Fred's dismal condition, she feared the manatees and all the other animals would be disappointed. And if the water didn't revive him . . . That was too heartbreaking to consider.

Ppeekk sighed and wheeled her backpack across the deck, down the steps, and onto the sandy driveway, bumping over shredded twigs and leaves. She was anxious to get back to school and see her friends. She had taken only a few steps when a series of familiar honks startled her. She frowned and stopped, and turned around to see her dad driving the Yugo straight toward her. *Oh, no, here we go again.* The little car bounced over the ruts in the driveway and came to a stop right beside her.

Her father stuck his long arm out of the window. Ppeekk's eyebrows shot upward. Her dad was wearing a cool-looking T-shirt instead of a business shirt and jacket.

He offered a closed hand to Ppeekk. "Here's something for you."

He opened his fingers, revealing a pink scallop shell in his palm. "Take it. I found it on the beach this morning and wondered if you had one like it. I don't know whether it's rare or not, but it sure is pretty. It reminded me of the shells you collected on your first walk to school."

Ppeekk stared at the shell and then at her father.

"Go ahead and put it in your pocket, honey."

Could she believe what she heard? A few weeks ago he had forbidden her to carry shells in her clothes for fear of tearing them.

When she still hesitated, her dad got out of the car. He was wearing board shorts instead of dress pants. He wore flip-flops in place of the usual shiny black leather shoes.

"But, Dad, what if the shell tears a hole in my pocket?"

He swept his hand through the air. "Pockets can be mended." He smiled. "Clothes can be replaced. Who cares?"

Ppeekk eyed his new outfit while a smile tugged at her lips. "So I see."

She took the shell from him and gently placed it in the pocket with Dead Fred.

"What I mean is . . . clothes can be replaced, but daughters can't. Ppeekk, can you ever forgive me for being so stupid and self-centered and neglectful?"

Her voice caught. "Oh, Dad, I forgave you when you jumped into the raging waterway during the hurricane. I have to admit, that *was* pretty stupid."

They both laughed, but when he put his arms around Ppeekk, she encircled him with her own arms and hugged him back really hard. She didn't want to let go.

They both turned their heads when they heard someone humming. Mini Romey nonchalantly skipped up Ppeekk's driveway, stepping over the occasional fallen branch, as if nothing unusual had happened, as if the hurricane had been a minor blip in Mini Romey's world. Quatro was right behind her.

"Hi, Ppeekk. Hi, Mr. Berry. Why are you wearing clothes like that?" Mini Romey said. She didn't give him a chance to answer.

"Hey, Ppeekk, I heard about you and your dad riding out the hurricane near the waterway. Did the TV reporters come to your house? I saw you on the news."

Mini Romey babbled on and on. Quatro stood back several yards, as if he were unsure whether Ppeekk had really forgiven him.

Ppeekk walked over to him. "Hi, Quatro." She'd never forget how he had braved the storm to check on her. "Let's walk to school."

They exchanged smiles and set off for school. Mini Romey ran to catch up. "Hey, wait for me."

The three children turned and looked at Ppeekk's dad still standing in the driveway, expecting him to slide into the driver's seat of the Yugo.

"Dad, aren't you going to follow in the car?"

"I thought I might walk along with you, if that's all right with you guys."

Ppeekk and Quatro exchanged wary glances, but Mini Romey latched on to this new development with gusto.

She grabbed his hand. "Oh, good. I like your new clothes, Mr. Berry. You look like an old surfer dude. Aren't you more comfortable now? Ppeekk, I'm sorry I said your dad was weird. You're not so weird today, Mr. Berry."

Quatro sighed. "Hush up, Mini Romey. I know you're happy to have a new audience, but stop being so pesky."

She looked up into Mr. Berry's eyes. "I'm not being pesky, am I Mr. Berry? Did you know that some manatees can talk? Some fish can, too. We could show you. Would you like to see something magical?"

"You're too late, Mini Romey. I saw the giant shark chasing Ppeekk in the waterway during the hurricane."

The three children stopped in their tracks. Quatro and Mini Romey stared wide-eyed at Ppeekk.

Ppeekk flushed. "N-n-no, Dad, it wasn't a giant shark you saw. It was just part of a roof floating behind me while I was holding on to a cypress log."

"That was no roof. It was some kind of large sharklike creature, and it was after you! I know what I saw."

"Lots of things looked strange in that weather with all the rain and mist. Anyway, how could a giant shark get into the waterway?" She laughed and tried to make light of it.

Mini Romey dug her hands into her hips. "Did Megalodon chase you in the waterway? That's not fair! You get to have all the adventures."

Ppeekk and her dad had a long, loud laugh. She knew she could never tell her parents the whole truth about Megalodon and the danger she'd put herself into. They wouldn't be able to handle it. Maybe someday she would tell them about Dead Fred and the manatees and the giant clam and the Eternal Life Circle, but not now.

They crossed the street to the paved path alongside the nature preserve. Ppeekk's Path was still there, but many of the trees had been twisted and wrenched out of the ground. Broken trunks and shattered tree limbs lay scattered everywhere. Shreds of colored cloth—red and black and white and brown hung from the branches, like someone's laundry had been ripped and torn and draped over the nature preserve's trees.

"Looks like the hurricane messed up those swamp creatures," Mini Romey said.

Mr. Berry smiled, but Ppeekk and Quatro grinned and whispered a fast "Yes!" under their breath, making a pumping motion with their fists.

"But the gumbo-limbo trees are still there," said Mini Romey, skipping. "Look! The hurricane didn't get them. I love those gumbo-limbos, especially the one that rescued us."

Ppeekk remembered how a gumbo-limbo had helped save her and her dad during the hurricane as well. It had even provided them with shelter. Drinking from the waters of the cavern that held the Eternal Life Circle made its roots stronger. *What if touching the Eternal Life Circle had been what saved her from Megalodon and the hurricane?* Maybe the Eternal Life Circle had given her and Quatro and Mini Romey a kind of immunity against evil and danger. She hoped it was so. If only she could manage to use its magic to save Dead Fred.

A car waited at the intersection. Frizz and Little Feet jumped out and ran over to them. Frizz wrapped Ppeekk in a hug.

"Well," Little Feet said, "you're the biggest celebrity in town. You're famous, Ppeekk. Everybody saw your interview on channel five."

McFlyo and Firecracker sauntered up the sidewalk, followed closely by Danimal and GJ.

McFlyo spoke to Ppeekk, turning his back to her dad. "I can't believe you did it. You really rode that hurricane out under a tree by the waterway?"

"That's right, McFlyo."

"And floated down the waterway on a tree trunk during the hurricane?" he asked.

"Didn't you hear her say so on TV?" Little Feet said.

McFlyo swept his hand through the air like he was swatting a pesky fly. "Yeah, yeah. I just want to hear it from Ppeekk herself."

Danimal sized up Ppeekk's dad. "Is this the dude you pulled out of the water? Man, what were you two doing out in that monster storm? Did you lose your marbles or something?"

Ppeekk hooked her hand through her father's elbow. "You guys, this is my dad."

"Hey, where's the little car?" Firecracker said.

"I left it at home. Thought I'd tag along on foot with all of you."

"Good idea. You never know what might happen walking to school with Ppeekk," Firecracker said.

Ppeekk's dad looked at her with raised eyebrows. "Is that right?"

McFlyo slapped Ppeekk on the back. "Ppeekk, you are one tough kid. Never believed you had it in you. Who would have thought the new girl in town could ride out a hurricane on the waterway and save her old man, too?"

Ppeekk would have been supremely happy in that moment if not for her worries about Dead Fred.

A school bus passed them on the street, reminding them where they were going. They neared the end of the sidewalk and approached the drawbridge and the Good Luck Circle. Ppeekk wondered if the hurricane had damaged it.

But no! There it was, shining like silver glitter on the rough pavement. When they reached it, she debated whether or not to tell everyone about it.

As usual, Mini Romey broke from the group and ran forward to be the first one to enter the circle. She looked with large questioning eyes at Ppeekk, who knew what the little girl wanted. She nodded her head yes.

Mini Romey danced an Irish jig. "Hey, everybody, I have an announcement. This is the Good Luck Circle!"

They gathered around Mini Romey standing in the shining circle on the sidewalk.

"See? There's Ppeekk's name. Ppeekk drew the circle in the wet concrete and then she wrote her name inside it, and the next day it was shining and magic. It gives you good luck if you dance in it. Isn't that right, Ppeekk?"

Ppeekk tried to keep her voice calm. "That's right."

The kids already knew magic existed in the waterway. They'd seen the clown fish and the flying fish, and they knew about Dead Fred. They believed in the magic just as she did. But Ppeekk could tell by the odd look on her father's face that he was unsure about the Good Luck Circle. Maybe he thought it was just a continuation of Mini Romey's imagination. Surely he didn't believe in it, did he?

Quatro brought out his extra-large water bottle and poured water onto the circle. The metallic flecks shimmered and glimmered like hundreds of tiny prisms. Quatro gestured for Ppeekk to go first.

She stepped inside, and her feet began moving. At the same time she turned around, twirling her whole body, picking up speed and then whirling round and round, her jumper skirt ballooning and her hair flying. She lifted her arms in a V above her head and spun like a top, sparks of colored light crackling all around her. She spun like the waterspout that lifted and tossed the evil Megalodon out of the waterway and into the ocean.

Ppeekk stepped out of the circle, dizzy but elated. Each of the kids took a turn dancing in the circle, showing off their different styles. Even Mr. Berry danced a few, old-fashioned waltz steps that made the kids giggle and him smile. Ppeekk felt happy; Dad would have good luck now whether he believed in the circle or not.

Ppeekk walked out onto the drawbridge. It was nothing short of miraculous that the old bridge survived the hurricane. She leaned on the rail and took it all in. The sky was the same ethereal blue it had been in the eye of the hurricane, a blue so intense and bright it hurt her eyes. It resembled a bright blue canvas with a few wispy clouds stretched across it like frothy shawls from angels' shoulders.

The waterway glinted like liquid sapphires, reflecting the blue of the sky. The green banks were greener than ever, as if the hurricane had washed everything clean and clear.

Even the old drawbridge, missing a few slats, seemed brighter. The bridge house roof had lost a few shingles, but everything else about it was the same. Maybe they did build things to last in the old days, as her father said. Ppeekk wondered if old Bridget had been blown away by the storm. Not that Ppeekk cared.

The others soon joined Ppeekk. McFlyo had a pocket full of pitch apples, and he and the boys started throwing them off the bridge. They tossed coconuts, too, to see who could throw the farthest. Ppeekk's dad, looking like an old quarterback, threw a long bomb and impressed the boys with his technique.

"Hey," GJ said, "remember when those clown fish teased us into tossing our lunchboxes off the bridge here and those flying fish came out?"

Mini Romey bounced up and down. "Yeah, let's do that again!"

Ppeekk convinced GJ and Mini Romey to throw crackers to the gulls. While dozens of white gulls squawked and swooped just over the children's heads, catching crackers in their beaks, the door to the bridge house slammed open. Bridget stomped across the bridge toward them.

"Uh-oh," Quatro said. "Here comes trouble."

Ppeekk bit her lip and clenched her fists, trying to control her anger. This was the woman who had raised the drawbridge on her and forced her to jump.

But now Bridget looked different. She didn't have a cigar in her mouth, and the corners of her mouth were turned up into a kind of a grimace that resembled a smile. *How odd.* Ppeekk backed up as the old woman neared.

Giving a wink, Bridget glanced over the kids' heads back toward the Good Luck Circle. "Old Bridget stumbled through that there circle of yours as she escaped the hurricane. Helped me get to safety. Haven't felt this good since my high school prom."

When her dad saw Bridget, he broke away from the group to shake her hand and talk to her. Then the old woman smiled for real, and her whole face instantly brightened.

Ppeekk stood with her mouth gaping. Dad put his arm around Bridget's shoulder and the two of them walked off the bridge together toward the marina. Ppeekk shook her head. Now this was a kind of magic she had not expected!

Quatro smiled wryly. "Strange things have been happening around here since you arrived."

She watched McFlyo, Frizz, and the others dangle their lunch-boxes off the bridge, trying to get the attention of the clown fish and the flying fish. "That's for sure." Ppeekk held her breath as McFlyo, of course, was the first to launch his lunchbox over the water. Were any of the animals of High Voltage still alive down there? Had the flying fish been swept out to sea? This was just fun and games for her friends, but for Ppeekk it was a moment of truth.

Then as the lunchboxes sailed through the air over the water-way—red, blue, green, and pink squares—gleaming flying fish rose from the water and guided each one toward the T-rock on the bank. The children clapped and cheered. Soon orange clown fish leaped and wobbled in crazy arcs near the rock. They chanted their funny taunt, and then Mini Romey and GJ joined in. Ppeekk had used that taunt just days ago in the tunnels to make

Megalodon mad enough to chase her.

Then stingrays appeared, silently gliding on the blue surface while electric eels wove among them like green ribbons, and jellyfish floated here and there. Fat and funny puffer fish and porcupine fish bobbed to the surface and rolled like little balls as the kids dissolved in gales of laughter.

Just beyond, a dozen dolphins leaped out of the water one after the other, their sleek gray bodies arching in perfect semicircles from head to tail. The dorsal fins on their backs seemed to salute the passing animals. The fast little dolphin, Flash, soared higher than all the others, flipping in an aerial somersault before diving again.

"Hey, Ppeekk," Little Feet said, "I wonder what happened to that monster shark we saw here one time?"

"Do you think maybe the hurricane got him?" GJ said.

Ppeekk threw a sideways smile at Quatro. "I guess we'll never know."

When Ppeekk spied three gray whiskered faces rising to the surface to breathe, she knew she had to go down to the water and see them. Quatro saw her sprinting down the boulder steps and followed. Mini Romey straggled behind him, but the others were still busy feeding the gulls and tossing lunchboxes.

Ppeekk knelt on the grassy bank beside the manatees. All three were there—old Mr. Mann, Anna, and little Manny, too. They squinted their small eyes and looked directly into Ppeekk's.

"The gulls have told us how you fought Megalodon during the hurricane and steered him away from High Voltage," Anna said. "They say a waterspout threw him into the sea, where he drowned. Now High Voltage is safe forever. Thank you, Ppeekk."

"I tried to destroy Megalodon. I tried to trap him in the tunnels, but I failed. And now Dead Fred is lost. Because I was too late."

"Nevertheless, you have cared for King Frederick. For this, we are immensely grateful," said Mr. Mann. "How can we repay you?"

"Well," Mini Romey said, "*I'd* like to take another ride through High Voltage."

"I'm afraid that cannot be," said Mr. Mann. "We dwellers of High Voltage must use all our energies to recover and rebuild after the long siege by Megalodon."

"I'm sorry, Mini Romey," Manny said.

Anna's small dark eyes twinkled. "But the clown fish have prepared something special for you, which we hope you will enjoy."

Manny spun in a circle. "You're gonna love it!"

Then the two adult manatees faced Ppeekk again.

"But we need one more creature before High Voltage is complete," Anna said.

Ppeekk gulped, knowing full well what she meant.

Mr. Mann nodded. "We are ready to receive our king."

"Have you got him, Ppeekk?" Quatro said.

Ppeekk nodded her head as a single tear trickled down her cheek. He had not moved in the last twenty-four hours, so she knew he was dead. This was going to be harder than she expected. Her mind reeled in a confusion of questions and emotions: What would High Voltage do if Dead Fred were indeed lost forever? How could she bear her own sorrow and that of the animals of High Voltage? Who would she confide in now? Who would be there to cheer her up and encourage her? But she knew what she had to do.

She reached into her jumper pocket and brought him out. The little fish lay on her hand, completely lifeless. The ever-present sparkle in his eye was reduced to a hazy film covering those once beautiful windows to Dead Fred's warm soul. Mini Romey whimpered at the shock of seeing him so shrunken and faded. Ppeekk was glad her dad and Bridget were at the marina and not around to witness this crucial moment. She could not have handled it if her father or Bridget had interfered.

Ppeekk gently placed Dead Fred on the surface of the water. The three children watched in silence as he lay floating on his side, rising and falling with the ripples. The manatees backed off and let the smaller fish approach. They swam around him as in a funeral procession while Mini Romey and Ppeekk openly wept. Even Quatro had a tear in his eye.

Ppeekk tucked her head into her chest. *I failed. It's too late.* Dead Fred had been too long out of the water of High Voltage. They had not been able to rid the waterway of Megalodon in time. It had taken the combination of all the creatures in High Voltage and the hurricane to do that, and their efforts had come too late. The fish swam in circles around their dead king, using their fins to gently splash water on him, bathing him with the waters of High Voltage. Ppeekk shook her head. *All useless.*

Ppeekk choked when she spoke to Anna. "What will happen to him now?"

"We will take care of him. For all prior rulers, we have a sacred resting place in the secret cavern just beyond the Eternal Life Circle."

Quatro tugged on Ppeekk's arm. "Come on, Ppeekk."

The three children stood to go. But something inside Ppeekk rebelled, refusing to accept failure. Why should she give up now when she'd worked so hard to save Dead Fred? She had to find something else she could do. Ppeekk jumped up with a sudden brainstorm. "Wait! Anna said it!"

Before Quatro and Mini Romey could grasp what was happening, Ppeekk was in the water, Dead Fred cupped in her hand. Her eyes flashed. "We're not taking Dead Fred to the sacred resting place. But we are taking him to the Eternal Life Circle."

Quatro shook his head. "But Ppeekk . . ."

Mini Romey flung off her shoes. "I'm coming, too."

Quatro stood with his hands on his hips. Then he sighed and removed his shoes. "Well, I guess that means I've got to go with you."

Ppeekk smiled, grabbed Flash's fin, and she was off. Two more dolphins picked up Mini Romey and Quatro, and all three children were quickly fitted with air bubble helmets.

Ppeekk held on to the dolphin's fin with one hand and cradled Dead Fred in the other as they swam past what was left of the underwater grate that Megalodon had destroyed. Then she on Flash and her friends on their dolphins maneuvered through the tunnels quickly and smoothly.

They wiggled through the half-blocked entrance to the secret cavern and then once more were in the extraordinary chamber, swimming down, down, down to the giant clam, where the light of the Eternal Life Circle illuminated it from within and cast a glow over the children and sea creatures gathered around.

Ppeekk leaned toward the giant clam. "Please, Pa'ua, open your shell. We haven't much time."

Mini Romey tapped on the shell.

From deep within, the clam rumbled, and Mini Romey jumped back. The ground and walls trembled. Even the tentacles of the jellyfish quivered in the wake of the clam's movement. Slowly, the shell opened. The children closed their eyes against the intense light. When they could open them again, they saw the dark purple lips of the clam waving in the water. "What brings you here again so soon to disturb my rest? I trust it is important."

Ppeekk's love for Dead Fred overcame her fear. "Yes, very, very important." She extended the palm where Dead Fred lay. "Here, I present you with the king of High Voltage. I want to place him within the Eternal Life Circle for its benevolent power."

"Approach."

The shell opened even wider, and out of the depths rose the spongy purple tongue bearing the magnificent Eternal Life Circle. Ppeekk was so blinded by the light she had to grope her way forward. Her hand followed the increasing warmth. When she touched the circle, she felt an electric shock shoot through her. Surely, the power of the circle could save Dead Fred. She opened one eye for just a second and quickly placed the small fish within the circle. Then she stepped back.

The children and the animals waited. It seemed like the whole underwater world was holding its breath. Dead Fred lay inside the embrace of the Eternal Life Circle on the clam's tongue, still lifeless.

After a while, Mini Romey spoke. "I don't think it's working."

Quatro pressed his finger to his mouth. "Let's give it another minute."

Mr. Mann nudged Ppeekk's arm. "You have done your best."

Anna's voice was heavy with sorrow. "Sometimes even the greatest powers are not strong enough."

"We have done all we could. It is time to depart," Mr. Mann said. "Leave him here, and we will prepare his burial chamber."

No, this can't be the end. He can't truly be dead. I only called him that to be clever and funny. Please, Dead Fred, don't die.

Ppeekk burst into tears.

After a moment, when she had quieted her sobs, she turned to swim out with the manatees, dolphins, and her friends. She glanced down once more to say good-bye forever to her beloved friend. Then she blinked several times. *What?* Was it just the light of the Eternal Life Circle that was reflecting off his lifeless little body, or was something happening? Instead of dull gray, he was turning pale yellow. As she continued to gaze at him, the yellow shifted to brown, which then slowly transformed into a deep burnished bronze. Was this the end or a new beginning? The surrounding sea creatures perked up and swam back down.

The cracks and tears in Dead Fred's fins seemed to slowly knit together. Dead Fred wiggled a tail fin. Then his side fins twitched. Suddenly, he flipped over from lying on his side to swimming upright as all fish did. Yes! The Eternal Life Circle was working its magic!

Then with a shift of his beautiful eyes, Dead Fred was transformed into a glossy, beautiful creature. Each scale shone like precious gold leaf, outlined and stenciled in intricate patterns of darker gold. His now flexible fins waved in the water like gold filigree. He grew plumper and more solid, fleshed out and healthy. He radiated the magical spark of life.

Then Dead Fred swam directly to Ppeekk and hovered in the water in front of her. His eyes shone bright, intelligent, and wise.

She met his gaze and felt a surge of gratitude and joy. She was in the presence of love. "You're back! And better than I've ever seen you. Thank goodness, Dead Fred! We didn't know if you were going to make it."

"Thank you, Ppeekk Rose Berry, for keeping me safe and for saving High Voltage from its certain demise at the fins of Megalodon."

"But I didn't really do much of anything," Ppeekk said. "All I did was pick you up from the bridge and keep you in the coatroom and the tree house. I tried to make High Voltage safe for you by destroying Megalodon. It was the sea creatures and the hurricane that finally got him."

"Ah, my dear, you have done more than you know. Because of you, Megalodon's strength was weakened, and you helped force him into the waterspout that ended his evil reign." His voice waxed stronger. "Sometimes we must swim into the waters of not knowing. You did this when you dove into the waterway to lure Megalodon into the tunnels. You did it when you and Flash swam through the looping tunnel. You did it when you were swept down the waterway in the hurricane and managed to save both yourself and your father. You did it by showing the inhabitants of High Voltage that they could combine their strength and defeat the evil they thought greater than themselves. And you did it today when you brought me to the Eternal Life Circle. You have shown great courage in all of these endeavors by facing the unknown."

"Thank you, Dead Fred, for everything," Ppeekk whispered.

"Remember, Ppeekk, what a wise teacher told me some years ago: 'Our greatest glory is in rising after we fall, standing again each time we stumble, not giving up in the face of what appears to be failure.' You can live your life now in the wisdom you have earned by your own courage and hard work and in the magic bestowed upon you by the shining circles of good luck and eternal life."

Dead Fred darted up through the water, swimming faster than Ppeekk would have ever guessed he could. Then he darted back down to her. "Let us go up to the surface of High Voltage and rejoice in the waters that are now safe from Megalodon."

Ppeekk, Quatro, and Mini Romey held on to their dolphins and zipped out of the cavern through the tunnels, this time not in panic and despair, but in triumph.

When they broke the surface, the other kids were still hanging out on the bridge. As soon as the trio stepped on land, their clothes and hair dried. They sat down on the ground, laughing, and laced up their shoes as King Frederick the Ninth, or Dead Fred as Ppeekk would forever call him, swam out to the middle of the channel.

All the animals of High Voltage rose to the surface and swam around him. The water sparkled with the gilt and shine of the Good Luck Circle, like a hundred interconnected Good Luck Circles, all created by the living, breathing animals of High Voltage. A general cheer erupted from the animals in the water and the three children on the bank. The kids on the bridge joined in, too.

Then Ppeekk's dad appeared on the bridge, waving a sheaf of vivid orange papers. Bridget shuffled behind him. Reluctantly, Ppeekk rose from the bank and followed Quatro and Mini Romey up the boulder steps to the bridge. Ppeekk paused and glanced back over her shoulder, but Dead Fred was gone. He had slipped into the magical waters of High Voltage, the place where he belonged. She wondered if she would ever see him again. The last of the High Voltage animals turned up their tails and dived down into their watery world, leaving only faint ripples behind and a wavery echo of a song: "O beautiful, for sparkling shells . . ."

CHAPTER TWENTY-FOUR

A TWENTY-SECOND
7-ELEVEN SHOPPING SPREE

Up on the bridge, the group of clamoring kids surrounded Ppeekk's dad and Bridget.

Mini Romey bounced on the balls of her feet. "What is it? What is it?"

"Looks like that orange paper we scooped out of the waterway a few weeks ago," Quatro said. "You know, the one that promised free treats at 7-Eleven."

Firecracker's eyes widened. "Free treats?"

"You got it! All the candy, ice cream, Slurpees, chips, and sodas we can grab in twenty seconds."

"Hey, one of those papers belongs to us," Mini Romey said. "Bridget took it from Quatro a few weeks ago."

"I want one, too," GJ whined.

Ppeekk's father held up his hand like a traffic cop. "Hold on, now. I have nine certificates here, one for each of you."

The kids cheered and whistled.

"But where did they come from?" Frizz said.

Bridget swiped her mouth with the back of her hand. "Found 'em on the bridge after the hurricane. Like they'd just dropped out of the sky. Ya know, that there hurricane stirred up a lot of mysterious things."

Bridget winked. Ppeekk's eyebrows shot upward. Had Bridget winked directly at her?

McFlyo threw Mr. Berry a sidewise glance. "Who would give away free treats? Nobody's going to do that. Who signed these papers? Let's see."

Ppeekk's dad smiled at Bridget. "Says here, these certificates are the gift of the clown fish. Probably just a clever way for an anonymous donor to bestow some gifts."

"What's that word mean—*anonna*-what?" Mini Romey said.

Quatro rolled his eyes and sighed. "Anonymous. The word's *anonymous*. It means the giver doesn't want to be known."

Mini Romey ran and leaned over the railing. "But we know who the clown fish are!" She pointed. "They're right down there in the waterway. Thank you, clown fish!"

Danimal stuck his hands in his pockets and shook his head. "I don't care who's giving away free treats. I'll take 'em!"

"Me, too!" chimed in GJ.

"How do we know it's for real?" Little Feet said.

Frizz ran her hand over her hair. "Can we go to 7-Eleven now and see?"

"How about I meet you right after school and we all walk over to the 7-Eleven store together?" Mr. Berry said.

Nine children went to school very happy on that first Friday of the month of September after Hurricane Lars struck southern Florida. Nine children had a hard time focusing on math and history and science all that long school day. And at 3:00, nine children waited at the front of the school.

When Mr. Berry strolled up right on time, the group walked together and chatted excitedly the one block to the neighborhood 7-Eleven.

Ppeekk's dad stopped outside the store's glass doors. "Okay, you know what the certificate says. You'll each have twenty seconds, and *only* twenty seconds, to grab all the candy, chips, ice cream, soda, Slurpees, and whatever you want, that you can hold in your hands and arms."

McFlyo cracked his knuckles. "You mean I can grab all the candy I want?"

Mini Romey ran her tongue over her lips. "All the doughnuts and cakes?"

"I'm going to pour as many Slurpees as I can in twenty seconds and drink until I get a brain freeze," Firecracker said.

Quatro grinned. "Can I stuff my shirt?"

Ppeekk's father put his hand on Quatro's shoulder. "Absolutely. It doesn't say you can't use your shirt, socks, pockets, even underwear. I would really go for it if I were you. And somebody get me a package of Starburst, too. Are you ready?"

All nine heads bobbed in affirmation.

"All right. On your mark. Get set. Go!" Mr. Berry said as he clicked the stopwatch feature on his watch.

The clerk behind the counter with *Jackie* on the name tag pinned to her shirt popped her gum. "Whatever," she said, to no one in particular, as the mob of kids ran madly through the store, clutching Slurpees and sodas between their arms and chests, balancing stacks of ice cream bars and candy bars and chocolate snack cakes on their wide open palms. Some of them tucked bags of chips under their chins. Little Feet, Frizz, and Ppeekk stuffed candy bars in their kneesocks. Mini Romey balanced a box of doughnuts on her head. The boys' shirts bulged with packages and bags. Little GJ had cupcakes stuffed all around his middle in his underwear's elastic waistband.

Then Ppeekk's dad clicked his watch. "Time's up!"

As the nine children wobbled and shuffled past the clerk and out of the store, Mr. Berry presented her with nine bright orange certificates, each with its own unique barcode.

He smiled and squeezed Ppeekk around her shoulders. She bit into a chocolate-covered ice cream bar and pulled something out of her pocket. "Hey, Dad, here's your pack of Starburst."

"Poor Mr. Berry," Mini Romey crooned. "You only have one pack of candy. Here, have some of my jelly beans."

All the kids urged him to take candy and cookies and chips and drinks. As they walked through the parking lot, a yellow concrete truck pulled in, and a group of men clad in orange jumpsuits entered the store. Out of the corner of her eye, Ppeekk thought she saw the strange little man who'd blown the smoke wreath at her. But by then her dad and the kids had settled into two-by-two pairs on the sidewalk going home.

Once the concrete truck passed them on the street, Ppeekk got a better look. Sure enough, it *was* the strange little man. He hung onto the back of the truck with one hand, just like before. And in his other hand he held the same kind of Drumstick ice cream bar that Ppeekk was eating. The little man looked directly at her and lifted his treat as if making a toast. She smiled and lifted hers back at him. It seemed ages since she'd drawn the Good Luck Circle in the wet concrete.

The group of kids drifted back to Ppeekk's house and eventually wandered out to the beach. As the sun set, they sat on the sand munching the last of the chips and candy, taking turns tossing them into one another's mouths.

Mr. Berry proposed a game of tag, and he was off and running across the sand, the kids following him, energized with the sugar buzz of all sugar buzzes! Only Ppeekk and Quatro stayed behind, content and silent in a way that only true friends can be, just sitting there in the sand, knees to their chests, gazing out at the ocean.

"Ppeekk, this has been the best school year I've ever had, and it's only just started."

"Yeah, and I'm going to walk to school every single day."

"Every day? Even when it's raining?"

Ppeekk giggled. "*Especially* when it's raining. That's when it's most exciting. You never know. There might just be another hurricane brewing."

The two friends burst into laughter.

The light faded, and the waves calmed. Ppeekk and Quatro put their shoes back on, stood up, brushed off the sand, and gathered their wrappers.

Ppeekk dug her toe in the sand. "Quatro, you and Mini Romey are my best friends in the world. I hope we live next door to each other forever."

Quatro extended his hand, and color flushed his cheeks. "Me, too."

Their handshake transformed into a quick and awkward hug.

Ppeekk stared at the ocean over Quatro's shoulder. Two large waves on the horizon caught her eye. Loosening her hold on Quatro, she craned her neck to get a better look. *No . . . It couldn't be . . .*

She swung Quatro around and pointed. "Look there. Why aren't those waves breaking?"

Two black specks far out in the water moved quickly, swimming parallel to the shore, jagged fins slicing in and out of the water.

Ppeekk strained her eyes and ears, trying to see or hear anything that would give her a clue. Then the black protrusions halted. A terrible bellowing drowned out the crash of the waves. Ppeekk's mouth went dry, and a hard lump rose in her throat. She clapped her hands over her ears. She recognized the bellowing. It was that of Megalodon, and not one, but two . . .

Afterword

The story of *Dead Fred, Flying Lunchboxes and The Good Luck Circle* was born from my experiences walking my daughter Laura (Ppeekk) and her friends to school every single school day of her life. Since prekindergarten, she has never been driven. We walk from our old beach cottage, through a dense grove of trees, past a nature preserve, and over a drawbridge on the Intracoastal Waterway on the one-mile odyssey each day.

Since that first walk many years ago, we have collected a beautiful shell or unique rock to commemorate each adventure. We now have over one thousand of them, each stored in a special place and categorized by grade.

There is a real Dead Fred (you can see a picture of him at Dead-Fred.com), we step in the Good Luck Circle every day, and lunchboxes do fly off the bridge and land by the T-rock. I think we even caught a glimpse of Megalodon once. And 7-Eleven is a regular stop at 7:15 a.m. on the first Friday of every month when the kids are allowed to get one of *anything* they want. Sometimes up to forty of us gather around a bench by school and enjoy our ice cream, sour Gummi Worms, candy bars, donuts with sprinkles, and cherry Slurpees before the first bell rings. Those walks are the talk of the school.

I encourage kids to ask their parents to take the time to walk them to school. I decided to do this when Ppeekk was just four years old because I thought we would grow to cherish the time together. Setting aside fifteen minutes to share the magic each day is not difficult at all, and I had no idea how much fun we would have over the years.

Kids, don't let your parents tell you they are too busy. Tell them this is the most special time in your life, and that you want to create your own stories and adventures that will turn into memories for you both to share forever. (Not to mention the goodies even grown-ups enjoy at your local convenience store!) Work will always be there for your parents, but these days when you are young and full of youthful imagination might not. If your parents tell you that you live too far from school, then drive to the last mile and walk from there. You will be amazed at the stories imagined, wild adventures experienced, and the loving bond you create.

Please share your thoughts and your own walking-to-school stories with me, Ppeekk, and other readers at Dead-Fred.com.

ABOUT THE AUTHOR

*D*ead Fred, Flying Lunchboxes, and the Good Luck Circle captures the essence of Frank McKinney's deep, fantastical creativity. It is as if he were born to write young reader fantasy.

Renowned for his imagination, Frank McKinney has introduced his gift to a broad audience of children and the young at heart through his first fantasy novel, *Dead Fred, Flying Lunchboxes and the Good Luck Circle,* charging it with fairy-tale wonder, enthralling magic, page-turning suspense, and a storyline that will race and gladden the heart.

In *Dead Fred, Flying Lunchboxes, and the Good Luck Circle,* McKinney brings parents and children together in a whimsical fantasy story inspired by McKinney's real-life experiences walking with his daughter, Laura (Ppeekk), and a larger group of children (up to forty at a time!) to school every morning for the past seven years (one thousand-plus times), and the adventures, stories, and whimsical games they create as they navigate their way to school.

For nearly a quarter century, best-selling author, philanthropist, and real estate "artist" Frank McKinney has been creating art in the form of the world's most magnificent multimillion-dollar oceanfront estate homes, each set on the sun-drenched canvas of Palm Beach on Florida's gold coast.

His gift and passion for extraordinary homes extends to his role as the founder and director of the Caring House Project Foundation, a nonprofit, 501(c)(3) organization he founded in 1998, which provides a self-sustaining existence for the most desperately poor and homeless families in Haiti, Honduras, Nicaragua, Africa, Indonesia, and the United States. The foundation develops entire communities, complete with homes, medical clinics, orphanages, schools, churches, clean water, and renewable agricultural assets, including both livestock and crops. The foundation started domestically with purchasing rundown, single-family homes, refurbishing them, and then renting them for one dollar per month to elderly people who were homeless, completely redefining "affordable housing."

What is most paradoxical about Frank McKinney is that he graduated from his fourth high school in four years with a 1.8 GPA (he was asked to leave the first three), never went to college, nor did he receive any formal training in literature, writing, design, architecture, building, business, or marketing. Yet he is the creative force behind the design, creation, and ultimate sale of some of the most magnificent homes in the world, runs a large nonprofit organization, and has now written five wonderful books.

McKinney is without a doubt one of the most visionary, courageous, and "contrary" business leaders of our time. His latest stateside creations include two of the world's largest and most opulent certified "green" (environmentally responsible) homes, priced at twenty-nine and thirty million dollars.

If there were a swashbuckling modern-day Robin Hood, McKinney would be him, selling to the rich and providing for the poor. Armed with rock star looks, a disarming personality, and a willingness to attempt what others don't even dream of, McKinney has defied both conventional wisdom and the predictions of others to achieve success on his terms. Because of his prior best sellers and the magnificent properties he builds, *USA Today* has called him "the real-estate rock czar." The *Wall Street Journal* dubbed him "the king of ready-made dream homes."

In 2009, against common practice in the publishing industry, McKinney released and toured three new books simultaneously: *Dead Fred, Flying Lunchboxes, and the Good Luck Circle, The Tap,* and *Burst This! Frank McKinney's Bubble-Proof Real Estate Strategies.*

Frank McKinney writes all of his books from a tree-house office overlooking the Atlantic Ocean. He lives with his wife, Nilsa, and their daughter, Laura (Ppeekk), in that old beach cottage just over the bridge near the Intracoastal Waterway in Delray Beach, Florida.

ACKNOWLEDGMENTS

Having written five books, I can say without question that creating the characters and storyline for *Dead Fred, Flying Lunchboxes, and the Good Luck Circle* was the most fun I have had since pretending I was Robin Hood in the backwoods of Indiana in grade school. Writing this book has permanently solidified my relationship with the little boy inside, who once went by the childhood nickname "Mickey."

In gathering the material necessary for such an epic story, I had many who helped draw out the imagination, creativity, and fantasy you hold in your hands.

The primary inspiration came from my daughter, Laura, and the hundreds of classmates and other children who walked the nearly one-mile journey from our house to school every school day of Laura's life.

First, moms and dads had to get these children ready, sometimes very early in the morning, so they could be at our house by seven a.m. I thank each parent who allowed his or her child to participate in these ritual walks. You are wonderful parents.

I especially want to thank Toast, Toad, T.O.A.D., Beans, Beanie, Nilda, Computer Wife (aka Nilsa McKinney). Yes, all of these names belong to one wonderful person, my beautiful wife, Nilsa. After twenty years even my wife has been bestowed with many nicknames. Without fail, Nilsa got Laura ready every morning (pancakes and bacon . . . again) for our walks. When I was out of town, she filled in and experienced the walk with Laura and her friends. Thank you, honey, for all your support in helping me to create this book.

I want to thank Big Romey and CD (Mini Romey's and Quatro's mom and dad). We went through many of Quatro's and Mini Romey's ties, shirts, shoes, and lunch boxes on our daily adventures. Thank you for your patience and for sharing your children every morning.

I want to acknowledge the children, by first or nickname only, who made numerous walks to school with Laura and me. Many of these children's personalities were developed into some of the characters in the book. I may be leaving some children out, I'm sure, and others aren't as fond of their nicknames as I may be, but through your eyes I experienced this book. Quatro and Mini Romey, although you are kids, I consider you my friends. I know we will stay in touch long after the pages of *Dead Fred* have curled and turned yellow. I have had such fun walking to school with you and also wrecking around in your golf cart. Some of the other wonderful children who participated in this book are Han the

Man, Alexandra Graham Beck, Charles the Surfer, Izzy, Zach Attack, Carson the Math Whiz, Frisbee, Frizz, Reils, Spencer Eye Lash, Anthony the Great, Jules, Firecracker, Zach Attack II, Jenibug, Michael the Chairman, 3-M, Amanda the Fish, Alysa Miss USA, Livy, All Hail Hailey, Sean Pop Star, Cole in your Stocking, Devin from Heaven, John Skating Rink, Maia on the Playa, Nick Tallabani, Christian of the Dogwood, McFlyo (Pants Boy), Little Feet, B-rad, Kate the Golf Pro, Kelly Don't Touch the Hair, Katherine Tippie Toes, Danimal, Peyme, Winner B, Nelson B, Hayden B, Sophie B, Sophia R, GJ (aka Boom Box Boy), Meaghan D, Erin D, James Scott, Goalivia, Jules D, and many more.

I must acknowledge and thank all the teachers and other faculty who were patient enough to listen to the children's stories about *Dead Fred* since we started walking to school way back in prekindergarten. You certainly encouraged the children to dream and use their imaginations. Thank you Vicki Delgado, Kathy Pollett, Jean Maffetone, Fran Allibaster, Sue Merrill, Kathy Savage, Kathy Viola, Delina Youngs, Martina Williston, Connie Prichard, Carri Gerasci, Kitty Crawford, Jill Broz, Coach Burke, Coach Debrecht, Angela Belmonte, Ilse Mish, Angela Garcia, Diane Rapp, Susan Lueken, Spring Transleau, Joan Lorne, Margaret Statler, Nancy Godden, Elizabeth Shannon, Marjorie Miarka, Molly Rocha, Mary Rodriguez, Lou Finelli, Sister Paula, Ana McNamara, Barbara Swiatlowski, Mr. A, Susan Grant, Jerry Bishop, Moji Doyle, and all those who have since retired.

I want to thank Ruth Fuller for keeping all the kids in check after our first Friday visits to 7-Eleven.

A special thanks to the past principal of the children's school, Sister Mary Clare, for tolerating our antics and loving the children. You will never be forgotten.

I want to thank all of my nieces and nephews for the many times we played together, especially the question game. You, too, allowed the little boy in me to flourish. Thank you Sebe, Gabblet, Noah the Boa, Leo sans underwear, Katelet, Magglet, Juan Julio, Indy, Huge, Madry, Audison, Cammadaud, Recammadaud, and Lars the Star.

How about my brother and four sisters, for allowing their kids to play with "Uncle Mickey?" My sisters referred to "You don't always have to do what Uncle Mickey does" as the "Uncle Mickey" talk before we would gather for a holiday event. I want to thank Martie, Marlen, Madeleine, and Heather for all the imaginative games we played growing up. I especially want to thank my practical-joking partner and brother, Bob. Wish I had the space to share some of our practical jokes with you; they were quite unusual. "Chook," as I call him, is my best friend.

Because I have been blessed with the ability to relate to children, much of what I learned has come from my beautiful mother, Katie. I have never witnessed such magnetism when it comes to Mom and children. She is the perfect concoction of Mr. Rogers, the Pied Piper, and Mother Goose. Children sense a warm soul, and hers is the reason children flood her lap. I am sure there are still times when she wishes I would "grow up." Sorry, Mom, but at least I now have an outlet.

I want to thank all of the imaginative people at Health Communications, my publisher, for their belief in the *Dead Fred* story and for their support of my commitment to this genre. Life is enhanced only through risk, and Peter Vegso, Thomas Sand, Pat Holdsworth, Paola Fernandez, Kim Weiss, Carol Rosenberg, Michele Matrisciani, Andrea Gold, Kelly Maragni, Lori Golden, Sean Geary, Mike Briggs, and Manuel Saez certainly took one when agreeing to take on *Dead Fred* as part of the "three headed monster."

When you graduate high school with a 1.8 GPA and don't pursue higher education, literary collaboration is critical. Even more important is to learn from those who know children's fantasy fiction. I want to thank Kate Mason, Jennifer Elvgren, Erin Brown, and Kathy May for their guidance and invaluable input. You helped me bring all the characters to life and taught me to love writing young reader fiction.

Just take a look at the book cover! When I asked Erik Hollander for a movie poster for the jacket art, boy, did he deliver. Thanks, Erik, for sharing your unbelievable talent. The movie poster is now ready for *Dead Fred,* the movie.

Books don't just jump off the shelves; their merits must be shared with people like you. Jane Grant of Pierson Grant Public

Relations, my publicist, has done a masterful job with all the media surrounding this book. Thank you for your tireless efforts.

Last, my lovely daughter, Laura. As you someday read this book to your own children, and tell of the adventures you had on your daily walks to school, know how much they meant to Daddy over the ten years that we will have experienced them. By the time you graduate from eighth grade, we will have walked nearly 1,700 times to school! Know that the half hour we spent together was the most important time of the day for Daddy. Remember, "Take care of the kids, take care of your teachers, laugh and giggle, don't worry about anything, and just be a kid."

DEAD-FRED.COM

Check out Dead-Fred.com where you'll find many interactive and updated features, including ways for you to: enter contests and treasure hunts, comment on your favorite characters and find out which one is most like you, share your walking-to-school stories (you gotta get your parents to do this with you!), find out when and where Dead Fred and other characters will be "on tour," help me create future villains, get sneak peeks at future books, and much more.

RIGHT NOW: AN ENCRYPTED, 3-HEADED TREASURE HUNT...?

Ppeekk and her friends invite you to play the 3-Headed Treasure Hunt and be one of nine kids to win the Grand Prize!

Ppeekk has hidden words inside your book. They're the titles of two other books I wrote and released at the same time as Dead Fred, Flying Lunchboxes, and the Good Luck Circle.

Here's what you're going to uncover: The names of the books are *The Tap* and *Burst This!*

Using those four words, Ppeekk has a challenging Treasure Hunt with exciting prizes for you: Can you locate the page numbers in Dead Fred where "The Tap" and "Burst This" can be found? The two words for each title must be found in sequence. *Clue #1:* The words "The Tap" and "Burst This" (all four words) are not found together. *Clue #2:* They do not have to be capitalized.

Now for the "3-Headed" part of the challenge: To be eligible for the Grand Prize below, you must perform the same Treasure Hunt in two other books I wrote.

You must find the words "Dead Fred" and "The Tap" inside the *Burst This!* book and find "Dead Fred" and "Burst This" inside *The Tap* book. *Another clue:* The words are harder to find in *The Tap* and *Burst This!*

THE GRAND PRIZE . . .

If you think you've found the treasure—all six book titles in the three different books—then e-mail the page numbers and the sentences where the words appear to me at Frank@Frank-McKinney.com. Be sure to include your name and phone number, along with proof of purchase for all three books. You can buy *The Tap* and *Burst This!* from us here: http://www.frank-mckinney.com/books.asp, at Amazon, from another online retailer, or at your favorite bookstore.

On August 1, 2009, 2010, and 2011 Ppeekk will pick three winners who will receive the following Grand Prize sometime before school starts each year in 2009, 2010, and 2011:

- Round trip airfare for you and one of your parents from your home state to Delray Beach, Florida.
- Accommodations for the two of you on the ocean for two nights in Delray Beach.
- Just like in the book, you will get to walk with Ppeekk, Mini-Romey, Quatro and Mr. McKinney (Edward) along the same path they take to school!
- Just like in the book, you will get to meet the actual Dead Fred, maybe even Megalodon!
- Just like in the book, you will get to step inside the Good Luck Circle!
- Just like in the book, you will get to launch a lunchbox off the famous drawbridge!
- Just like in the book, you will get a twenty-second shopping spree at 7-Eleven! That's right, you'll grab all the candy, ice cream, or Slurpees you can in twenty seconds!
- That night, you and your parent will be treated to dinner on the beach where Ppeekk and her friends will discuss stories about the book.

Review the Treasure Hunt directions and clues, find the titles in all three books, and send in your page numbers, sentences and proof of purchase for all three books . . . and GOOD LUCK!

THANK YOU!

Proceeds from the sale of this book benefit the Caring House Project Foundation (CHPF), http://frankmckinney.com/caring_project.aspx.

Our Mission Statement. "The Caring House Project Foundation shall create projects based upon self-sufficiency by providing housing, food, water, medical support, and opportunity for the desperately poor and homeless from around the world, particularly in the Caribbean, South America, Indonesia, Africa, and here in the USA."

The Gospel of Luke teaches, "Much will be required of the person entrusted with much, and still more demanded of the person entrusted with more."

I like to say, "Each of us is fortunate to be blessed with the ability to succeed at some level. This success is not for our sole benefit, however, but so we might apply the result of our success to assist those less fortunate."

We founded CHPF in 1998 on the simple idea that *stability begins at home.* Without the most basic needs of shelter being met, there's often little hope. The foundation provides for entire communities, donating homes, medical clinics, orphanages, schools, churches, clean water, and agricultural assets, including both livestock and crops.

We started in the United States, purchasing run-down single family homes, fixing them up, and renting them for $1 per month to elderly people who were homeless, completely redefining "affordable housing." As we moved to much poorer regions like Haiti, where 80 percent of the population lives on less than $2 a day and 22 percent of children won't see their fifth birthdays, CHPF works to bring home stability and security to the world's most desperately poor and homeless.

Won't you consider supporting CHPF, or better yet, go out and share your blessings by sharing the three "T's," time, talent or treasure?

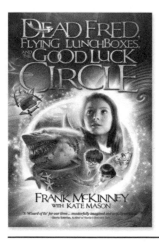

If you enjoyed reading
Dead Fred, Flying Lunchboxes and the Good Luck Circle . . .

Consider giving copies of this book to your family, friends, and classmates . . .

Hardcover book (HCI, 2009)
Available at Dead-Fred.com • $25

You or Your Parents May Also Enjoy These Other Exciting Offerings from Frank McKinney

Bestselling author Frank McKinney introduces **The Tap**, a profound spiritual practice leading to success in the business of life. Your prayers for more are answered! **The Tap** shows how to sensitize yourself to feel and then act on life's great "Tap Moments," embracing the rewards of a blessed life. **The Tap** shows that the promises of an enriched life come with astonishing speed and size to those who act on the greater responsibility that comes with greater resources, giving you confidence in your ability to handle your "more," whether it's more wealth, health, happiness, or relationships.

Hardcover book (HCI, 2009) • Available at The-Tap.com • $25

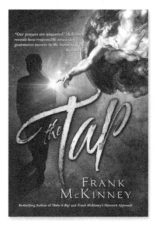

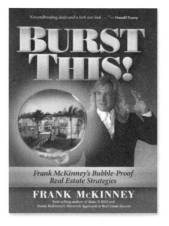

Burst This! Frank McKinney's Bubble-Proof Real Estate Strategies continues Frank McKinney's international bestseller tradition of delivering paradoxical perspectives and strategies for generational success in real estate. Tired of all the "bubble" talk, all the doom and gloom? Here comes McKinney in his unassailable fear-removal gear and hip boots to help you wash away the worry—the anxiety that financial theorists and misguided media constantly dump into the real estate marketplace. During his 25-year career, this "maverick daredevil real estate artist" has not only survived but thrived through all economic conditions by taking the contrarian position and making his own markets.

Hardcover book (HCI, 2009) • Available at Burst-This.com • $30

Frank McKinney's Maverick Approach to Real Estate Success takes the reader on a fascinating real estate odyssey that began more than two decades ago with a $50,000 fixer-upper and culminates in a $100-million mansion. Includes strategies and insights from a true real estate "artist," visionary, and market maker.

Paperback book (John Wiley & Sons, 2006)
Available at Frank-McKinney.com • $25

Make It BIG! 49 Secrets for Building a Life of Extreme Success consists of forty-nine short, dynamic chapters that share how to live a balanced life, with real estate stories and "deal points" sprinkled throughout.

   Hardcover book (John Wiley & Sons, 2002)
   Available at Frank-McKinney.com • $30

Frank McKinney's Succeeding in the Business of Life—The Series™ was recorded in Frank McKinney's tree house by Frank McKinney himself. Twelve hours of audio and video are based on content found in his first two bestsellers, *Make It BIG!* and *Frank McKinney's Maverick Approach*, plus new and expanded information found nowhere else.

Compact Discs • Available at Frank-McKinney.com • $249

The Frank McKinney Experience, Public Speaking, Appearances and **Personal Success Coaching**
One-on-one or group events
Prices and schedule available through Frank-McKinney.com

Please visit Frank-McKinney.com to peruse our entire online store at http://www.frank-mckinney.com/entire_store.asp and take advantage of savings with assorted-product packages. **It's important to note that proceeds benefit Frank McKinney's nonprofit Caring House Project Foundation** (http://www.frank-mckinney.com/caring_project.aspx).

Dead-Fred.com